Across the Inlet

A STORY ABOUT UNCONDITIONAL LOVE IN ALASKA

Gail Summers

THE ALYESKA SAGA: BOOK 1

ISBN: 1505206448
ISBN 13: 9781505206449
Library of Congress Control Number: 2014921323
CreateSpace Independent Publishing Platform
North Charleston, South Carolina

Part 1

WASILLA

Fire

> My name is Father's Joy. This is a story about a jour-
> ney across the Inlet where volcanoes smoke, oil
> platforms burn off scarlet sunsets, fireweed blooms,
> and midnight suns bore holes right through you.
> In the end I will answer any questions. For now
> I tell you this story so you might understand fire,
> how a single flicker against flint or a gentle kiss
> into tinder turns to rage. To face this heat, we must
> fly across the Inlet. As we fly over, look down. If you
> see Beluga, it is good luck. If you see a halo, it's a
> warning. When we land, look up. If you see a baby
> black bear in a tree, you are safe. If you see a red
> sea of salmon up river, it means death. I'm sorry
> if death offends you. But this story stalks death. It
> follows the ash over open water to the Valley of No
> Return to where the answers lie. But for now I tell
> you this story.
>
> —Abby Miller, morning pages

3 March
Welcome Back

My name is Abigail Miller. Family and friends call me Abby. In
Old English, Abigail means father's joy. But my father called me
a dumb-ass girl instead. So when I learned my beloved stepdad,

1

the man who loved me, whom I wanted for my real father, would die very soon, I flew to him as fast as I could. Back to Alaska to say good-bye to my Bill. To hold his hand. To be there.

I don't remember the plane ride from Albuquerque to Anchorage or the car ride from the airport to Wasilla. I blinked, and here I am in my sister's house, walking up the steps to the landing leading to the living room. There's Bill in a hospital bed. There's Mother.

"Bill pooped his pants," Mother tells me quietly so Bill can't hear. She stands in the living room wearing blue latex gloves and seems confused.

I put down my suitcase and hug her. I haven't been back to Alaska in two years, and except for the hospital bed in the living room, my sister Aurora's house seems the same.

"He is a little stinky right now," Mother says. There's strangeness in her voice. She's embarrassed for Bill to be seen in this state and to have to say such words.

"It's OK, Mother." I try to ignore the smell, go over to Bill, lean down, and kiss him on the forehead.

"Hello, Roadrunner," Bill says.

Though tired, he seems happy to see me.

"Howdy, Billiam." I hug him the best I can while he lies there in his soiled bed.

Though Mother has tried to clean Bill, I suspect she can't clean him well because it's difficult for her to reposition him. If she tried to move him around too much, she might end up rolling Bill right off the bed. And clearly Mother can't lift Bill from the bed to the wheelchair or move him to the shower. Aurora can't lift Bill either because of her bad knees. Why don't we have safety rails on the bed?

Bill's hands, knees, legs, and feet splay out in awkward forms and directions. The smell is hard to ignore.

Aurora prepares to give Bill a bath, getting the wheelchair in place; the water temperature adjusted; the towel on the chair; and more towels, soft sponges, gentle soap, creams, codeine pain killer, and clean clothes nearby. Meanwhile, Mother gathers fresh sheets, trash bags, paper towels, and moist towelettes. Aurora strips down to her underwear.

Aurora asks Ray, the handyman, to help. Why does Aurora have a handyman? Aurora's husband, Tim, arrives home, and the two men move Bill to the wheelchair. I'm assigned vehicle duty and scoot the wheelchair under Bill. Only Bill notices that Aurora is running around in her underwear.

"So I have to be eighty-nine years old and an invalid before girls will dance around in their underwear for me," Bill says.

We all chuckle. Mother immediately and discreetly pulls a sheet over the soiled bed and glances at Bill. She doesn't want Bill to see the mess.

We remove Bill's dirty clothes. For a few seconds, he is exposed, naked, adorned in a variety of redness and blotches, a catheter tube dangling, a thin body devoid of muscle. A leather lift strap circles his chest. The content of the catheter bag is dark brown. Dark urine is one of the signs of the dying noted in the hospice booklet.

I cover Bill with a blanket, move him down the hall, and wait by the bathroom. Bill's hands begin to tremble.

"When he trembles like that, he's in pain," Aurora whispers to me.

Bill continues to tremble. I lean down and put my arms around him and hold him until Aurora is ready.

Down the hall, in the living room, Mother cleans up the bed. Ray, the handyman, helps her. They clean up the poop in silence, an odd reverent silence. They ask Aurora which garbage can to use for soiled paper products and bed pads. Aurora has a plethora of garbage cans, each specialized and reserved for a specific use. When Aurora is ready, I move Bill into the bathroom, and she administers codeine to Bill. Ray and Tim come into the bathroom and carefully lift Bill by the leather strap onto the stool in the walk-in shower.

I get the clean nightshirt, bring it to the bathroom, stand there in the doorway, and watch my stepdad sit on the shower stool. His hands tremble less. Aurora washes him down with the soft sponges. She winces as she shifts her weight or maneuvers around Bill on her bad knee. She will undergo knee replacement surgery in two days.

"It's OK," Aurora keeps telling Bill.

"Welcome back, Roadrunner." Bill looks over at me and winks.

4 March
Cold Feet

Yes, Aurora's house is still the same, a large log home with two levels, the main living areas and bedrooms upstairs on the second level and the garage, utility rooms, furnace room, and large game room downstairs on the first level. The logs always need maintenance. The game room is always cold and drafty, and the plumbing and furnace still need updating, if not replacing. Up in the living room, big windows surround the room on three sides, and we can look down onto expansive views of Aurora's large yards and the wooded areas at the edge of the yards. The one wall with no windows is mostly taken up by a giant river-stone fireplace with an equally giant raised hearth and mantle, very Alaskan. Baskets of kindling and piles of firewood are stacked near the hearth. A fire crackles in the fireplace, a warm, homey sound.

I help Mother put socks on Bill, whose feet are swollen and bend unnaturally. Mother struggles to pull on the socks. This sock routine must be painful, but Bill doesn't complain. We pull the socks up over Bill's deformed, gnarled toes. One of Bill's feet is cold.

"I miss meals the most. We used to eat together at the dining table," Mother says. "I don't need help with breakfast. I need help lifting him." I'm not sure if she's talking to me.

Bill's cold foot concerns me. I know what it means to have cold feet. I remember reading about cold feet in the hospice booklet.

"I miss my friends from the pantry." Mother goes on to talk about her volunteer work and her friends at the Homer Food Pantry. I keep thinking about that cold foot.

After everyone goes to bed, I go to Bill and watch him breathe. His breath comes so shallow and subtle that I watch him long enough to be sure he is really breathing. He stirs slightly and continues to sleep under a codeine canopy. Codeine and morphine are the only medications that have been prescribed. The pneumonia won't be treated. The urinary tract infection won't be treated. The collapsed lung and the paralyzed right side of his abdomen can't be treated. The DNR order is in place. With the codeine Bill can sleep and be lucid by morning. With the morphine he can sleep and might never be lucid again. We won't start the morphine until we must.

I check Bill's feet again and close my eyes to get a better reading on the foot temperature. One foot is warm; one foot is cold. I sleep on the couch but wake to the sound of Aurora's dog, Bear-Bear, an extralarge German shepherd, charging through the dog door downstairs and barking. I get up and look out the window. There is a moose in the front yard.

5 March
Twelve Minutes

In the waiting room, I wait while Aurora is in the operating room undergoing knee replacement surgery on her second knee. She had the first knee replacement three months ago. Mother and Bill wait back in Wasilla. I'll call when Aurora gets out of surgery.

We drove into Anchorage this morning with two feet of snow fresh on the ground and with more snow falling, which pushes the moose into the roads and made us twelve minutes late for Aurora's check-in time.

Everyone's late today," the hospital staff says. "Besides, what's twelve minutes?"

Twelve minutes? I think of Bill, how Aurora called me in New Mexico and said Bill was dying and had only two weeks to live. What's twelve minutes to a dying man? Is it twelve minutes of life to be preserved at all costs? Is it twelve minutes that prolongs the unavoidable? Is it twelve minutes of not living life as before, becoming more helpless each minute to even the most basic life need? What could happen in twelve minutes? Bill had laughed this morning when I told him a funny story about Aurora. The story took one or two minutes, but the memory of the telling and the laugh could last a lifetime. For Bill a lifetime could be just twelve more minutes.

Aurora's surgery goes well. The snow stops. The cloud ceiling lifts. To our surprise the late winter sun reveals itself and, in turn, reveals a virgin-snow-covered Anchorage, sparkling with the snowcapped Chugiak Mountains behind us and the glinting ice-covered Cook Inlet in front of us. Aurora is moved to a private corner room with views of both the Inlet and the mountains. She smiles when she sees the views.

"I am a cyborg," Aurora mumbles before falling asleep.

She has a leg brace, an IV tube, a cryo machine with foot pumpers to keep the leg cool and moving, monitors of all sorts, and whatever machine it takes to heal the new knee with its Rolls-Royce ball and socket.

I admire the view of the Inlet and listen to Aurora sleep, the strong steady sounds of her sleep. It seems that now I find myself listening to sleeping people.

6 March
The Tipping Point

Mother prepares Bill for bed. She wants to clean him up first. This requires the roll procedure: rolling Bill, rolling the bed pad, unrolling the bed pad, rolling Bill another way. I'm not sure of the procedure. Mother wears blue latex gloves. I reach under Bill's arms and roll him. It's not enough. I roll more. Not enough.

I roll more. Still not enough, but we've reached the tipping point—the point of no return, the point where the tide can't be turned, where one extra inch could result in a fall. This is probably the point back at the Homer house where Mother accidentally rolled Bill off the bed onto the floor.

She wasn't strong enough to deflect the tipping point, and she wasn't strong enough to lift Bill back onto the bed. She told me she did the best she could, tried to make him comfortable on the floor, placed a pillow under his head, and covered him with a blanket to keep him warm until morning when she could find someone to help her. She was afraid to call 911.

Bill's hands tremble.

"Am I hurting you?"

"No," he answers. He feels the tipping point, too.

I draw closer to him and hold him so close it seems perverse.

When Bill seems calmer, I try to roll him again. It's still not enough. We both feel the approach of the tipping point. If we continue, we'll roll him right off the bed.

Bill's hands tremble again.

"It's OK," I say, and I carefully roll him back to the original starting position.

"Not OK," Bill says.

I don't understand the procedure. Mother explains again, then again. I'm frustrated. Mother is talking too fast, too vague in places, too specific in other places, too desperate in all places. My mind isn't working fast enough. I fight an age-old need to seem smart and to know the answers. I fight the urge to say, *Yes, I understand.* Should I pretend to know what I'm doing?

"Mother, I don't understand," I say.

Mother finally stops explaining the procedure, looks at me, and realizes I don't understand. She explains the procedure differently, and we succeed in rolling him.

"Help," Mother says suddenly. "Give me the trash. I need the trash can." Mother holds a soiled towelette in her blue-gloved hands. There's no trash can near me. She frantically looks around. She seems afraid of the towelette.

"Throw it on the floor," I tell her.

She visibly recoils at my suggestion.

"It's nothing that soap and water can't fix."

She doesn't move. I grab the towelette and throw it on the floor.

We hug afterward in front of Bill. Then we look at pictures.

"I'm sorry I got so grumpy with you," I tell her. "But I really didn't understand."

"You didn't want to understand," she tells me.

At her words the age-old childhood resistance returns. I breathe in so that I can't talk, and the resistance is forced to stay inside.

"Mother, would you like to go somewhere tomorrow after Bill's caregiver, Carol, gets here?" I ask. "Perhaps, we can go see Aurora in the hospital."

"No, I can't leave Bill."

"Carol will be here," I counter.

Mother's eyes fire up. "I don't trust Carol. She doesn't know what to do. I don't trust any of the caregivers or home health aides. They're not trained. I'm the most trained. I've seen what the Homer nurses do, and I've..." Her voice trails off.

Mother thinks she is the most trained person to care for Bill? Does she think she can don blue latex gloves and become a trained health care giver?

"That's fair enough." I pause and lower my voice. "But tell me, if you had more confidence in the home health aides, would you be more comfortable going out?"

"Yes, yes, I would." There's no hesitancy in her voice.

I hear a train whistle far off, probably going through Wasilla on the way to Fairbanks. Mother goes to bed. Tim is still visiting Aurora at the hospital. I read to Aurora's dog.

8

7 March
Poop Is Love

Bill's caregiver, Carol, doesn't show up. Mother seems agitated. I want to get out of the house. We learn later the caregiver had several doctor appointments today. She had informed Aurora, but Aurora never told us.

When the time comes, I lift Bill, not smoothly or artistically, to the portable toilet. Mother stands ready with all the cleaning supplies. Again, she wears the blue gloves.

Poop seems to be everywhere. I tell mother we'll get it all clean. We don't use bleach like Aurora wants us to. The bleach smell is obnoxious, more obnoxious than the poop smell. I hold Bill steady as Mother cleans him. She seems disgusted.

"It's just poop, Mama," I say. "Nothing soap and water won't fix." Normalize the poop.

We get the toilet mission accomplished, but it exhausts Bill.

During the cleanup ritual, we notice Aurora's new carpet is soiled. Mother seems worried. I get a basin and hot soapy water and scrub the carpet, scrub it twice, counting sixty seconds for each scrub. The carpet comes beautifully clean.

Don't tell Aurora," I say.

"You know, Aurora says cleaning up someone's poop is an act of love," Mother says.

"Aurora is right." I marvel at this new piece of knowledge. Poop is love. "We only do poop for those we love—for babies, puppies, old dogs, and old folks." We chuckle.

"You should wear gloves," Mother says.

"I'm OK with not wearing gloves," I answer. "We are not dealing with a contagious disease here." Any other person, any other time, yes, I'd wear gloves. This is just old age, the fading of a soul to the next dimension. This is family. He needs fresh sheets and a fresh bed shirt. The towelettes don't clean well.

"Use real washcloths, Mama," I say. "They'll come clean in the washing machine." Normalize the poop.

Later, I prepare the guest room for the arrival of Alice and Palmer, my other sister and her husband. Mother stands in the doorway with a quizzical look on her face.

"We're not dealing with a contagious disease here," she says.

"Mama, remember when us girls were babies?" I ask. Of course, she remembers. "Did you wear gloves or fuss about our messy diapers? Plus, how many puppies have we all cleaned up? Heck, I've been totally covered in puppy poop before." We laugh big laughs together.

Yes, Aurora is right. Poop is love.

8 March
The Bookkeeper

"Do you want some chocolate cake?" I ask Bill.

His eyes light up. "Ice cream, too," Bill says.

"He likes to feed himself," Mother says. "I give him foods he can eat with his hands."

"So it shall be." I spread a beach towel like a giant bib over and around Bill with great formality. Then I place a hunk of cake on a paper plate on the towel, an ice cream bar in his shaky hands, and a travel mug of strong coffee on the little table next to the bed. "Enjoy. Make as much mess as you want. When you're done, we'll clean it all up."

Bill drops the ice cream bar several times and squeezes chunks of cake between his long gnarly fingers as he pushes the cake toward his mouth. Most of the cake falls apart and lands on the towel in a pile of chocolaty crumbs.

"Hmm, it seems half the cake is not reaching my mouth. That means my efficiency quotient is only about fifty percent," Bill says.

"Doesn't seem like good quality control or something like that." I chuckle.

"You'd better bring me another piece of cake. Then I'll get fifty percent of each piece in my mouth, which gives me one hundred percent of a piece of cake."

"Hmm, it sounds like a trick to get more cake," I say. "Do you need another ice cream bar, too?"

"Nope, my efficiency with ice cream is much better," Bill says. Bill spends the next twenty minutes savoring the cake and the ice cream bar. When I clean him up, I note his fingernails. The color is good. Bill falls asleep, leaning against the safety rail I attached to the bed earlier this morning.

I join Mother in her room, and we sit on her new bed. The bedroom is full of moving boxes and stacks of clothes. When Bill's condition worsened and it became too much for Mother to handle by herself, Aurora went down to Homer and moved them and all their belongings up here to the Wasilla house. For Bill this meant living in a hospital bed in Aurora's living room. For Mother it meant living in Aurora's master bedroom.

"Fancy bed," I say.

"I mentioned I was thinking about a memory-foam bed, and Aurora shows up with this bed," Mother says. "Of course, I paid three thousand dollars for it."

Mother's voice seems strained. Something is wrong.

"I calculated what I will lose when Bill passes away, and it's a lot of money," Mother says. "I'll lose his air force retirement, which is over sixty thousand dollars a year."

I'm amazed Mother is fretting about money right now, and then I remind myself that Mother's a retired bookkeeper and does volunteer work as a bookkeeper for the Homer Food Pantry. Knowing where the money is or is not is Mother's business.

"I keep asking to see the balances." Mother's voice becomes shrill.

What is she talking about?

"I don't have control over my own finances. Aurora has the power of attorney for Bill." Mother's eyes glisten. "I'm paying the bill for Jessica."

Who's Jessica?

"I'm not sure what I'm paying for anymore."

Aurora has control over their money? Why? Mother is an excellent bookkeeper. In fact, Mother is more qualified to handle money than any of her three daughters.

"I don't know what's happening." Mother suddenly pounds her fist on the bed.

I'm stunned.

"I know Aurora and Tim have been good to us and they're struggling." Mother breathes fast, and I see her chest heaving. "I want to help them, but I need to control my own finances."

I don't quite understand what Mother is talking about, but I understand that something's wrong and Mother's probably too emotional to talk right now.

"Yes, you should control your own finances," I say. Why isn't she? "We'll talk to Aurora when she gets back from the hospital and get this figured out."

Mother looks relieved.

I really don't want to be in the middle of this. I want to run.

"Let's go get Bill ready for bed," Mother says.

Mother tucks the sheet around Bill, covers him with an extra blanket, turns out the lights in the living room, and pads down the hall to her room. The full moon glows off the snow outside in the yards. The whiteness of clouds resembles the northern lights, the aurora borealis, for which Aurora was named. The mother moose is back in the yard.

"Sleep well." I kiss Bill on the forehead.

He's awake and seems alert. I pull up the stool to his bedside, hold his hand, and wait for him to go back to sleep.

"How's Matt?" Bill asks.

I talk about my husband.

"How's John?" Bill asks.

I talk about my husband's father, who had a stroke recently. "He has trouble with his speech. It's slow, and he struggles now,"

12

I say. I describe how John is starting to forget, to repeat, to forget again, and to suddenly remember but remember wrong.

"Oh no," Bill says. His voice rings of sorrow.

"I don't know what is worse, to lose the use of our minds or our bodies," I say.

"Our minds," Bill says. His voice sounds surprisingly strong. "I can't move or take care of myself, but my mind is still here."

"Yes, we still have you with us." I stroke his hand, expecting him to fall asleep, but he continues to talk, clear and coherent.

"I'm so tired of lying in this bed," he says. "I'd like to go for a car ride."

"We can," I say. "We could take your Malibu, put you in a parka or even a sleeping bag." Can we? Can we bundle him up, prop him up, and take him for a ride? "Why not?"

"Why not?" Bill responds.

"Where would you like to go?"

"Across the Inlet," he says. "Can we go now?"

Across the Inlet. I resist saying the obvious, that you need a boat or plane to go across the Inlet. I sense he has wandered out of this world.

"Should we bring Mother?"

"Oh, yes, bring Mother," Bill says. "Can we go now?"

It's close to midnight. It is eleven degrees outside. The snow still lies too thick in the woods, and moose wander into the roads. Bill seems coherent and lucid. His words flow clear and strong, and he seems to mean what he says. There's no slurred speech, no odd phrases, no incoherent babbling to cue me this isn't real. But I sense this is not real.

"We'll go in the daylight, so you can see better. Sleep now," I say.

He seems happy. He kisses my hand too long—then again, then again. The kisses become strange and uncomfortable, almost sexual. Or am I overreacting? I notice his other hand slides down to his groin area. This is not real. I don't know what I'm observing. Perhaps the sundowner's syndrome I've heard

13

about or perhaps a reflex action that speaks to or from a world gone by.

"Sleep good." I touch Bill's cheek and go to the window and watch the moose in the yard. I glance back at Bill. His hands pick at the sheets, and his mouth makes soft kissing sounds.

9 March
Laundry

The home health aide, Carol, arrives at 9:23 a.m. So this is Carol. She's young, strong, tall, and pregnant. She immediately tends to Bill—a shave, a tooth cleaning, a face wash, a catheter-bag emptying.

Carol scolds me for giving Bill coffee. "Coffee is a natural diuretic," she says. "We shouldn't be giving it to him."

I think of yesterday's coffee and chocolate cake. He's dying. He can have anything he wants. I go to the computer room to check my e-mail and try to work on a consulting project. Mother plays a card game on her computer in the opposite corner. Her e-mail doesn't work. She can't print. I try to fix it.

"Abby, I notice that you snore," Mother says abruptly. "Have you tried using those snore strips?"

"They don't work." I cut her off. Mother snores, too, but I don't say it.

"But the new strips are supposed to open up…"

"They don't work." I cut her off again and say it harshly.

I hate her pointing out my flaws and feel that age-old resistance again and the urge to go into the kitchen to eat the rest of the chocolate cake. This is my issue, not Mother's.

"The snoring is weight related. I need a special machine."

"Oh." Mother's voice softens.

"I cured the snoring when I lost seventy pounds two years ago. Unfortunately, I gained all the weight back, and the snoring came back," I continue.

I'd named the machine "the Snout" and remember the humiliation of having to use it. I tell her about the Snout. I hate being home because it means being reduced to the sum of my flaws. It's why I ran away.

"Do you wake up tired?" Mother asks me.

I wonder at her question, a valid question about snoring. How much does she know about snoring?

"I wake up exhausted, with a big headache from the low oxygen count," I say.

"That should be good incentive to lose weight," she says.

Mother is overweight, too, but I don't say it. In another part of my mind, I consider going to the bed-and-breakfast down the road where I can snore in privacy.

"Yes, but it's not that easy. It's an emotional issue. I joined Overeaters Anonymous. The weight issue isn't what you think it is," I say.

We all have weight issues. Aurora has been overweight all her life. Alice is sometimes overweight. Currently, Alice has reached her ideal weight, and I'm envious. We are all tall and have a somewhat similar bone structure with strong shoulders and hips, though we carry our weight differently. Aurora carries her weight in voluptuous curves with an enticing allure in spite of her one hundred extra pounds. Alice carries her weight in almost a straight line from her chest to her hips, in a sporty youthfulness. I carry my weight evenly, though it is most noticeable on my hips and my face and in my snoring.

The story of the Snout seems to diffuse the tension. I try but can't fix Mother's e-mail or printer problems, and I attempt to work in spite of the interruptions and questions and comments. Mother continues to play card games on her computer.

When I don't feel like doing e-mail or other work or watching Bill sleep, I do laundry. For some reason I feel compelled to finish all the laundry before Aurora gets home from the hospital. The laundry ritual starts with towels and lots of rules for the towels. A white bucket for white towels. All Bill's towels are white and are bleached, dried on medium heat, and folded in neat stacks according to size.

The buzzer goes off to the washing machine, and I put the second load of white towels into the washer. After folding, the white towels are then placed in the towel cupboard on shelf number two, which is labeled "Bill's towels." All other towels are stacked separately on different shelves, all labeled accordingly: good towels, hair-color towels, or guest towels. A small sign is posted on the inside of the door of the towel cupboard with instructions on using, washing, folding, and properly storing towels.

Except there are exceptions to the rules. Exception: kitchen wash towels are also white and look just like Bill's white towels. Exception: the kitchen towels are folded in squares and stored in kitchen drawer number two instead of on bathroom shelf number two. Exception: Bill's big bibs, which are officially considered white towels, are not white. Exception: all white towels get bleach unless the white towels are kitchen towels. Other towels don't get bleach.

I throw them all in the washing machine together, don't use bleach, and fold everything the same. The buzzer goes off to the dryer.

Laundry continues with linen napkins, which need starching and pressing. There's a special laundry basket for napkins, labeled "to be ironed." I throw all napkins into this basket. I don't iron. I don't press. I don't starch. Note to self—buy paper towels.

The ritual goes on with sheets, nightshirts, bed pads, and small blankets for Bill. There's an assortment of throw rugs and more blankets. I don't see any clothes. Where are the clothes? Are people wearing the same clothes every day? The buzzer goes off to the dryer. Keep folding.

There's also a variety of hampers and baskets for each type of laundry. Exception: a forty-pound dog-food container is also located in the laundry room, and it resembles the hamper for white towels. Sometimes I accidentally throw a dirty white towel into the dog food.

The laundry ritual closes with a crystal candy dish strategically placed on the laundry room floor to catch the drips that sometimes dribble down from the plastic liquid-detergent bottle. Another buzzer goes off. Keep folding.

Mother joins me in the laundry room and helps me fold.

"I know one thing. I'll never get married again," Mother tells me. "It's too much."

Mother tells me a story about a lady friend who'll never remarry because she can't endure the torture of burying a second husband.

Her story reminds me of a big white dog, a Samoyed Husky named Spot. The dog was my only friend for many years, traveling with me though Europe, through the divorce of my first husband, through the journey to New Mexico and starting over. Most importantly, whenever I ran away, he ran away with me.

The dog lived to be almost fifteen years old, past the age big dogs are supposed to live. His dog body finally wasted away with thyroid and spinal cord disease and cataracts and, finally, paralysis. The day I had to put him down, I cried into the night and into the next day when I woke up and found myself alone. I vowed I'd never have another dog. Certainly a dog is not worth the same as a human, but I understand Mother's lady friend. It's too much. We both don't want to wake up alone again.

"My life will never be the same," Mother says.

I put the stacks of towels away, hopefully on the correct shelves, and we go to the computer room.

"I don't know what to do," Mother says. "I don't know what I want."

"Mother, remember what I said once about one foot in the old world and one foot in the new world?"

She nods.

"Well, you're not supposed to know what you want right now."

I see a hint of hope in her face.

"Mother, is there something you'd like to do but never had a chance to do?" I ask.

"I can't think of anything," she says.

17

For a fleeting moment, I sense defiance in her and a hint of rebel spirit.

"I always liked to travel," she says. There's a faraway look in her eyes. "Bill and I used to go on adventures." But that faraway look is not about adventures with Bill.

"Where would you like to go?" I ask.

"My friend LeeAnn does missionary work," Mother says.

The buzzer to the dryer goes off.

10 March
Carol

It's lunchtime. I've not worked much on my consulting project or checked my e-mail. I missed my morning snack and am now overly hungry. Mother informs me Bill needs to poop.

Because Carol's pregnant, she's not allowed to lift heavy objects, especially not Bill. After just one day, I resent Carol. She's paid to help us, but she can't help us because she's pregnant. Why doesn't home health send someone else? I help Mother lift Bill to the portable toilet, not smoothly and in fear that I'll lose my grip and drop him.

Later, I cook dinner. Bill sleeps to the sound of the cowboy channel on the television.

"I think I'll go home early," Carol says. "No sense in Aurora paying me to sit around and watch Bill sleep."

"Actually, I pay you." Mother enters the kitchen.

"Oh, whoever," Carol says. "My back hurts. I think I'll go now."

11 March
Signs

Bill sleeps most of the day and when awake, doesn't say much, but he surprises us by waking hungry. I feed him finger food, which he relishes, and a big cookie, which he gobbles. He seems momentarily more energetic before falling back to sleep.

We know from the poop smell that Bill needs to be cleaned. He sleeps now, and we wonder if we should wake him to clean him up. We decide cleaning him is the right thing to do. During the cleaning I notice our pace is less frantic and Mother wears only one blue latex glove.

At night I go to the couch and try to sleep as I listen to Bill breathe, hearing the congestion in his throat and a subtle whistling. Is this the death rattle? He picks and jabs at the sheets, and his trembling hands reach out as if he's trying to touch something.

His breath comes shallow and labored. Sometimes he emits a sigh or a low whine. I go over and check his feet. They're warm. All night he reaches and struggles to touch something, making trembling, jerky movements in the air. Are these are the signs of the dying I read about in the hospice booklet?

12 March
Pain in the Shoes

I need help," Bill cries, loud enough for us to hear from Mother's bedroom.

I rush down the hall to Bill. "What's happening?" I ask.

"I have a pain in my shoes," Bill says. He's not wearing shoes.

"Dementia." Mother shakes her head.

"I'm at my limitations." Bill's entire body shakes. He clutches the safety rail. "I want to get out this situation."

"He thinks he's in a cage," Mother whispers.

"Why am I here?" Bill cries. "Why are you whispering? What have I done?"

"You haven't done anything, William. You're safe now." Mother tries to dislodge his grip on the safety rail.

"I'm at my limitations. I want this situation to end," Bill continues to cry out. "There's pain."

"Bill, where's the pain?" I ask.

"In my shoes, in my goddamned shoes!" he yells.

"Dementia," Mother whispers.

Not sure what else to do, I check Bill's feet and discover the lower safety rail jammed between two of Bill's toes. A large red bruise is evident. Bill pushes his toes against the rail.

"Aha, we do have a shoe problem here," I tell Bill. "Hold on."

It takes me several attempts to free Bill's toes. The skin between his toes is rubbed red and almost raw. It's not dementia. It's a different interpretation. Pain in the shoes. Pain in the feet. Pain in the toes. What's the difference? It's our literal interpretation that's flawed.

I see Bill still clutching the safety rail, still shaking. I sit next to him on the stool.

"I'm scared," Bill says.

I don't want Bill to be in pain. I don't want him to be scared. Above all, I don't want him to be scared.

13 March
Mashed Potatoes

Tim brings home Aurora with her new knee wrapped in a stiff black brace. I help her remove the brace, change into pajamas, and go to the toilet.

"Give me your hand," Aurora says.

I give her my hand to help her up. But she leans her entire weight onto my hand as she stands up, and I'm not prepared to support her, causing Aurora to fall back on the toilet.

"Get out of here. Go get Tim," Aurora says. "I can't trust you to help me."

A few minutes later, Aurora hobbles up to the living room. "I'm home," Aurora calls.

Bill perks up and seems instantly alert.

"Make mashed potatoes," Aurora tells me. "He looks depressed. He needs his medicine." She gives Bill medicine. "Make brownies," she tells me. She feeds Bill the potatoes. "Get fresh blankets." She strokes Bill's hands. "He needs protein.

Cook some bacon," Aurora continues to order. "He's exhausted. Has he been sleeping? Have you been giving him his sleeping pill?" Aurora demands.

Color returns to Bill's face. He eats large amounts of food. He relaxes. His shaking hands turn calm. The warmth in his eyes returns, and then his head drops to one side as he gently falls asleep. What did I just witness? By the end of the day, I've eaten an entire bag of potato chips. Nothing else.

"I need to talk to you about Mother and money," I say to Aurora.

"Not now!" Aurora snaps.

I sleep on the couch and wake up at midnight to the sounds and smells of Aurora cooking ham and eggs for Bill. The smell makes me hungry. I go looking in the kitchen cupboards and find a cabinet full of chips and crackers and a drawer full of diet milkshakes. There are four refrigerators and two large freezers in the house. Under one refrigerator I find a drawer crammed with bags of candy. I grab several handfuls of mini chocolate bars.

14 March
Rise and Shine

It's morning and time for the usual hygiene rituals. Carol's late again, or perhaps she's not coming today and Aurora hasn't told us yet.

"Don't suffocate me," Bill tells me as I reach under his arms and around him to lift him.

"Don't do it that way," Aurora yells.

"Don't fight me," Bill tells Mother as she tries to loosen his grasp from the safety rail.

"We need to move you to the toilet," Mother tells him.

"I'm just going to move you over here, Bill," I say.

"You're doing it wrong," Aurora insists. "Use the chest strap."

"Bill, let go of the rail," Mother says.

"Wrap your arms around me," I say to Bill.

"For heaven's sake, use the chest strap," Aurora says.

"William, you need to help us help you," Mother says.

"Stop. One person at a time," Bill commands us in a booming voice.

We stop moving, stop talking.

"I'll move him." Tim appears and deftly grabs Bill by the chest strap and moves him to the portable toilet.

15 March
Alice Arrives

"Alice and Palmer are here," I announce.

They've come to say good-bye to Bill. According to Aurora, there is only one or, possibly, two weeks left.

Bill perks up like he perked up when Aurora came home from the hospital. Alice immediately goes to Bill and flutters around him. She feeds him and talks and talks and talks while Bill laughs.

It's bath night. Alice puts on a swimsuit and takes over wash duty. Palmer, Alice's husband, takes transport duty. I do safety and temperature control. Aurora takes an imaginary platform and gives commands and tells Mother to get out of the way.

"Lift up your butt cheek, Bill," Alice instructs. "I need full access."

"That area's restricted. Do you have a security clearance?" Bill grumbles cheerfully.

During the washing I visually inspect Bill from where I stand holding a stack of towels. His nail beds are pink. Good. His lips are pale gray, almost blue. Not good. His hands and arms are pink. Good. One foot is beginning to darken. Not good. The conflicting good and not good confuses me. I don't know what it means.

"Those are the wrong towels," Aurora tells me.

Bath completed, we sit around the living room and watch Alice feed Bill. Mother stands in the hallway, watching, too. Aurora turns the television to the cowboy channel and then disappears down to the game room where she and Tim have moved their bedroom. I follow her downstairs to talk about Mother's money.

"Get lost," Aurora tells me.

16 March
Rally

Today is Bill's best day. He seems alert and coherent, talking and sitting in the big blue recliner. Napping soundly one minute and engaging a conversation about the stock market in another. Eating a large supper. Watching an old Western movie. Alice sits next to him after feeding him two servings of meatloaf and potato salad. On this night Bill is happy, noting new sounds and footsteps coming down the hall or up the stairs or wondering what the dog is barking about.

Mother sleeps on the sectional sofa all day. This is her worst day.

17 March
Sleeping

I oversleep, feel anxious that I have slept too long and will appear in my pajamas too late in the morning. However, it is my first restful sleep since I've been here.

It is one in the afternoon, and Mother sleeps on the couch in the living room. She's still in her pajamas. Just days ago, Mother was active all day, doing things, cleaning the refrigerator, sorting through boxes, playing card games on the computer, and conducting long conversations with me. Now, she sleeps most of the day.

Bill sleeps in the recliner. When sleeping, his mouth hangs open, his hands tremble, and sometimes he seems to make gestures to people not there. When awake, he's especially alert to sounds of people coming and going. I think about how Aurora called Alice and me, telling us Bill would die in two or three weeks. Yet here he is, holding court in the living room.

Aurora sleeps down in the game room, the cryo machine cooling her knee. Her dog, Bear-Bear, sleeps nearby. Her leg has begun to turn purple from the knee surgery stress. When not sleeping, she hobbles around and up the stairway, cooks, directs the affairs of her house, mostly ignoring the pain and taking a pain killer when the pain becomes unmanageable or when she needs to sleep. Her snores are a variety of sounds that range from groan-snores to the basic snores of air going in and out. Her dog snores, too, but soft and low. Aurora and her dog sleep and snore like a snoring duet. And with sleep Aurora can heal better. With sleep she feels no pain. Perhaps it is the same with Mother. With sleep she feels no pain.

Then again, with sleep Aurora doesn't have to talk to me about Mother and money.

When I was a child, sometimes Mother would sleep on the couch all day, in her pajamas, oblivious to the world around her, sometimes waking and making contact with the nonsleeping world to say how tired she was or how she could not get an uninterrupted night's sleep because of the window.

"Geese were honking outside my window."

"Moonlight was too bright in my window."

"Cold air was coming through my window."

"The dog was under my window."

Sometimes she was unaware of us, almost catatonic, with me wanting her to get dressed, to move around, to have energy, to be our mom, but she could not. I don't remember why. Perhaps problems with JB, our biological father. At eleven years old, I became thirty years old, taking care of my sisters and mother, still in her pajamas. To this day I feel its impact. I don't linger in pajamas in the morning. I don't put on pajamas early in the evening. If there is a logical reason to put on pajamas at an illogical time, I ask permission.

And to this day, I feel protective of my mother and sisters. Also to this day, I watch and listen to people sleep, for the act of sleeping is more than sleep. It reveals how we are and the world we are in.

Meanwhile Aurora continues to avoid any conversation about money.

18 March
Lunch with Mother

Bill sleeps into the late afternoon. When awake he continues on, coherent, funny, with good appetite. "Why are there rails on my bed?" he jokes. "To keep me in? Or you guys out?"

Aurora and Tim sleep all morning and will probably sleep all day. Alice and Palmer work in the computer room. When not on the computer, Alice tends to Bill. Alice is now the chief caregiver for Bill, giving orders to us and the home health aides and assuming control of most activities. Palmer tries to stay out of the way. Tim has a job, but his schedule is so odd that I just recently knew he had a job at all. He works weekends and long hours on Mondays and Fridays, coming home to change into his pajamas, grab a plate of supper, and go downstairs.

Sometimes we hear Aurora calling, "Nurse."

We go downstairs, where she lies in her bed, to see what she needs. It may be her leg rubbed or a bowl of rice or a pill or another blanket or to give orders for what to cook or instructions for Jessica, who will be back from spring break soon.

"Who is Jessica?" I ask.

"My little helper," Aurora says. "I pay her to come on weekends to help with the chores, clean up the yard, and help me with other stuff."

"Oh, that's nice," I say.

She pays someone to help her with chores? Then there's the handyman. Things don't make sense.

"You seem to be feeling better," I begin. "Can we talk about finances?"

"Yes, of course," Aurora says. "How much do you want to contribute?"

"Contribute to what?" I ask.

"The expense of having so many guests in the house," Aurora says. "My utility bills are skyrocketing."

"No, I'd like to discuss Mother and Bill's accounts and the power of attorney that Bill gave you." I try not to react to her comment about contributing.

"Go to hell," Aurora says and rolls over in the bed, her back to me now.

"Well, understand this," I say to her back. "We will talk."

Aurora does not say anything to me. She calls her dog. "Come up here, Bear-Bear." The big dog jumps up on the bed and sidles next to Aurora.

"Also understand this," I add. "I'm not your nurse."

I take Mother to lunch. She takes three hours to get ready, but I don't rush her, so it's actually close to suppertime by the time we leave. Mother hasn't been out of the house since she moved up here from Homer.

"Where would you like to go for lunch?" I ask.

"How should I know?" Mother says. "I don't know this place." Harsh white light glares off the snowbanks and fields on each side of the road. Because of the glare and the layer of snowpack on the road, the painted road lanes are difficult to see. Sometimes I can't tell what part of the road I'm on. We squint even with dark sunglasses.

"I don't have any cash," she says.

"I have money," I say. "If you want, I can take you to a teller machine."

"How?" she retorts.

"What do you mean how?" I ask.

"How am I going to get money? I don't know the balance," she says. "I keep asking Aurora for the balance."

"We'll get that fixed," I say.

Her conversation continues in short, shrill statements of helplessness: "How should I know?" "Don't ask me." "I don't know this place." I know these are all good signs. She's still in my world and has not retreated into her pajamas to sleep on the couch until the world softens and becomes safe again. So I'll bear the shrillness of her retorts until she feels safe.

Just listen. Offer suggestions? No, just listen.

"I'm angry at Bill." Mother stabs a tomato. "He did this to himself. We've spent the last seven years trapped because of his health. I tried to get him to do something. I'm so angry. The overall money situation unnerves me. I don't know what's going on. I don't have a penny in my purse. I'm so scared. My life will never be the same. I can't lift him. I told Aurora *that* money is my retirement money. Aurora has power of attorney."

Mother looks at me. "You're the executor of our wills." She searches for some response, some indication of an ally, testing the ground for safeness.

"Mother, you told me you don't know what's going on," I say. "Tell me what you do know."

Mother looks out the window for the first time. She comments about the fabric store, the ice cream shop, and the UPS store. She comments about the parking lot and snow in the road that blurs the lane markings, and then there's a long pause.

"I don't want to be a bag lady," she says.

"Mother, what's going on with your money?"

"I don't know how much I have," she starts. "Ever since Aurora brought us up here from Homer, she's been buying things for us and using our accounts."

"Mother, first, you'll never be a bag lady," I say. "Second, you have plenty of assets."

I'm exhausted from listening, worn out from not running away, and weary from wondering what's happening. The world seems a blur, just like the road lanes. I'm not aware of the restaurant or what's going on around me.

"What exactly is Aurora spending money on?" I ask.

"I don't know," Mother says. "That's the whole point. She won't give me my bank statements so I can check the balances."

"I think I'm paying for the handyman, but I don't know why. I pay for Carol, and then there's the stair lift and the new television and the expenses for moving us up from Homer," Mother says. "Then Aurora and Tim are struggling to make ends meet, and they always need help. There are all the groceries and the big blue recliner, and Tim needs medications for his shoulder and doesn't have health insurance, and Aurora needs gas to put in her truck and new tires and…"

The list goes on and on, and this and that and this, too. I'm aghast. Stair lift?

"Mother, are you giving Aurora money for all this?" I ask. I dread the answer.

"No, she has her own debit cards to our accounts. The bank issued them to her when Bill gave her the power of attorney."

"Are you telling me that Aurora has full access to your accounts?"

"Yup."

19 March
Rally II

The calm before the storm, one last hurrah, a rally before death. Is this what's happening? Did Bill rally when we three girls gathered here in Wasilla? I don't understand. Bill seems to be getting better.

Perhaps Bill isn't close to death, but I recall Aurora's telephone call distinctly—how she said the doctor had told her Bill had only one or two weeks left, possibly three. And Bill had pneumonia and a collapsed lung and a urinary tract infection, plus a paralyzed right side. No curative measures would be taken. Morphine has been prescribed. I've been here in

Wasilla over two weeks. Bill seems no worse than two weeks ago. My husband, Matt, wants to know when I'm coming home.

And what is Aurora doing with Mother and Bill's money? I need to look at Mother's accounts myself, make a mental note to set up Internet access for Mother for her bank accounts. I need to know what's happening with Bill.

I go to my computer and read about death. Death is sometimes preceded by a rally, and a rally will use up any remaining energy reserves. If this is a rally, then in a few days, Bill will deteriorate. The surge of a rally is usually short, and soon after, the signs of death will become more apparent: increased darkening of the feet, sleeping longer each day, picking at the sheets, brain stem reflex actions, darkening of urine, incontinence, disorientation, the confusion of sundowner's syndrome. How long does this process go on? It's different for everyone. It could take days or weeks or months.

It's three degrees outside and clear. It's so cold that the moisture in the air forms tiny ice crystals that sparkle and flutter in the sunshine.

20 March
Unpacking Boxes

It's said our lives flash before us in the moments before we die. This is a romantic image of death, probably from the movies, to help disguise our fear of it. In the real world, if we live long enough to die of old age, death will probably be humiliating, not romantic. Ask Bill, sitting there on his portable toilet in the living room with a house full of strangers and young girls coming and going. Here is your bowel movement for the whole world to see.

I think it's more plausible that our life flashes before us when we unpack boxes of stuff that belonged to our parents. My mission today is to start unpacking Mother and Bill's boxes and help get Mother settled in Aurora's house. They've been up here since last Thanksgiving, living out of boxes and suitcases. Bill doesn't really care. Mother does.

Alice and I go out to Aurora's extralarge, detached garage. It is twenty degrees outside, and we hope today will warm up enough to melt another layer of snow. I remember Aurora saying this past winter produced the heaviest snowfall on record in years—125 inches! The snow crunches under our feet, and our breath puffs out in white clouds when we breathe. Shining translucent icicles hang from the eaves of the detached garage all the way to the ground.

Moving boxes line the walls and fill the garage—box after box after box moved here from the Homer house, from Mother and Bill's former life, a life of certainty, to this new life now altered and so uncertain.

"We need a plan for opening and organizing these boxes." Alice surveys the area.

"Can't we just open them?" I ask.

"I'll go get a clipboard." Alice leaves. Her feet crunch on the snow as she goes outside and walks back to the house.

I start opening boxes, and with each box a snippet of my life flashes before me. Here are the Asta pots and pans I gave Mother when I went to the factory in Germany. Here is the cuckoo clock and the collection of nutcrackers and the wooden Madonna from Oberammergau when Mother and Bill came to visit me. Here is a copy of my dissertation. I remember how Mother and Bill came to my graduation. How proud they were. Here is Bill's diploma from Purdue. Here is his college ring. I remember the stories he told us about going to school, how he developed a horseradish business to pay for school. Here is a picture of us with King Kong.

Here are Bill's Shriner hats. Here is his Masonic apron. Here is his Mason ring. Here are his air force pilot wings and his gold oak leaf clusters. Here is his air force ring. I don't remember Bill wearing all those rings. Here is the coffee mug with the C-130 logo. I remember how Bill carried that mug every morning to the Motley Moose to drink coffee with the guys.

Here is the carved platter from Haiti, a gift to my mother from my first husband. I remember Bill walking me down the aisle. I remember when I filed for divorce and flew to Homer, ashamed that my marriage failed and embarrassed to tell them. Bill hugged me and said, "Try again," and "Go walk by the Inlet."

Here are dozens of delicate china teacups we gave to Mother on every birthday and holiday even though she didn't collect teacups. I remember Alice coordinating a plan to create a teacup collection for Mother so we'd always know what to give her. Here are suitcases of Bill's clothes. What should we do with his clothes? Here is a box with the Christmas, Easter, Valentine, and birthday cards we sent Mother and Bill. There are so many cards. Here's the pink pillow I made for Mother. Here's the brown lap quilt I made for Bill. Here and here and here in this box and that box and another box, our lives flash by. I hear a moose outside the garage. Back in Homer moose always ate my mother's tulips.

21 March
Wells Fargo

Done. The Wells Fargo account is ready for Mother to manage online. I'm concerned about what Mother will see when she looks at her bank statement. Aurora has power of attorney and uses this account, allegedly on behalf of Mother and Bill. What has Aurora really done?

"Are you ready?" I ask.

She nods.

I show Mother how to enter her user name and password. "OK, you just need to log in."

Mother doesn't move. She looks at the login page on the screen. "Does Aurora know we are doing this?"

"No. Why should she?"

"I'd like her to know we're doing this," Mother says.

There it is. I should have guessed it. Mother's afraid of Aurora.

"Mother, it's your account."

"I need her to know we are doing this before we do it," Mother says.

I feel Mother's fear. She's not ready for this.

"You're right," I say. "We'll coordinate with Aurora."

Mother looks relieved.

"Mother, this isn't so much about what Aurora has done with your money," I say. "It's about getting your life back in order."

Again she looks relieved.

22 March
Scam

Today there are mixed signs. Bill's feet are pink, which is good. He seems lucid and funny and complains about the slow chef in the kitchen, me. All good signs. His eyes are red and seem to sink into the sockets, and his nail beds are gray. These are not good signs. The mixed signs confuse me. It's been this way since I arrived.

Does Bill really have only two or three weeks to live? Does Bill really have pneumonia, the collapsed lung, the urgency, the finality? We go to sleep each night wondering if Bill will be here in the morning. Each morning, we sigh and wonder why Bill is still here and then feel the guilt of wondering and play nurse to Bill and, yes, play nurse to Aurora as she recovers from knee surgery. How long will this go on? When will Bill die? Then there's the guilt of just thinking it, the collective unsaid question that only my husband asks.

"When are you coming home?" Matt asks every time we talk on the phone.

"I don't know," I always say.

In these past weeks, we have also come to know the exhaustion of caregiving.

"I don't want him to linger," Alice says.

I'm not sure this is for Bill's sake or Alice's, and I don't want to know and don't ask.

Carol comes for two hours three days week. But we need more help. Alice is helping Aurora develop a plan and coordinate with the hospice folks and the VA folks to get more home health aide hours.

"Nurse," Aurora calls from downstairs. Alice goes downstairs.

"Aurora wants you to make her a bowl of rice with butter," Alice tells me when she comes back.

"Nurse," Aurora calls from downstairs. Alice goes downstairs a second time.

"Aurora wants us to give Bill a bath," Alice says when she returns.

Something's not right. I go to the computer room and look in Aurora's file cabinet where she keeps important papers. There is a file labeled "Bill." In the file is a copy of the power of attorney that Bill granted Aurora, Bill's medical record, his record of military service, and the results of Bill's last doctor's appointment. I read about the pneumonia, the collapsed lung, the paralyzed right side, and the urinary tract infection. I note the doctor's recommendation for Bill to be entered into hospice care for "six months or less." Six months. Not two or three weeks.

I go back to the living room where Alice feeds Bill fried chicken and corn. He eats with gusto and later will use the toilet with gusto, not the final signs of the dying described in the hospice booklet. Why would Aurora tell us that Bill had only two or three weeks left to live?

"Nurse," Aurora calls again from downstairs.

"You go this time," Alice tells me.

"I'm not her nurse," I say.

"I think she needs help putting ice in the cryo machine." Alice gives Bill more chicken.

"Handy, isn't it?" I blurt out. "How Aurora got us to rush up here just in time for her knee surgery?"

Bill winks at me then continues smacking on his chicken.

"I want you to spend time with him before he dies," Aurora told us, and we felt the urgency and flew up here as soon as we could—Alice from Seattle and me from New Mexico—because we wanted to spend time with him, to say good-bye, to be here when it happened.

"Oh, I'm having my knee surgery," I remember Aurora saying. There it is. Aurora's scheme is about me and Alice being here to play nurse to her and take care of Bill because Aurora would be recovering from surgery. And the home health aide only comes two hours three days a week, and it isn't enough. Bill's immediate dying is a scam.

23 March
The Eyes Have It

"What's wrong with his eyes?" I ask.

"We need to call the hospice nurse," Alice says.

Bill's eyes seep fluid, and it dries and turns crusty all around them. We gently clean his eyes with warm water and a soft sponge. We drop liquid tears into each eye, but they continue to seep fluid, and the fluid continues to crust over.

"Does it hurt?" I ask Bill.

We watch Aurora go to a drawer and retrieve a small container of special eye drops.

"These are atropine eye drops," Aurora says. "Tad, the hospice nurse, prescribed them in case we needed them."

"How are they different from regular eye drops?" I ask.

"Well, they manage the fluid from Bill's eyes. According to Tad, it's not normal eye fluid." Aurora carefully puts a drop in each of Bill's eyes. Aurora replaces the cap on the container and lowers her voice. "Tad says the fluid coming out isn't normal eye secretion. It's something called terminal secretion."

Terminal? I don't want to know any more.

24 March
As the World Goes By

Today I realize I'm back in Alaska, have been here over two weeks, and haven't gone to the Inlet. The time has been a blur of taking care of Bill, rarely taking a moment to go outside. Sometimes I go over to the detached garage to unpack another box or take the Malibu and drive to Fred Meyer for groceries.

The morning comes with blue sky, dazzling white snow over the Knik hayfields, craggy and sharp Chugiak Mountains, and two moose chewing the bark off the birches in the front yard. I serve Bill two small sausage patties, two scrambled eggs, half of a perfectly ripe pear, and a slice of sourdough toast with the crust trimmed, all presented on the plate to look like a clown. The morning cleanup procedure will begin in about ninety minutes.

"I have to go," Bill tells us only two or three minutes later, not ninety minutes.

Alice and Palmer handle the procedure. Bill's exhausted after Palmer lifts him to the portable toilet. I'm glad Palmer is here to do the lifting. Bill sits there on the toilet, sagging to one side, shoulders drooping, chest heaving, panting. Alice covers Bill with a blanket.

"Nurse," Aurora calls from downstairs.

Mother goes down.

Alice proceeds with a sponge bath for Bill while he sits on the toilet. I clean the kitchen and cover Bill's breakfast with tinfoil to keep it warm. Aurora's weekend helper, Jessica, a sweet, slender sixteen-year-old, arrives and begins to tidy up the living room. Palmer works on his laptop in the big blue chair, on standby to transport Bill from the toilet back to the bed. Carol arrives, says good morning to Bill, and changes the sheets on Bill's bed. Mother returns with instructions from Aurora on how to cook Bill's breakfast. Mother stiffens when she sees Carol. Bear-Bear arrives and plops down in the kitchen, waiting for someone to feed him.

Bill sits there, sagging even more, on the portable toilet in the living room as the world goes on. He passes gas profusely with great noise. We say nothing and continue our activities.

25 March
Family Meeting

"Call the troops. I want to have a meeting. Get her," Bill tells us.

He seems lucid, but I know he's not. He's in that other place. I listen for the essence of what he says and not to the words themselves, trying not to interpret literally. I sense Bill means "family" when he says "troops," and "her" is Mother.

"When do you have go back to work?" Bill asks each of us.

His worlds have collided, and he's only half talking to us, half talking to people from another world. Perhaps people he remembers from his air force days.

"Next Tuesday," Tim says.

"Then we'll have a meeting next Tuesday," Bill says.

Though he hears the answer from Tim, I sense Bill's responding to people in that other world.

"Tuesday at ten hundred hours." Bill pauses. "Where shall we meet?"

We agree to meet here at Aurora's house. Bill seems pleased.

"I need you to draw up an agenda and a list of action items." Bill looks at Alice.

She's interpreting literally. She doesn't understand Bill is trying to tie up loose ends.

"What action items do we have?" Alice asks.

"There will be changes," Bill says. "I have to catch a train."

I sense Bill is preparing to leave this world. Or is he preparing us?

"When is the date?" Bill asks Tim.

"What date?" Tim asks.

"For the milestone," Bill says.

"For the action items?" Alice asks.

"No, the date. When is it?" Bill says.

It's something about Aurora.

"Aurora and Tim will be setting a wedding date very soon now," I say to Bill, and he seems pleased. Everyone else in the room gives me a quizzical look.

"Let's talk about financial matters. We moved up here from Homer in a hurry," Bill goes on.

Yes, he is tying up loose ends.

"I want to make sure each one of you has a little gift from me," Bill says.

It's not about money.

"That's very generous of you," Aurora says.

"I need to talk about my will," Bill says.

"Your intention is to leave everything to Mother?" Alice asks.

"We need to do the preflight. We have to do the preflight," Bill says.

This time, it's about Mother.

"Bill, we will take care of Mother. I promise," I say.

Bill seems extra pleased, and everyone gives me a second quizzical look.

"What about the stair lift?" Bill asks.

"What stair lift?" Alice says.

"Stair lift?" Palmer adds.

Mother purses her lips. Aurora and Tim exchange a quick look.

"I paid twelve thousand dollars for that stair lift. I want to know the status," Bill says. He's lucid in this moment. There's coherence in his words.

Another shared look passes between Aurora and Tim, and then I realize that Bill gave Aurora $12,000 to get a stair lift for Aurora's house. Why does Bill need a stair lift? He's bedridden. Oddly, nobody addresses Bill's question.

"I don't know about the stair lift; however, I'll take the action item to get the status and get back to you," I say to Bill and look straight at Aurora. Sooner or later, I'll reckon with her.

Alice and Bill speak briefly about taxes. Bill looks tired, falls back onto his pillow and goes to sleep.

"What's this about a gift?" Aurora asks.

26 March
Relapse

"I'm very uneasy," Bill says. "My feet are so cold."

I check his feet and they're warm, but now a dark-gray, almost blue, mottled color. I get out the heating pad, slide it under Bill's feet, and turn the heat on low.

"Thank you, Roadrunner." Bill sighs and falls asleep.

"Look, his lips are blue," Mother whispers.

We watch Bill's breathing turn irregular and louder than normal—then quiet, then louder, and then quiet. There are pauses between the louder breaths. We count three seconds between breaths. The Cheyne-Stokes breathing has started. We know what that could mean. According to the hospice book we read, this breathing pattern often occurs within eight hours of death. We decide to stay up all night to keep vigil.

Mother, Alice, Palmer, and I gather in the living room while Tim and Aurora sleep downstairs. Alice and I watch a movie about dragons. Palmer works on his laptop. Mother knits. We don't talk much. The questions we have are probably similar, just as the embarrassment we feel for having the questions is similar. Will he die tonight? When? How much longer? It's been almost three weeks since Aurora called us and told us Bill was dying, though we now know that phone call was a scam. Bill could take many months to die, and I instantly feel the guilt for thinking this. Aurora! Right now, I hate her.

"When are you coming home?" Matt keeps asking during our nightly phone call.

I want to say I'll come home when Bill dies. I want to be here when it happens. What if I go home and Bill dies? What if I stay here? What about Matt? What if Bill lingers on and ultimately needs six more months to die?

"I don't want him to linger," Alice keeps saying.

There's also the money issue between Mother and Aurora, the stair lift, and the reckoning that needs to be done with Aurora. What do I do? There are no answers, and we continue to listen to Bill's irregular breathing and count the seconds between breaths, still three seconds. Perhaps he will die tonight.

Just past midnight, Bear-Bear charges out the dog door down in the landing and starts barking. I go to the window and see two moose sleeping in the front yard, a cow and last year's calf. I check Bill's feet again. Cold, but no longer gray. These mixed signals of the dying continue to confuse me. Perhaps Bill's circulatory system is breaking down. I adjust the heating pad. We watch another dragon movie.

During the next foot check, Bill's feet are warm. I turn down the heating pad and put balm on Bill's lips. We count seconds between breaths, still three seconds. Mother sleeps intermittently in the big blue chair.

"Why don't you go to bed, Mother? I'll come get you if anything happens," I say.

"Let me know if the breathing gets worse," Mother says and trudges down the hall.

Alice and I watch another movie. At three in the morning, Bill's breathing becomes regular, the Cheyne-Stokes pattern stops, and his feet are warm and pinky. Bill will not die tonight.

27 March
Sunrise

The sun is almost up, and Bill and I drink strong coffee. His eyes have sunken further into the sockets. He seems so weak. He savors his coffee, a treat only I offer.

"Everyone's always so serious," Bill says.

We're alone, and we chat in code and in and out of our private realities.

"Do you have half the table?" Bill asks.

"Sure do," I say and push aside the tray and various things on the bedside table and put down my coffee cup.

"We had to move those big buildings," Bill continues. "We used an apparatus similar to a bicycle chain."

I know Bill is referring to something back in his air force days. It doesn't matter what. I get the gist. "Isn't technology amazing?"

"When do you have to go back?" Bill asks. "Is Matt is getting restless?"

"The other night you were talking about horseradish in your sleep," I say to deflect the question. I don't want to worry Bill about issues between Matt and me.

"It's how I made money to go to school," Bill says. "You know, I keep asking about the stair lift."

"I'll find out about it."

"Made a good business out of horseradish. Now I won't eat the darn stuff," Bill says. "You're going to have to go home, Roadrunner."

"It's OK," I say.

"Not OK." Bill slurps the last of his coffee, shakily hands me his cup, and asks for more. I go to the kitchen with its small east window over the sink and morning light. No moose in the yard.

"You can walk on those walls to get to the basement," he says when I return with more coffee.

He's talking about the stairs outside. Those stairs go from the deck, down the side of the house, and down to the driveway. Very much like walking on the walls to get to the basement.

"Yes, but there is no ramp. It would be tough for you."

"That's right, that blasted stair lift," Bill says. "I paid twelve thousand dollars for it."

"I know. I'll check into it and get back to you."

"Want some coffee?" Bill offers.

"Who are you talking to?" I ask.

"My good buddy Slim," Bill says.

Red streaks of light appear through the big east window of the living room, bringing the sunrise as Bill deals with sundowner's syndrome. This is the first time the sundowner's has come at this time of day. Soon, the sundowner's and the sunrise will merge, and Bill will no longer be confused or struggle with code. He'll communicate clearly again, just not with us.

28 March
The Stair Lift

It's not easy to talk to Aurora. Yes, I'm thankful she has created a nursing home for Bill in her living room and a new home for Mother in the master bedroom, accomplished when Aurora herself is dealing with double knee replacement surgery.

Even so, I dread asking about the stair lift. I know for each question or smallest inquiry, Aurora's response will be swift, hissing, and snakelike and will involve an implication of my own incompetence, stupidity, or inability to remember. In the past her responses to questions usually involve a barrage of explanations fired so fast and with such overwhelming force that she will subdue the person asking questions, her perceived attacker, so decisively and with such finality that the person usually won't ask for further explanation.

When we have the energy, Alice or I might try to debate or argue or present a differing opinion to Aurora. This usually results in Aurora overreacting, and her onslaught becomes even more ferocious and ear piercing, bombarding our senses, ripping away at our defenses until we attack back just as ferociously and nothing is gained. Mostly, we don't risk the battle. We avoid her. We stay away from important issues. We let her dictate. It's a strategy that has served Aurora well.

I go downstairs. Aurora lies on the bed, her legs wrapped in support stockings, the new knee strapped and wrapped to the cryo machine to keep her knee cool and control the swelling. She seems calm. Bear-Bear snores in the corner. We chat in small talk, but I hope not so small that she suspects I'm preparing for something larger. I keep the pace slow and observe her reaction to the questions amid the small talk.

After ten minutes I feel safe enough to talk about the stair lift. I fully understand that I'm afraid of my own sister. I steer the conversation toward Bill and hopefully create a window of opportunity to talk about the stair lift.

"You know, Bill has asked me about the stair lift a couple times," I begin. I try to keep my voice slow and soft. I wait for it.

"How many times do I have to tell them?" Aurora's reaction is fast and sharp.

I see her clenched jaw. She stares at the television and offers no further details. Her sharp voice and tone pierce me, and I feel myself react to her, wanting to respond just as sharply.

"Well, Bill doesn't seem to remember," I say. "And I need to know so I can report back to him."

"Bill doesn't remember, Mother doesn't remember, and now you need to know." Aurora throws me a disgusted look.

You bitch. Careful. This is a crucial moment, another tipping point of sorts, a point of no return so fragile that the outcome could be changed in one slight movement and so imperceptible we could deny it ever happened. Breathe.

"I know," I lower my voice. "I'm sorry. There are so many things happening, and I really don't understand the deal with the stair lift."

"Like I told Bill, it's about the disability and the VA and the percentage!" Aurora barks at me, staring at the television. She folds her arms across her chest.

"I don't understand," I say, but slow, so very slow. And low. Keep it slow and low and calm and nonthreatening. With luck she'll respond the same.

Aurora explains that Bill paid $12,000 for the stair lift because originally the VA would not pay for it. Bill is now being reevaluated by the VA. She expects the reevaluation to reflect 50 percent disability, which means the VA will pay for 50 percent of the stair lift, which means Bill will be reimbursed $6,000.

"So we are awaiting the results of the evaluation?" I ask.

It seems odd that Mother, the bookkeeper, doesn't remember this detail or that Bill, the man who invests in stocks, doesn't remember it. I dislike family drama. I'd prefer to run away or walk along the Inlet. I've been here three weeks and have not walked along the Inlet.

"That's how it is," Aurora says. She readjusts the blankets on her legs and loosens her barricade-arm stance.

"That's pretty cool, if you can get Bill reimbursed six thousand dollars," I say.

Aurora relaxes because she thinks I believe her.

"You betcha," Aurora says.

I know she's lying.

29 March
The Inlet

> My name is Father's Joy. When the wind whispers answers, I go to the Inlet to ask what will happen. In the wind I can hear. "You will sleep in a painted house over the Knik. You will climb to Eureka. You will sing with snow goose in spring. You will take tea with moose and bear."
> Where will Bill go? "To Denali the Great One. To Resurrection Bay to kayak. To Hope to swim with beluga. To Eureka—you will see him there." Can you ease his pain? Give him one easy breath? Another chance to say good-bye? "He'll feel no pain across the Inlet. He'll smell sea grass. He'll say good-bye when the fireweed blooms." Why do I struggle? Sink hip-deep in mud? Race against high tide? "It is the universe. It is life. It is one precious moment."
> —Abby Miller, morning pages

I'm exhausted.

"When are you coming home?" Matt asks every night.

The hospice nurse, Tad, arrives, and Aurora sends him upstairs to the living room. Tad wears his long black hair pulled back in a ponytail, dresses in black, and wears bold silver and turquoise jewelry. He hails from New Mexico. Of course, I instantly like Tad. Aurora stays downstairs. Tad goes to work. Alice comes in and begins talking with Tad.

Alice describes the situation. Palmer confirms. Alice describes what is needed. Mother hangs off to the side. Nobody talks to Mother. Alice is still talking. I know Mother has her own concerns, but she is not consulted. I know Aurora is coordinating many different agencies and services, but now Alice seems to be recoordinating. She is still talking. Bill is quiet and listening to what Alice says he needs.

Alice appears in front of me and says something.

"Damn it, can't you just shut up?" I'm so tired. I want to go home. Don't think I want to stay until…

Alice stares at me, wide-eyed. "It's OK. Calm down."

Her voice feels patronizing, solicitous, and dismissive. I'd like to slap her.

"No, it's not OK. I don't know what's happening, and everyone is coordinating and saying what needs to be done, and I want to help but don't know how and don't know who is doing what!"

I go outside into the sharp, cold white air and take Bear-Bear for a walk. The craggy Chugiaks are bright above the trees against the clear sky, and the Inlet lies beyond those trees.

When I return to the living room, Alice tells me the hospice nurse believes Bill's time is in months, not days.

"Is this a surprise?" I say.

I hear Aurora whisper to Tim, "Take her to the Inlet."

We drive to Anchorage, toward the Inlet, passing the new moose gates at Eagle River, the snow dumps, and the ice sculptures. Tim drops me off at the Anchorage Museum. We arrange to meet in four hours at the Cabin Fever Café.

Clothes make a difference in Alaska, and I'm wearing sissy clothes. I go to Nordstrom and buy long underwear, a scarf, and extra socks, all on sale.

"Can you tell we are ready for spring?" The clerk points to racks of summer clothes.

I walk toward the Inlet, past L Street where the sound of traffic disappears and the air turns quiet. And there it is, the Inlet, full of ice floes and bergs. Mt. Susitna looms on the horizon. I walk along the Toni Knowles Coastal Trail. A man sits on a park bench.

"Is it Spring yet?" the man asks. He's obviously delighted for this sunny day.

A baby moose appears in the trail. Stop, freeze, and watch. The baby reaches up and pulls down birch branches and chews away. Where's the mother moose? Two large ears appear behind a huge snowbank. Don't move. Back up slowly. Baby moose climbs up and over the snowbank to join the mother moose. Baby sinks, at times, up to its hips in powder snow and struggles to keep its balance. Once reunited, the baby and mother moose munch bark off the birch trees.

The Alaska Range sprawls across the north horizon. Sunlight on the south face creates shadows on the north sides that seem to move. The snowy peaks and glaciers contrast smartly against the sky's blueness. Denali appears, but only for a moment, and most people in Anchorage momentarily stop and stare toward the mountain. The Chugiaks sprawl along the horizon far to the southeast.

I walk toward Ship Creek and pass children sledding down the slope. The sledding is marginal with the snow inconsistent down the slope, crust giving way to powder, then wet, then melting, then slushy, then hard packed, and then more crust giving way to powder. Yes, this is spring with the annual flocks of birds and broken ice floes. Ah, the Inlet. It renews me.

30 March
A Lucky Man

The priest from Mother's church, Father Steve, arrives to talk to Mother and say a blessing for Bill. After he leaves, the hospice chaplain from the VA, Ron, arrives to talk with Bill. Mother serves pie and ice cream. Alice feeds pie and ice cream to Bill, one spoonful for Bill, and one spoonful for Alice. We all sit there in the living room with Bill in his hospital bed, a fire crackling and our lips smacking on pie.

"You are a lucky man," Chaplain Ron says. "You get to die at home surrounded by family."

"Yes, these are precious moments that most people don't get," Aurora coos.

Fraud.

Bill and Chaplain Ron talk about their military days. It's five o'clock in the afternoon, the time when the moose come out, so I sit on the couch, watch the yard below, and look for moose. The wind is blowing harder than usual—the spring wind that blows like a demon down the Knik.

31 March
Needs of the Family

It is six in the morning. I get up to work on a consulting project. Bill is awake. I give him water and juice. He's still groggy, and perhaps he'll sleep more. The home health aide will be here in two hours and will prepare breakfast for him. But Bill doesn't sleep.

"My feet are cold," Bill says.

I check his feet, and indeed his feet are cold. "I'll get the heating pad."

"My shoes hurt, too," Bill says.

"No wonder, you've got the wrong shoes on. You need your sleeping shoes."

"Roadrunner, I don't feel good enough for funny stuff," Bill says simply and matter-of-factly. I instantly feel bad because Bill feels bad.

"I'm sorry, Bill. I was just—"

"I know, Roadrunner. I know." The fatigue in Bill's face becomes more apparent.

"My knee hurts," Bill says quietly, again a simple fact, not a complaint. His eyes are crusty at the corners again, and his lips look parched.

"Do you want some pain medicine?"

"No, not yet," Bill says. "Music?"

I play a choral piece by the Anchorage Arctic Ensemble. Bill loves the Ensemble. He and Mother would buy tickets whenever the Ensemble came to Homer. Sometimes the Ensemble would play out on the Homer Spit, and the sounds of waves or wind or birds would become part of the concert. We listen to the music as I put the atropine eye drops in Bill's eyes, wipe his face with warm wash towels, and apply balm to those parched lips.

The home health aide is late again, so I prepare breakfast for Bill and Mother. After breakfast Bill informs us he needs to use the toilet. After sitting on the portable toilet for an hour, Bill cannot produce the bowel movement.

"I'm too tired to poop," Bill says.

I'm not sure if he's trying to be funny, so I don't laugh. We put him back in the bed, but the move exhausts both Bill and me. Bill no longer has the strength to hold onto me when I move him. Aurora is still downstairs asleep. She has missed two doctor appointments. I think I heard Tim leaving for work earlier this morning. Where are Alice and Palmer?

At eleven thirty Aurora comes upstairs and asks us all to join her in the living room. She's still in her pajamas, and her hair flies wild all around her head like a hair halo. She informs us that Tim's soon-to-be ex-wife has accused Tim of molesting their young daughter, that the state troopers went to Tim's workplace just a couple of hours ago and arrested Tim for several counts of child abuse. Tim is in the Palmer jail right now. Funny, I didn't hear any phones ringing. How was Aurora notified?

Tim is not divorced yet? Child abuse? Why would Aurora tell us here in the middle of the living room with Bill listening? Throughout her explanation Aurora pauses and bursts into tears. She feeds off the drama; she craves it. The drama queen. The drama pig.

"The divorce lawyer will give us a package deal," Aurora explains. "He will handle the divorce and the legal stuff for the child abuse charges for fifty-five thousand dollars."

Mother's lower lip begins to quiver. I don't know if Bill is listening.

"I'm not going to let Mother give you fifty-five thousand dollars," I say quickly.

"I didn't ask for fifty-five thousand dollars," Aurora snaps. "I can put a second mortgage on the house." Aurora's cell phone rings, and she goes over to the dining table to take the call.

The home phone rings. I look at Mother on the couch. Her face is pale.

"Yes, I'm working it now. Bye," Aurora says in the voice she uses when talking to Tim. Aurora's cell phone rings again.

We hear the doorbell ring. Bear-Bear runs downstairs and barks aggressively.

"Someone get the door. It's the hospice social worker," Aurora yells.

Social worker? Mother doesn't move.

"Someone get Bear-Bear," Aurora yells again. Why didn't she tell us the social worker from hospice was coming today?

The home phone rings again. I hear a car drive up when I go downstairs to contain the dog and greet the social worker. In a few minutes, I hear the voices of Alice and Palmer outside by the car.

"Hello, I'm Renata." The pretty woman, about thirty years old, introduces herself and shows me her identification badge.

"Hi, I'm Abby," I say. "Bill's upstairs."

We go upstairs, and Mother is still on the couch, very still, almost frozen to the couch. Bill is awake, and I introduce Bill to Renata. Alice and Palmer appear and more introductions follow. Aurora stays at the dining table and talks on the phone. She makes no move to greet or even recognize Renata.

"Aurora must have coordinated your visit with us, but she is unfortunately handling an emergency right now," I say. "I assume you are here to check on Bill?"

"Yes, and to evaluate the needs of the family." Renata takes out a notebook and pen.

"We're all family here," Palmer says. "We can speak for the family needs."

"We need a plan for taking care of Bill," Alice says. "We need more coverage with the home health aides, and they need to be strong enough to lift him from the bed to the toilet or to the shower," Alice says.

Renata writes notes. Aurora continues to answer the phones at the dining table. At times her voice grows loud and rises above our conversation in the living room. The noise of the different conversations and the phones and the dog barking makes me dizzy. All this noise and confusion doesn't bother anyone else?

"Yes, I told you, I'll use the truck title," Aurora says. "Yes, I have the money."

"Can we have a home health aide come every day?" Alice asks.

"Why are you here?" Bill asks Renata.

"I'm here to make sure everything is OK," Renata says.

"What about respite care for the weekend, perhaps on Sunday?" Alice asks.

Bear-Bear continues to bark downstairs where I locked him in the game room. The phone rings again. I turn off the music.

"The real problem is lifting him," Palmer adds. "It's not much help when our home health aide is pregnant and can't do any lifting."

"Plus she's always late or sick or going to a doctor's appointment," Alice says.

"Not OK," Bill says.

I sit next to Bill on the little stool and realize I haven't brushed my hair for two days.

"Damn it, I'll get the money. Just stop calling every five minutes so I can do what I need to do," Aurora shouts into the phone.

Renata glances over at Aurora and writes a note.

"What about the pain medications?" Alice asks.

"How about something to calm him down?" Palmer says.

Renata continues to write notes.

"Why don't we ask Bill what he needs?" I ask.

1 April
The Balance

Tim has to stay in the Palmer Jail for at least four more days because of legal complications or documentation. I'm not really sure which or what, and I don't really care. Visiting hours at the jail are at six in the morning and again at six in the evening. Each time, visitors are allowed thirty minutes, and each time, Aurora is there in a nice dress and fresh makeup, using her cane to assist her new knee.

Meanwhile, I search the boxes in her bedroom for the titles to the Homer house and the Malibu. I don't want those documents falling into Aurora's hands. Alice folds napkins on the other side of the bed. An old western movie plays on the television on the highboy.

"We need to give the lawyer a retainer." Aurora enters the room, just back from visiting hours. She leans on her cane, breathing heavy from the exertion of coming upstairs on that new knee and looking down at the floor.

"I thought you were going to get a second mortgage on the house," I say.

"The bank won't do it because the house note is in arrears," Aurora says.

"You're late on your house payments?" Mother's eyes widen.

"Don't worry. You have to be at least six months behind in payments before the bank will begin foreclosure proceedings," Alice says.

"It's been almost seven months," Aurora says and sits on the edge of the bed and faces the television.

"I thought I gave you the money to bring your house note up to date." Mother's lower lip twitches.

"No, you didn't. That money was for something else," Aurora says.

"But I don't know the balance," Mother says suddenly, and her lip twitch turns into a quiver.

The hairs on the back of my neck stand up and vibrate. Mother has refused to go online to check her bank balances. But I will.

While they talk, I retrieve my laptop, sit on the floor, and position myself so nobody can see the laptop screen. I log in to Mother's Wells Fargo account and immediately see the balance is $425. That seems low to me, and soon the reason is clear. The balance was $50,000 five weeks ago. The list of debits astounds me: $7,000 to Aurora's psychiatrist, $7,000 to Tim's lawyer, $5,000 to a second lawyer, several entries around $500 to the commissary for groceries, $2,000 to a men's clothing store, several withdrawals for $1,000 in cash, many entries for restaurants and gas stations, another $5,000 for a third lawyer, and a long list of entries for items purchased at Fred Meyer on almost a daily basis. Plus there are entries where Mother wrote checks to Aurora for large amounts. My head swims. Three lawyers? A psychiatrist? Over $2,000 in groceries?

"Can't you and your lawyer come up with a payment plan?" Alice asks.

"He won't do it," Aurora says, watches the television, and waits.

This is part of her strategy. She will wait and play her passive-aggressive game, sometimes in sharp, short telegraphic sentences that force us to pump her for information, until we ultimately offer to pay for whatever needs paying.

"Why not?" Alice asks. "Lots of lawyers do payment plans."

"It's like a down payment to show good faith," Aurora says.

What do you know about good faith? You just siphoned $50,000 out of Mother's Wells Fargo account.

"That money was for you to bring the house note up to date," Mother says.

"No, it wasn't. You're thinking about something else," Aurora says. "Tim has to stay in jail until we pay the lawyer."

Oh, let him rot in jail.

I quickly scan the list of entries in the Wells Fargo account and look for an amount big enough to pay for six months of house payments. I figure the amount would be about $15,000. Nothing. I check last month's entries. Nothing. I check three months ago. There it is. I see the digital copy of a check written to Aurora for $16,000. There's a note on the check that says, "House." I see another copy of a check written to Aurora. This time the check is for $19,000, and the note on the check says, "Truck payoff." I add up the numbers and realize Mother has given Aurora, knowingly or not, almost $75,000 in the last three months. Sadly, I realize it isn't enough money. It will never be enough. Never.

"Get a new lawyer that will work with you." Alice studies the stack of napkins she just folded. She rearranges the blues from dark blue to light blue and then restacks the napkins with the folds lying all in the same direction. She studies the napkins again. "You probably want them ironed," Alice says to Aurora.

"He's the best lawyer in town," Aurora says.

I understand now why Mother didn't want to see the balance on her bank accounts. She probably had an idea of how much money was slipping away. Then there's the Aurora outburst, that quick, sharp, attacking response that causes most of us not to question Aurora. I suspect Mother writes the checks so Aurora won't have an outburst, so Aurora won't think Mother is a mean mom or ungrateful for helping out with Bill, and then, with a sinking feeling, I realize Mother is afraid say no to Aurora.

"Let me get this straight. Tim has to stay in jail another four days, maybe longer, because of legal issues or some sort of legal paper work," Alice says. "And you are saying this guy is the best lawyer in town?"

"Has the bank initiated any foreclosure proceedings?" Mother asks. "What if the bank takes the house? Where would we take Bill?"

"He'll be dead by the time the bank foreclosures," Alice says. She flushes and looks down at her napkins.

"Why don't you just use your debit card for Mother's Wells Fargo account?" I want to see how she responds because I know she knows there's not enough money in that account.

"Well, I need to talk to Mama first," Aurora says. "Oh, Tim had big bruises on his face tonight."

I've seen this tactic many times. Aurora will feed our guilt or our fear until we have no choice but to pay. If she plays the tactic well enough, we will volunteer to pay. Do what I want, or I'll kill myself. Do what I want, or you'll pay the consequences. Or, even more merciless, do what I want, or I won't love you. Merciless because it never ends.

"Plus, they won't let him have his meds," Aurora says, and her eyes swell with tears.

How does she do that, cry on demand?

"How much is the retainer?" Mother asks.

"Why does he have bruises? Is Tim getting beat up?" Alice asks.

"Ten percent." Aurora sniffles.

"How much is that?" Alice asks, but Aurora ignores her.

"Well, he needs a lawyer, of course," I say.

Aurora's shoulders relax slightly.

"Mother, are you OK with Aurora using the Wells Fargo account for the retainer?" I watch for Aurora's response.

"I guess so," Mother says and seems confused.

Alice glances up from her napkin folding and refolding. Aurora looks at me sideways and narrows her eyes.

"Never mind, I'll use the fucking title to the truck." Aurora stands abruptly.

Checkmate.

She leans on her cane to half walk and half limp out of the room. "Never mind that Tim's in jail getting beat up by other inmates and can't get his meds."

"You just said it was OK for her to use the Wells Fargo debit card," Alice says after Aurora is gone. "Why is she all mad?"

"Gather around, folks." I get up off the floor and go sit on the bed. "I'll show you why."

"What about the house note?" Mother says.

"Dunno, Mother, but look at this first." I point to the laptop screen. "This is your Wells Fargo account." I give Mother and Alice time to squint and study the laptop screen.

Oh, Mother, what happened between you and Aurora after I went away to college? Does it matter? Does it only matter that you still feel guilty and Aurora still feels unloved?

I'd like to choke Aurora, call the troopers, and have her arrested for bilking my eighty-year-old Mother. Oh, Mother, Aurora will take every dime you have. She'll always burst out and react and feed off your guilt and make you pay.

Mother quickly sees the balance of the Wells Fargo account is $425. She does not look over the expenditures, where the money went, or how much money is gone. She cares only about the balance. Incredibly, she seems satisfied.

"Are you interested in recouping any of this money?" I ask Mother.

"I don't think so. It's too much stress," Mother says. "Besides, I have to live here."

"It looks like a big chunk of this money was spent for Tim." Alice shakes her head.

"Did you give Aurora permission to spend all this money?" I ask.

"It doesn't matter," Mother says, and an eerie glassiness comes over her eyes, as if she sees something we can't see. "What if she goes out and kills herself?"

2 April
JB

"All these checks you wrote to Aurora—if you wanted to say no, what made you say yes?" I ask Mother.

"I didn't feel I had a choice, and I don't want Aurora to think I'm mean," Mother says. "Plus I don't want to seem ungrateful for all she's done for me and Bill."

All that Aurora has done for her and Bill? What would that be? Create a crisis everywhere she goes? Anger rises in my throat. Focus. Control the anger.

"She gave me a list of other expenses she needs." Mother hands me a list.

On the list, Aurora notes she needs $1,575 for the Wasilla Funeral Home, another $7,500 for Tim's divorce lawyer, and $5,296 for the house. Mother is not sure what is meant by "the house." I discover Mother has already written the check for Tim's divorce lawyer. Aurora told us yesterday that she needed $55,000 more for Tim's divorce lawyer. I'm dizzy with the numbers and the staggering amount the numbers represent, even more dizzy with why the money is needed. It seems like Mother's paying for the same thing over and over.

"I need to balance my checkbooks," Mother says.

She then balances the Wells Fargo account, never once questioning the low balance but fussing for over an hour about two missing pennies. She finds the two pennies and sits back satisfied.

"Mother, aren't you concerned that over fifty thousand dollars has been drained from your account in the past three months?" I ask.

"What can I do?" Mother says. "Now I need to balance the USAA checkbook."

Mother balances her USAA checking account, which also shows large checks written to Aurora for lawyers and psychiatrists and items so similar to the entries in the Wells Fargo account that I think I'm seeing double. Mother balances the checkbook to the penny.

"Why does Tim need all these psychiatric evaluations? Why do they cost so much?" I ask. "Who are all these lawyers?"

"I don't know." Mother shrugs. "I don't know—I never know." Mother's voice becomes shrill. "I only know it's always an emergency. She always needs the money *now*. She only tells me not to worry. Last year we paid off her truck and all her debts. Four years ago we did the same, and four years before that we did the same. I keep trying to help her, but she doesn't listen, and there's always a new emergency or a new crisis and never an explanation. When she wants money like that and then says don't worry, it triggers memories of Jared."

I gasp. Jared is my biological father. I refer to him as JB, and he's the man I've hated most my life. I hate him for how he treated Mother, how he left her penniless, left her with the IRS pounding on the door and seizing the house and everything she had because that damn miserable JB never paid the taxes.

"I'm scared she'll force me to sell the Homer house, and I'll have nothing." Mother's voice becomes an ear-piercing shrill, and then she stops talking and starts rocking back and forth.

Oh, Mother, what are you trying to prove? That you love Aurora? I know Aurora came along too late, an unwanted pregnancy after your marriage to JB went wrong, after the priest told you that your marriage was your cross to bear. You stayed with JB and gave birth to Aurora, who represented that cross. You stayed until JB abandoned you, and then when you realized Aurora was Aurora and not JB, it was too late, and the guilt consumed you. Does Aurora know? Of course she does, and she makes you pay. Just like JB did.

3 April
A Precious Moment

I'm tired of cooking and keep the cooking process simple, and meals emerge from whatever is available or requested. Corn chips and chocolate milk are perfectly fine for breakfast, Riesling and cookies are reasonable for lunch, and anything with pears is organic. Tonight we are having heart-shaped pancakes with blueberries and vanilla ice cream, except for Alice and Palmer, who are having protein milkshakes.

I plate up for Bill. Mother serves him while I finish plating for her and me. I take our plates to Bill's bedside table. I pull up a chair, and we have supper together. Bill lies in his hospital bed, head propped to one side so he can swallow without choking. Mother helps him to eat between bites of her own meal. I sit on the opposite side of the table with the drugs and the tissue box and the eye drops. For a moment we are a normal family having a normal supper together. This is a precious moment, a real one, and the rarity is I know it in this very moment of its happening.

4 April
White Envelopes

> My name is Father's Joy. I was my mother's joy instead. On the day I was born, she made a white envelope for me. Then out on Ninilchik cliff, she faced the wind, called my name to the Inlet, and held out that envelope. "This is for her college," she said. She managed all her money in white envelopes—for birthdays, Christmas, the Sears order. Each month she scrimped, saved, and siphoned from other envelopes for my envelope.
>
> The spring I graduated from high school we celebrated next to the Kenai all iced over, creaking and moaning and ready to break up. Trees glazed in ice sparkled like diamonds. She gave me a pink mug with my school logo and the worn white envelope with my name. And the pride in her eyes out-sparkled the ice glinting on the Kenai, out-twinkled the diamond trees.
>
> —Abby Miller, morning pages

"Palmer and I are going home tomorrow," Alice announces. "Everything seems in order here, and Bill isn't going to die anytime soon."

I'm envious because I want to go home, too.

We now have additional home health aides, which gives us professional help for four hours daily and eight hours on Sunday for respite. Along with the pregnant Carol, we have Darlene and Mike. The hospice nurse comes weekly. The VA chaplain, Ron, also comes weekly. The hospice social worker comes every two weeks. Mother's priest, Father Steve, comes intermittently.

Jessica, Aurora's weekend helper, comes on Friday and stays until Monday morning. Aurora's handyman comes and goes. Once a month, the mobile dog groomer comes to wash and tidy up Bear-Bear. Aurora leaves every day at six in the morning and six in the evening to visit Tim at the Palmer Jail. This is order, the new normal.

"When are you coming home?" Matt continues to ask.

"I'm worried about leaving Mother here alone with Aurora," I say.

"I understand that," Matt says." But when are you coming home?"

I think about what leaving Mother alone up here with Aurora might mean. Probably Aurora will try to get more of Mother's money. I'm not sure how much money this involves. I know Mother has investments and retirement accounts. The Homer house and the Malibu are paid for, and she has no debt. I still haven't found the deed to the Homer house.

"No, I didn't authorize my daughter Aurora to liquidate any of our assets," I hear Mother tell Ben, Bill's investment broker of many years.

"I'm sure it's a misunderstanding," I hear Mother later tell the lawyer who's been their family lawyer for over twenty years. "No, I'm sure I don't want her having full access to Bill's estate."

I need a plan. I need to put Mother back in control of her finances and protect her from Aurora. I need to tell

Aurora that her manipulation of Mother stops now. I need to run away, get away from this drama and crisis. I need to hate Aurora. I have not felt hate like this since JB. Yes, and I need Bill to die. I'm embarrassed to think this part, so I continue sorting through Mother and Bill's piles of papers and documents.

I find old checks, bank statements with Mother's careful notations on the back where she reconciled her checkbooks, stock reports and notices, and receipts for carpeting or appliances. Then I find the envelopes—worn, yellowed envelopes with notes or names or dates written on them. An envelope marked "1979" with a canceled check inside written for $2,500 to Aurora. An envelope marked "Aurora" with over a dozen canceled checks, each written for $1,000. Envelopes marked "Truck—2000," "Truck—2006," and "Truck—2011." Bill and Mother never owned a truck, so I look inside the envelopes and see canceled checks for $13,000, $15,000, and $18,000, each featuring the note, "pay off Aurora's truck." Envelopes marked, "Anchorage house," "Wasilla house," "lawyer—Aurora," and "therapist—Aurora" and another envelope for the Wasilla house.

Seeing these white envelopes reminds me of that envelope of long ago with my name on it. Mother had taken out an annuity when I was born. She'd put the annuity in an envelope and gave JB twenty-five dollars every month for eighteen years to pay on it. She did the same for Alice. Mother gave us those envelopes for high school graduation gifts. The annuities should've been enough to pay for our college. But in all of eighteen years, JB never paid once on those annuities.

"What should we do?" I had asked Alice.

"We make a plan," Alice said calmly.

And we did. We didn't waste time hating JB. Besides, Alice could never hate him. Our plan was to apply for scholarships, take out student loans, get part-time jobs, and manage what little money we had in white envelopes.

We never told Mother. How she beamed when she attended our graduations. Later, she beamed even more when she slipped the doctoral hood over my head.

To this day I bristle when I think of JB and those envelopes.

I want to go home. That's not true. I want to run away. But there are other envelopes, ones that make me smile, and some still have money in them—envelopes that are marked "vacation" or "garden" or "Bear-Bear" or "anniversary" or "church."

But so many of the envelopes reflect how Mother's life is punctuated by one Aurora crisis after another. Surely Mother realizes this. Is she tired of it? I remember Aurora's phone calls at three in the morning with a crisis usually involving a man who was married, but not to Aurora, and, invariably, he would be abusive to Aurora. I would talk to her, sometimes for hours, until she felt or seemed calmer, years and years of this. When I first moved to New Mexico, I remember too vividly talking to her one late night, music and sounds of water in the background, how her voice slurred and the phone went dead as it fell from her hand into the bath water. I remember calling 911 in Anchorage and saying the critical words "danger to self or others" and how they called me from Aurora's house in less than five minutes and said they found her in the bathtub with her wrists slit, unconscious.

"It's close," they told me. "She might not make it."

I authorized Aurora's commitment for psychiatric evaluation at Providence Hospital and then requested protective custody for her dog. When Aurora was stable, I told her what I'd done.

"Every time you do that, I'll have you committed." I can still hear and feel myself saying it. To my knowledge Aurora hasn't done it again.

5 April
Jessica

I sleep until eight and wake to a morning headache and an overall stiffness from lack of exercise.

"Alice and Palmer have already left for the airport," Jessica tells me.

Still groggy, I check on Bill. "I'll be back after I take a shower and make you some breakfast," I say, but Bill's asleep.

Foot check: one foot warm and one foot cool. His lips are pale blue. A faint stinky smell lingers around him. I hesitate to disturb him to clean him up. There, he's awake now. I don't think he's aware he needs cleaning. Oh, he sleeps now.

"Aurora told me to make breakfast," Jessica says.

She is a slender, pretty sixteen-year-old with short boyish hair. She first seems quiet and even, meek, but that's only an outward appearance because Jessica is tougher than she seems, spending her weekends working and doing chores for Aurora. These chores are never soft or delicate, rather the chores of teenage humility and embarrassment—gathering trash, going to the dump, shoveling piles of dog poop, scrubbing toilets, washing strange underwear, and making breakfast for old people. Defying the nature of the chores, Jessica works in a soft and delicate manner. Her movements are subtle and accomplished in a series of small, quiet steps. She brings grace to the trash.

"If you want to do some other chore that Aurora gave you, I can make breakfast." I start planning what to cook.

"No, I'll do it," Jessica says. She continues her work in her quiet, elegant manner. She takes out three plates, one for Bill, one for Mother and I assume one for me.

I pour coffee and am embarrassed she's cooking for me and because I'm still in my pajamas.

"You don't need a plate for me. I don't eat breakfast," I tell Jessica. "I usually just have a protein bar." My manner is not graceful or subtle. I feel clumsy and should thank her for cooking, but I don't. I take my coffee and retreat into the computer room where I hide in my pajamas.

There's an e-mail from Matt: "Come home."

I hear Aurora's voice in the kitchen. Her voice is light and easy as she gives directions to Jessica on peeling carrots and stacking pans correctly. I think of the faint stinky smell that lingers around Bill.

6 April
Rally III

Mother and I are alone with Bill. Darlene, the new home health aide, does not show up. Aurora doesn't explain why. We do our best to provide care for Bill. Aurora stays downstairs and hasn't talked with me much. In past times Aurora and I drank coffee together, wandered around in flea markets, and went on adventures. I miss Aurora.

We finally see Aurora when she comes upstairs to rearrange the furniture because the hospital bed is too close to the window.

"Everyone keeps closing the curtains to keep the glare off Bill, which puts my plants in the shade," Aurora explains and moves the furniture and Bill's bed, with Bill in it. She hobbles and hops around on her new knees, a woman with a mission to save her plants.

I'm happy to see Tad, the hospice nurse, when he arrives for his weekly visit. Bill's asleep, and I feel comfortable telling Tad about Bill's blue hands and feet and the Cheyne-Stokes breathing and all the signs of dying.

"Isn't the time close at hand?" I ask.

"Hmm, not soon," Tad tells me. "Possibly months away."

Months?

"In fact, the pneumonia is gone," Tad says after listening to Bill's lungs.

"But those blue hands and feet."

"When the time comes, yes, the hands and feet usually become mottled blue, but they will be very cold, almost ice cold," Tad explains. "And they'll stay that way, not turn blue and then turn pink or warm again. And it's different for everyone. There are tendencies and signs we often see, but in reality the process can be different for every person," he adds.

"But what about the Cheyne-Stokes breathing? The hospice pamphlet says—" I pause.

"Just normal apnea, or it may be diminished breathing due to diminished lung function, which means Bill is not getting enough oxygen, which means his feet and hands and lips may come and go blue," Tad says. "See how it all works together?"

"And the decreased urine output?"

"Probably dehydration," Tad says.

"And the decreasing BMs?"

"Probably constipation," Tad says.

"And the picking of the sheets and the grasping and clutching of the rail?" I continue.

"Probably a normal reflex action related to the fear of falling off the bed," Tad says. "I'll show you how to use a draw sheet to safely roll him."

"And talking to and seeing people at night who aren't really here?" I ask.

"He's talking to those on the other side," Tad smiles.

The other side? Why didn't I think of that? I wonder who waits for Bill on the other side.

"But how will we know it's time?" I ask. "How will we know, when the signs are so confusing?"

"The signs are only half present. What you have observed is indeed accurate, but what you're seeing is a body slowly fading and shutting down, not a body actively dying," Tad says softly. "That's why the signs are only half there. When the time comes, look for two blue feet that are very cold and stay that way. Then it's probably time."

"How long does he have?" I ask.

"We can't be sure. A lot depends on his genetics, his will to live, his desire to fight," Tad says. "Bill's strong for his eighty-nine years. A lot will depend on Bill."

I walk with Tad downstairs and thank him. Bear-Bear runs in through the dog door and starts to bark, but when he sees Tad, Bear-Bear stops barking. Tad gives me and the dog a hug.

"You folks are doing OK," Tad says. "This sometimes tears families apart."

I go back upstairs and sit on the stool next to Bill's bed in the new, not-so-sunny place in the living room.

"Psst," Bill says, and I look at Bill. "Both my parents lived to be one hundred years old, so I've got strong genetics." Bill chuckles. "I may be around for a while."

7 April
Dust

Coughing. Everyone coughs here. Everyone says, "It's the dust." Odd. Out in the yard, the last layer of snow still covers the ground, which means there is no bare ground, mud, or dirt or any other thing that creates dust.

"When are you coming home?" Matt asks again.

I keep telling him I don't know. How long will he accept that answer?

I clean all the surfaces in Aurora's house, wash the knick-knacks, wipe the dust off the plants, clean the mirrors, and clean out the fireplace. Bill watches me.

"Watch out for those people in the fireplace," Bill says.

"They're not here right now," I say.

"Come here," Bill says.

He holds out his shaky old hand to me, and his hand is warm. My own hand is cold. His hand is blue and trembles. My hand is pinkish and is shaky from the nervous agitation of the dusting.

"How are you doing?" he says.

"OK."

"Not OK," Bill says. "Stop the dusting and go home."

8 April
Jennifer

In the living room, a new person arranges blankets around Bill. "Who are you?

"I'm Jennifer, from hospice." She moves around the bed to check the catheter bag.

I notice Bill watching Jennifer. He seems confused. He looks at me, looks at Jennifer again. "Have we met?" Bill asks Jennifer.

"No, I don't think so," Jennifer says.

"You were here before?" Bill asks. He picks at the sheets and blankets, pulling them up into a wad.

"I'm pretty sure not." Jennifer finishes arranging the sheets and blankets.

"Yes, you came once before." Bill seems agitated and picks at the sheets. "I remember you."

"Oh, yes, I guess I was here before," Jennifer says.

"I knew it." Bill stares at Jennifer.

"I must've made a mistake," Jennifer says.

"I don't want you here." Bill stares at Jennifer.

"OK," Jennifer says.

"Not OK. Go and don't come back," Bill says.

"What should I do?" Jennifer asks me.

"Apparently, you've been fired, and the man says to leave," I say.

"I'm so sorry about this. I came several months ago when Bill first came up here, and Aurora said I reminded Bill of someone he didn't like," Jennifer tells me. "Aurora asked me to come back and said that Bill had dementia and he wouldn't remember me, but he does."

Jennifer apologizes again and leaves. Bill remains agitated all day. He grows more agitated as evening approaches and sundowner's syndrome falls over him. I bring him cookies.

"I don't want you here," Bill tells me when I sit in my usual place on the stool next to his bed.

Is he talking to me?

"You're not listening." Bill's voice is strong and harsh. "Go away, and don't come back."

I stand up and watch Bill watch me, daring me, confronting me, demanding me to go away. I hide in the kitchen and eat cookies, noticing someone has spilled flour all over the floor. I sweep up the flour to calm myself, to avoid the realization that Bill doesn't recognize me.

9 April
Where's Your Mother?

"Did your mother get any sleep?" Bill asks.

"Did your mother get some supper?" Bill asks.

"Did your mother go to church?" Bill asks.

"This is the most intimate they have been in years," Alice says. What a dumb thing to say.

"Where's your mother?" Bill asks.

"She's sleeping on the couch," I say.

"Is she still in her pajamas?" Bill asks.

"Yes," I reply, and Bill seems pleased, and he, in turn, sleeps.

Perhaps Alice is right. There does seem to be an odd intimacy here.

"Where's your mother?" Bill asks when he wakes.

"She's taking a shower," I tell Bill. "She'll be right back."

"She'll be in there forever. Why do you women take so long to get ready?" Bill fidgets with the sheets.

"Well, you could use some cleaning up," I say. "You smell like a mule."

"Roadrunner, what in the blazes does that mean?" Bill says. "I've smelled some fine mules back on the farm."

I sponge bathe Bill and listen to his stories about mules and C-130s. I rub lotion on his skin, place a foam pad between his knees, and replace his bed shirt with a fresh one.

"Were you surprised at how big it is?" Bill asks me.

It? Oh dear. You can't talk about "it" to me. Is this the brainstem reptilian reflex that I read about? Though not sure what it means. The hospice literature says it's something patients say or do that might not seem consistent with a person's character, often involving basic human functions, such as the size of "it."

"I was both shocked and amazed," I tell Bill. He chuckles.

"Where is your mother?" Bill glances around the living room. "Is the car ready?"

"Yes. Where're you going?"

"Not sure," Bill says. "Slim wants to go fishing over by Seward."

"It's a bit early for fishing."

I can almost feel Slim here, egging Bill to take a quick fishing trip up to Seward or Anchor River or even out on the Homer Spit at the Fishing Hole where the tourists gather. Bill was heartbroken when Slim died two years ago.

"Where's your mother," Bill says again. "I've got to tell her Slim's here."

10 April
Darlene

"No, we don't want a replacement," Aurora tells the hospice supervisor. Darlene, the new home health aide, has caught the flu. "Bill likes Darlene."

Not long after, Mother comes to me, pale. "They sent Carol," Mother whispers.

"Talk to me, Mother," I say. "What's bothering you?"

"She can't help me. She's pregnant. All she can do is housework or cook," Mother's voice is still a whisper. "She costs me four hundred dollars a week, and all she does is sit around."

I go out to the living room. Carol sits on the couch, watching the morning news with Bill.

"Hi, Carol. We didn't know you were coming today," I begin.

"Oh." Carol seems surprised but not genuinely surprised—perhaps surprised that I talk to her or perhaps surprised I might interrupt her work of watching TV.

"Aurora said I should…" Carol describes a list of things that Aurora wants.

"You know, Carol, it's not about what Aurora wants; it's about what my mother wants," I say. "My mother pays your salary, not Aurora."

Carol looks more surprised—this time more authentically surprised.

"I believe my mother has told you this."

"Oh, I know," Carol says.

"And now my mother no longer needs your services. She needs someone who can help lift Bill and do heavy things. So your employment here is terminated."

Carol continues to watch the news.

"Effective right now." I dread the outburst from Aurora when she hears about this.

Carol stays on the couch, glances over at Bill, and sighs.

"Shall I inform the hospice folks, or do you want to?" I ask Carol.

"Whatever." Carol shrugs but remains on the couch.

"Get your ass out of this house," Bill says loud and clear.

So we will wait for Darlene to recover from the flu and will tend to Bill ourselves. We have become adept with the draw sheet and the roll technique and set the timer for every two hours to remind us to reposition Bill in the bed.

"I understand you let Carol go," Aurora says when she comes upstairs later that evening to feed Bear-Bear.

"Yes, is that OK?" I ask, but don't really care what she thinks.

"If Mama wants to do the caregiving," Aurora says to Bear-Bear, "she can."

11 April
Children of God

> My name is Father's Joy. I met God when we took a trout up to the ridge. We sat for hours downwind until five baby red foxes stuck out their noses, crept forward, and sniffed toward the trout. One step, one pause, one sniff, cautious nibble. Scruffy, not quite red. Ears too big. Nibble, nibble as the mother fox watched, as we watched silent and not moving. Not even a camera click. Each week-end all summer, watching them grow less scruffy, more red, into their ears. On Sundays they always came late. We said they were at church. We said

our own prayers out on the tundra with bugs buzzing our blessing. Afterward the foxes reappeared.
We decided they really did go to church, that the
mother fox was God and the pups were children
of God.

—Abby Miller, morning pages

The VA chaplain, Ron, sits with Bill for almost an hour. Sometimes
they chat about the air force. Sometimes Bill falls asleep and Ron
watches Bill sleep.

"Would you like to pray with me?" Ron asks when Bill wakes
up.

"I would like to go somewhere else," Bill says.

Ron proceeds with a prayer asking God to bless Bill and Bill's
family, Bill's friends, Bill's caregivers, Bill's doctors, and a litany
of other Bill's people. Chaplain Ron's voice is low and warm and
soothing, and soon Bill falls asleep again. When finished with
the prayer, Ron continues to watch Bill until Bill wakes again.

"May I come back and visit you?" Ron asks.

"No, don't come back," Bill says.

Chaplain Ron seems nonplussed. He stands slowly, watching
Bill, waiting for Bill, expecting an explanation from Bill.

"I don't want you here," Bill says. "I have no use for you."

"OK," Chaplain Ron says.

"Not OK," Bill growls.

As Chaplain Ron leaves, Mother's priest, Father Steve, arrives.
I ask Bill if Father Steve can say mass. We gather chairs around
Bill, and Father Steve leads the Mass and the anointing of the
sick. He takes thin communion wafers from a gold container
that resembles a pocket watch. The wafers taste like cardboard
and dissolve on our tongues, and we are granted a moment of
grace. Bill is granted sanctity, which means he is cleansed and
prepared to meet God.

I've heard people say that when we die, our hearts and
actions are weighed against a feather. I have an eagle feather,

light, delicate, strong. This feather weighs less than an ounce. My heart alone weighs about a pound. Add to that my past actions and my heart will always weigh heavy. I doubt if sanctity will ever be granted to me. No priest's blessing will transform and cleanse me, make my heart weigh lighter than a feather.

Out in the front yard, two moose lumber across the driveway. The sun is so bright that it refracts off the long icicles under the eaves of the detached garage, turning the icicles turn into giant crystals, bathing the yard in a dancing, sparkling brilliance. Over the treetops the snowpacked mountains are visible. Beyond the trees lies the Inlet, where I go when I stink of mud from Clam Gulch or reek of fish guts from Togiak because the Inlet washes all that away and blesses me each time.

Perhaps sanctity is only granted just prior to death. Once, I almost died in the Inlet. Aurora and I were salmon fishing on the beach with a gill net. I waded out and became tangled in the net as the tide came ripping through and pulled me under and out toward the sea. I fought to untangle myself, to pull the net back, but the force was too huge, and I saw death coming and saw Aurora coming and yelled at her to stay away. But she kept coming with her knife, yelling back at me to keep my head above water. As the riptide pulled and pulled and pulled me out, the net swirled under me, pulling me down, and I was terrified and amazed at the power of the tide's pull. She grabbed my leg and somehow managed to cut the net away and free my leg. The salmon churned around us, some struggling in the net. We made it to the shore, exhausted and shaking and worried that JB would get mad because we lost the net.

I let the communion wafer dissolve on my tongue and grant me its temporary grace. In reality, I don't feel any different.

12 April
Vulnerable Adult

I have decided to return to New Mexico this weekend on the regular midnight flight. Meanwhile I continue to help Mother organize her finances though I become angrier and angrier as I uncover the extent of what Aurora has done with Bill and Mother's money.

"What's done is done," Mother says. "I don't want to go there."

"Mother, what do you want?" I ask.

"I want Aurora to communicate with me," Mother says.

I sense, in this case, communicate is another word for love.

"When you say 'what's done is done,' what does that mean?" I ask.

"Start over, clean slate," Mother says.

"What about all the money she has taken?"

"Clean slate," Mother repeats. "Total forgiveness, a pardon so to speak."

"She needs to be held accountable," I object.

"Clean slate," Mother says.

I try to arrange a meeting between Mother and Aurora to discuss a clean slate. Aurora declines. I ask Aurora three times, and each time, she declines.

"We've already talked," Aurora says.

"Mother, Aurora says you two have already talked," I report.

"We have?" Mother says. "What did we talk about?"

"I dunno, Mother. I dunno."

"I don't care if it pisses Aurora off," Alice tells me on the phone. "Aurora isn't concerned about Bill anymore. She's only concerned about Tim's various legal problems and will stop at nothing to deal with those, even if it means stealing from Momma."

Alice is hot and rolling, but she is right. In the month I have been here, I haven't seen Aurora help with Bill. I've only seen Aurora worry about money, Tim's divorce, Tim's emotional state, Tim's court case, and more money. Then she worries about money some more.

"Mother is willing to forgive Aurora for all the money loaned or taken if only Aurora will communicate with her," I tell Alice.

"That's ridiculous, and we can't allow that to happen," Alice continues. "We need a plan. If we have to, we can rent a place and move Bill to a new location."

"Slow down. That's a bit drastic," I say.

"Can you cut off Aurora's access to Momma's accounts?" Alice asks. "We could find an ombudsman to look after Momma and Bill's best interests," Alice says. "It is negligence if we don't do this."

I discover it's also Alaska state law. I find it under the Alaska Adult Protective Services Division and read about vulnerable adults and mandatory reporting requirements. Hmm. The definition of a vulnerable adult is someone over sixty-five years old and in a certain income bracket, handicapped, or having mitigating circumstances. Mother has her own assets and is not handicapped, but she is eighty years old and has mitigating circumstances.

Mitigating circumstances involve Mother being afraid to say no to Aurora. Mother is basically a blackmail victim. She worries that Aurora will kill herself. Mother feels she has no choice but to give Aurora money whenever Aurora asks for it. Mother worries about the stress and trauma of moving Bill. Mother is watching her husband die in Aurora's living room. All that surely puts Mother in the vulnerable adult category. Alice agrees.

"I believe we have tangible evidence of exploitation or abuse," Alice says.

Later I discover I might be a mandatory reporter, someone in a position to give care, execute a will, or otherwise be responsible for or observe the treatment of a vulnerable adult. These people are required by Alaska state law to report any abuse or exploitation of a vulnerable adult.

"Then I'm a mandatory reporter, too," Alice says. "Oh God, do we have to report Aurora?"

"We certainly could," I say.

"If we could find a bed for him, do you think we could change Momma's mind about moving Bill to a nursing home?" Alice asks.

I open a bag of popcorn. "Slow down. Let's think about this," I say. "Mother seems to want to make it work here."

"It's not going to work. We need to make a plan to get Momma and Bill out of Aurora's house."

Report my own sister? Very disturbing.

"If we do move Mother and Bill, how's that different from when Aurora went down to Homer and moved Mother and Bill up here to Wasilla?" I ask.

"Our intentions are more honorable." Palmer joins in on the phone call.

"I've heard people say that the road to hell is paved with good intentions," I snap at Palmer. "Moving them anywhere against their will isn't honorable."

"We could put Momma on a waiting list for an apartment at the Homer Senior Center," Alice says. "She likes the senior center."

Alice goes on to describe the various logistics involved in moving Mother and Bill back to Homer and that there are more resources available for Momma and Bill in Homer. What's Alice saying? It's negligence to do nothing.

"If Momma stays there, Aurora will try to get Momma's every last dime," Alice says.

"Aurora has unlimited access to only one account," I say. "For all other money, Aurora has to ask Mother in person. The problem is Mother can't say no to Aurora."

It doesn't matter where Bill and Mother live. Mother still won't be able to say no. The real vulnerability is Mother herself. The popcorn is salty and soothing handful after handful until the taste is no longer discernible. What is an ombudsman?

13 April
Desperation

> My name is Father's Joy. My destiny came to me at Russian River by a clear eddy when fish fever hung heavy in salmon decay, and carcasses floated past or washed up on riverbeds. A water ouzel stood on a rock—dip, dip, dip. A quick fluty trill, and

then it dove down under to walk the river bottom. The ouzel saw me just before its quick faint blink, falling asleep as the river rushed over. A miracle to sleep so sound under the torrent. Maybe the ouzel's nest is here, mossy and cushy and cool in a small waterfall or rock outcropping. No nest. Ouzels usually travel alone. Another miracle to be so secure in solitariness. In that moment as the ouzel woke from its nap and spread its wings against the current to stalk the river bottom for itty-bitty larvae and water bugs, I knew I could go against the current, sleep sound in its torrent, and survive a deluge, too.

—Abby Miller, morning pages

The chatter in my mind is too loud today. Need coffee. Where is the deed to the Homer house? Bill would have kept good records and organized files. There're still a couple of boxes to unpack in the detached garage. I make extrastrong coffee and open a bag of chips. Did Aurora use the deed to the Homer house to secure a loan? Would that even be possible for her?

Done. Mother's forty-six crafts tubs are packed and labeled. The tubs are identical and easy to store. The labels are located in the same spot on each tub, centered off a seam line. The tubs are also transparent, making the contents easy to see. I plan to store the tubs in the downstairs garage, where Mother can easily get to her craft supplies.

"Put all those crafts tubs in the shed," Aurora tells me when I start stacking the tubs in the downstairs garage.

I see it clearly. Ice. Moose. Dark. Cold. Mother going out to the shed, falling, breaking a hip to fetch a darn knitting needle. It's just another way Aurora emotionally abuses Mother.

"I don't know why she is keeping all that stuff," Aurora says. "You should just put it all into the yard sale pile."

Mother can't live here.

Why is Mother's e-mail always malfunctioning? It's late afternoon, and I still need to brush my hair and wash my face.

"It's in the briefcase," Bill says when I ask him about the deed. "Why do you need it?"

"I'm helping Mother get all the important papers organized."

I know he doesn't believe me. What else can I say? I want to hide the deed to the Homer house so my sister won't steal it? Would I say that and have Bill worry? Never.

The chatter in my mind intensifies. Aurora's house is six months in arrears. Tim's in jail. They need enormous sums of money for the lawyer. The state is taking 40 percent of Tim's paycheck for child support. Both Tim and Aurora have numerous medical bills. Aurora has not hit rock bottom but will soon, especially if she can't pilfer anymore money from Mother.

What happens when someone becomes desperate, hits rock bottom, and there is nothing left to lose?

"What if she goes out and kills herself?" Mother's words echo in my head.

"Aurora is not concerned about Bill anymore. She is only concerned about Tim's various legal problems and will stop at nothing to deal with those, even if it means stealing from Momma," Alice's words echo also.

"Great! I'm getting excited. My sweetie is coming home!" Matt tells me on the phone.

Is it safe to leave Mother here with Aurora? What will happen if Aurora triggers too many JB memories for Mother?

Mother needs an escape plan, a current passport, a prepacked travel bag, and a prearranged ride to the airport. Once she gets to the airport, I can arrange an electronic ticket from whenever I am.

Finally, I find the deed to the Homer house in a box labeled "crafts." Desperation. Yes, Aurora lives in the realm of desperation. I remember how I once lived in that realm. I remember struggling through my undergrad years, even with student loans and a part-time job: selling my two gold chainsin the pawn shop, the payday loans that I took forever to pay off, and selling my own blood. I went out with boys just to get dinner. I well understand the inspiration of desperation.

I tell Mother I'll talk with Aurora and explain the new facts of life. First, she is to use Mother and Bill's money only for things directly related to Mother and Bill. Second, she is not to ask Mother for money. Third, she is not to ask Bill for anything.

I hide the title to the Malibu and the deed to the Homer house in Mother's closet out of sight from Aurora.

"I don't envy your position, having to talk to Aurora," Alice tells me when she calls to see how things are going. "They have guns and a history of mental illness."

Will they shoot me? Do they have the capacity for violence? Probably all people have the capacity for violence if they're threatened or desperate enough.

I call Shelly from Mrs. Taxi and arrange for her to pick me up at Aurora's house Saturday night at nine and take me to the Anchorage airport. After that, I don't want to ever see Aurora again. I hide the empty chip bag in the outside garbage can. How do I say good-bye to Bill?

"Mother, get dressed. We have to go to the post office."

"Why?" she asks.

"To apply for a new passport for you," I say.

"Why?"

"In case you want to travel," I say so Bill can hear, but in the car I tell Mother about the escape plan.

"You're not trapped here," I say. "If it gets too stressful, call me, grab your passport and your little bag, and call Shelly. I'll have a ticket waiting for you at the airport."

I dread the talk with Aurora. Everywhere I go, I smell poop.

14 April
Morphine

Two doses mixed with orange juice, one dose under the tongue, and Bill floats in and out of lucidity and euphoria.

"Don't be afraid to give him five milligrams," Tad, the hospice nurse, tells me. He sees me hesitate and hugs me. "Don't let him suffer. Give him two to five milligrams every hour until the pain stops."

It's not really the morphine I fear. It's the end it signals. Each time I walk by Bill, I look at his chest to see if his chest is moving. His soft breathing rhythm continues, but I want it to stop. I want to be here until the end. Foot check: warm and gray, probably due to poor circulation. Catheter bag check: urine darkening, probably due to dehydration. Poop check: no poop, probably due to constipation due to the morphine.

Mother has become the consummate nurse but only when we are alone, not when others are here, when she is pushed away. Pain check on a scale of one to ten: Bill says eight. I give Bill more morphine. I don't say the *M* word. I don't even think the word. I say pain medicine.

Outside, the last of the snow melts, the roads become muddy, and all the cars become muddy. Aurora's twenty-one begonias sprout. The moose nap under the birches. It might be an early breakup. In Alaska we are obsessed with spring and count the minutes when the ice breaks up in the rivers, breaks up the cabin fever, and begins the delirium of fish fever.

"Where is the loadmaster?" Bill asks.

He's an air force pilot again with good health and sharp eyes. The morphine brings Bill his own version of spring and a golden moment to be young again.

"How many souls are aboard?" Bill asks his loadmaster. "Let's hustle! I want wheels up right on schedule," Bill continues in a voice so clear and so distinct that I look around for the loadmaster. "Who are those people in the fireplace?" Bill asks.

Aurora eats supper upstairs. She seems calmer. Perhaps it's because I'm leaving soon. It's the first meal I've eaten with her. Bill isn't hungry. He gives more orders concerning the preflight of his C-130. Mother stands in the hall, looking into the living room. It's where she retreats to observe and not be seen by Bill.

"I am losing him." She wipes her wet eyes with the back of her hand.

15 April
The Talk

"Do you have to talk to her? What if she gets mad?" Mother says. "What if she insists that Bill and I move out?"

"Mother, listen to yourself," I say. "You're scared of her."

Mother pauses and looks down for a moment. "Can you talk to her gently?"

Of course. I hug her and go downstairs, wanting to go home, not wanting to leave Mother here unprotected, but wanting to go home.

I find Aurora in the downstairs bedroom and sit in the brown chair opposite her. She looks down at a stack of papers and envelopes that resemble bills and receipts. When she sees me, she eyes me for several seconds and sits the on the edge of the bed with her back to me.

"As you know, I'll be leaving," I begin. "First, thank you for everything."

Aurora nods, but doesn't look at me.

"It was very gracious of you to bring Bill and Mother into your home," I say.

"It was the least I could do," Aurora says. Her back and shoulders stiffen. She knows something is coming. She's as familiar with my tactics as I am with hers. She starts to rub her new knee with a slow rocking motion of her entire body.

This small talk annoys me. Go gentle.

"I noticed the Wells Fargo account is low," I say.

Aurora pauses; looks over her shoulder; and gives me a sideways, pickerel glance, eyes narrowing. She turns back, returning to her knee rubbing and rocking.

"So," Aurora says.

So? She just says "so"?

"As a matter of fact, it's more than low," I say. "Over fifty thousand dollars low in just the past few months."

"What's it to you?" Aurora replies.

"It's illegal for one thing," I say. Go gentle.

"Hmm." Aurora looks at one bill or receipt and sets it aside.

"Under the provisions of the Adult Protective Services, you can be arrested." I need her to react, but Aurora remains unresponsive, still sitting on the edge of the bed with her back to me.

"Like I said, so?"

"So it could mean you're a thief and an elder abuser," I say. Gentle. But this is gentle. I'd prefer to hit her on the head with a shovel.

"Fuck, I don't have to listen to this." Aurora storms out of the room.

I follow her out to the front porch. I'm focused, clearheaded, and without the usual chatter in my head.

The look on Aurora's face reflects anger. More so, she reflects the look of a threatened animal. I stay close to her face. I'm tired of her thinking that we believe her.

"You're gonna talk to me."

Silence.

"I'm not getting out of your face until you talk with me."

Glare.

"I don't care how long it takes."

Aurora lights up a cigarette. Since when does she smoke? I grab the cigarette out of her hand and throw it on the ground. Aurora's hand swings back. She wants to hit me. She's bigger and stronger than I am, but her new knee is vulnerable. A blow to her knee would take her down. Aurora pauses and drops her hand and fishes out another cigarette.

"I don't care how angry you are or why." I need her to respond. The hairs on the back of my neck tingle.

Stare.

"This is family."

79

Curious look.

"Families aren't always all pretty and nice," I don't know where all these ridiculous words come from. They just spew forth and blurt out.

Another curious look.

"Families come with the good and the bad,"

"I'm not a bad person!" Aurora shouts.

"I didn't say that." But I think it.

"You don't have any right to judge me!"

Aurora's face turns red, and she throws down the cigarette without lighting it. The cigarettes confuse me for some reason. Does she smoke now?

"You don't know how it is," Aurora shouts.

Bear-Bear comes through the dog door with a great clatter, positions himself between Aurora and me.

"Maybe not. But you can't be manipulating and stealing money from your own mother." My voice goes higher, and Bear-Bear's ears prick up.

"She owes it to me!"

"She owes you nothing!"

Something in my voice or body language triggers Bear-Bear, and the hackles on the back of his neck stand up.

"You're abusing a vulnerable adult. You can go to jail for that."

Bear-Bear opens his mouth just slightly, just enough to show a glimmer of teeth. I can't out-attack a 150 pound German shepherd. But the vulnerability is not with the dog. It's with Aurora.

"Control your dog. If he hurts me, I'll get a gun and shoot him."

"It's OK, Bear-Bear." Aurora looks momentarily scared, not sure whether to believe me. She then coos to the dog, stroking the back of his head. "It's OK."

"We're just talking," I tell the dog. Go gentle.

"What do you want?" Aurora asks.

"Stop taking money from Mother to pay for the problems you and Tim have," I say.

"Tim says we'll pay her back every dime," Aurora says.

"That's not what I said or asked for."

"Well, what do you want?"

"Mother wants a good relationship with you and to communicate openly."

I watch those Aurora eyes do their famous narrowing, like a cat about to pounce. I see the hate in those eyes, hate so deep it comes natural, hate that inspires and motivates and consumes in its quest for revenge. My god, Aurora wants revenge! What Mother wants will never happen. It's no use to continue.

"Very well. We'll start having Sunday meetings," Aurora says very slowly. She's so sly.

I go upstairs to brief Mother. She looks fragile and worn. Bill's having the worst day yet, with three doses of morphine. As I'm talking with Mother, Aurora comes into the room and hands Mother the Wells Fargo debit card, which Aurora has cut into little pieces. A stupid, meaningless gesture designed to manipulate.

"It was not my intention for you to give up the card," Mother says. "I just want to communicate."

Aurora tells Mother about the Sunday meetings. Mother seems genuinely relieved and even happy upon hearing this. I hate to leave tomorrow, but I want to go home.

"Aurora can get another card," I tell Mother. "Make it an agenda item for your meeting."

16 April
Anchorage Airport

"Good-bye, Billiam." I lean over to kiss him on the forehead.

"Bye-bye, Roadrunner," he whispers in that raspy voice. Weeping at the corners of the eyes. The smell. Crunched up in the odd fetal position, clutching the safety rails.

Good-bye, my Bill. I'm pleased he recognizes me through his half-lidded, morphine-laced eyes.

At nine o'clock at night, Shelly arrives with her taxi shuttle, Mrs. Taxi. I introduce Mother to Shelly. Part of the escape plan is for Mother to have a ride to the airport. Shelly can be that ride. A quick hug for Mother and me. Then I see Mother in the window watching me walk to the taxi, get in the taxi, and leave. I hesitate. Maybe I should stay.

Good-bye, Bill. It's too dark, and I probably won't see the Inlet. Will I see Bill again? After the Wasilla house is behind me and out of sight, I finally cry. I'm not sure why. Perhaps the relief of leaving, the concern for leaving Mother here, the fear of not seeing Bill again. I don't know. I just cry as quietly as possible in the backseat of the taxi all the way to Anchorage.

I cry and cry in the terminal, a gush of pressure letting off, looking down so people don't notice, looking away so I don't have to tell people I'm OK and say something like, "I'm just tired." Oblivious to people walking by, I'm crying for leaving. Crying for not saying a proper good-bye, though what is proper? Crying good-bye to a lingering soul.

"Are you ready to go?" Bill had asked me.

"Bags are packed," I said.

Why does everything have to be unfinished? Maybe I should go back. What happens if a passenger doesn't get onboard? Is it just one empty seat? Do I need to tell the airline? Bill, why couldn't you die on schedule?

It plays over and over, too much to hold in. Bill dying. Mother moving in with Aurora. Aurora's knee replacements. Tim's divorce. Tim in jail. The money issues. Alice. Matt. Mother's vulnerability. We are all burn victims, burnt to a crisp, fried so fragile we cannot be touched or we fall apart and cry for no reason, or we simply disintegrate. Panic. One hour before boarding.

What did Bill say? "Not OK. Stop the dusting and go home."

It might be OK. Aurora and Mother may need time to learn to live with each other. I watch two aviation security guards escort and transfer guns to a pilot.

"Is the preflight done?" Bill kept asking about his C-130.

"Yuppers, but where are you going?" I always asked.

"Across the Inlet," he always answered.

"Can I go with you?" I know I can't go, but he likes it when I ask.

"Nope. Only one soul on this plane."

Panic. Thirty minutes before boarding. In Anchorage the planes depart at midnight. This time of year, it is dark at midnight, and depending on the amount of moon and where I am seated on the plane, the Inlet may not be visible after takeoff. Once aboard, there's no turning back, and I leave without getting a last look at the Inlet and am no longer part of its universe.

Part 2

EDGEWOOD

---

17 April
Numbness

My name is Father's Joy. Can anyone hear me in this late storm, driving Turnagain Arm in white-out when the Inlet disappears into mountain-side? Focused on amber headlights ahead, red taillights, and orange balls on high wires. They're the clues I'm still on the road and not driving into the Inlet out where the tide moves between layers of ice sheets and frozen mud. If I drive off the road, which layer will take me? Where am I now? Perhaps Beluga Point. Are those trees drooping in snow or shadows from my life listening for an avalanche? Keep moving because there's no pulling over, no stopping in whiteout. No up or down. No ground. No way out. Keep moving. With steady studded tire-beats on snow, watch for tracks of vehicles ahead. Watch for vertigo. Control it. Freeze it. Feel no fear. Feel nothing. Focus. Keep moving.

—Abby Miller, morning pages

I wake up in Edgewood disoriented and startled to see the barren high plains of New Mexico after spending time in Alaska.

Everything is brown. The chatter in my head dulls and takes on a low constant buzz. So here, back home. So what? In my living room, Bill's dying is replaced with custom-made purple leather chairs. Who cares about chairs? My hands ache, swollen. I step on the scales and note my ten pound weight gain. I have not been to Overeaters Anonymous in over a month. Doesn't matter. Don't want to go.

I want to go back to Alaska, protect my Mother, and be there when Bill dies. Alice had said she'd "made peace with Bill." What does that mean? Is it saying good-bye? Doesn't matter. Nothing matters in this numbness. Matt plans a birthday party for his own father. I don't care. My clients need me to touch base with them. Don't care.

The day opens with warmth and sunshine and a clear view of the plains and South Mountain. On a monsoon day, we can see thunderstorms for fifty miles in all directions. But the Inlet is not here. I want to feel again, chase away the numbness, stand out in my garden, and face the plains like I used to stand out on the Kalifonski cliffs and face the Inlet to hear what it had to say and the answers it whispered in the winds and tides.

But today there is no sound, no whisper, no echo. Even the wind is quiet. I work in the garden all day, raking up debris, gathering up tumbleweeds, digging up dirt to stimulate wild verbena, picking up rocks one at a time, examining each rock, and repositioning each rock to catch the sunlight on its most sparkly side. What's happening in Wasilla? What's Bill doing? Did I leave too soon? Should I go back?

Back in Alaska the snow is still too deep in some places, and moose trample the gardens and wander the streets and don't know where to go, and moose are everywhere in the wrong places. People try helping the moose with feeding stations, special lights on the highway, a moose patrol car on the railroad. The moose learn to eat the wrong food, become confused by the lights, and get their spindly legs caught in the railroad ties because they run and stumble and fall when they see the moose patrol train. I feel like a moose. I never want to see Aurora again.

"Will you return for the funeral?" Matt asks me.

His tone reflects the casualness of asking will I check the mail or do I want more coffee.

"I don't know."

"Do you want to go to a movie tonight?" Matt asks.

I resent his nonchalance, his ability to be happy. Everything he says nips at me. At sunset the west sky glows red.

18 April
He Did Not Die

Tad, the hospice nurse, says all his clients die. But Bill did not die. What do I tell people? I went up to Alaska because Bill was supposed to die.

"Did you get a chance to say good-bye?" people will ask me.

In my mind I see Bill in Aurora's living room directing a preflight meeting. I see Mother afraid of Aurora, watching Bill slowly fade and certainly, but eventually, die in Aurora's house. Aurora will be hobbling upstairs with pain in her new knees with a new crisis, needing new money. I chase away this chatter and cluster of images, the same images I dreamt last night.

Sometimes when I stand in the hallway and turn back, I see Bill in our living room. I smell the poop.

I see a friend in the grocery store and hide, not wanting to see people right now. Returning home without buying the groceries, I hide in my away-room and work on our taxes.

I pick up the house phone to call the accountant and hear Matt's voice on the line.

"What should I do?" Matt asks.

"She knows what to do," the voice on the other end of the phone says. "Make her connect with people, friends, family, clients."

"I think she's sick of people," Matt says.

"Perhaps just e-mail," the voice says.

So I connect and write an e-mail to my friends and close colleagues. "Dear friends, I just returned from a month in Alaska helping out with my stepdad's journey through hospice territory. The process will probably take two or three more weeks, and I expect to have to go back soon, but I had to come home to rest and see my husband. My apologies for ignoring you and disappearing so suddenly. I really love you all. Abby." My friends immediately write back. Connection energy touches me, begins to bring me back to Edgewood world.

"Hoping all is well with you and that you don't get run down. Wishing the best for you and your family," Trish writes.

"Glad you can rest and see your hubby before heading back," Ildi writes.

"Thinking of you!" Judy says.

"Thoughts and prayers out to you and your mom and Bill," Shelby writes.

"Prayers for you and your family," Kerri writes.

"Bless you and your family," Jean writes.

"Stay well. We're thinking of you!" Joan writes.

"I miss you. Glad you are back. Can hardly wait to see you," Gladys writes.

"Our prayers with you and your family. We love you!" Charlotte writes.

"Hey, honey, I hope all is well. Call me," Tina writes.

"Hugs!" Sally writes.

"Miss you," Denise writes.

I miss her, them, too.

19 April
Reaching Out

Alice calls to talk about what's happening in Wasilla.

"I reached out to Aurora," Alice says. "I commended her for demonstrating her new commitment by cutting up that debit card."

"For heaven's sake, Alice, she only cut up and destroyed the debit card in a passive-aggressive fit, not a commitment!"

"Yeah, yeah," Alice goes on. "I suggested she have a discussion with Momma about a budget."

Oh dear. Alice is in her save-the-world mode.

"Tim's still in jail, and the doctor at the jail says Tim needs shoulder surgery, but Tim isn't healthy enough to have shoulder surgery," Alice continues.

Is anyone healthy up at the Wasilla house? I remember looking for Bill's morphine and discovering the house to be a picture of unhealth. I found the morphine stowed away in a basket with Aurora's drugs: for her knees, her hormones, her depression, her codependency, and her assorted other maladies. Next to this basket was Tim's basket with another selection of drugs: for his shoulder, his depression, his arthritis, his self-esteem, and his vertigo. Next to Tim's basket was a carton of menthol cigarettes. Next to the cigarettes was a bottle of bourbon.

The upstairs hall bathroom supports Bill: drawers and cabinets full of creams, lotions, ointments, powders, bandages, baby wipes, stacks of gauze, piles of the white towels, the A and B sponges, basins, ice packs, heat packs, bed pads, bed liners, boxes of latex and nitrile gloves, the atropine eye drops, and the pain medicines—codeine and morphine.

Mother has her own basket with vitamins, supplements, and drugs for her blood pressure and bones. I have small plastic bags with appetite suppressants and protein bars. Alice has plastic bags, also, with homeopathic hormone patches, vitamins, herbals, and protein milkshake mixes. Curious. Perhaps it's true: we all have our tic.

"I told Aurora to work this as a family team," Alice continues. "This is a way to control the spending, give Momma back some control over her life, and be transparent."

Does Alice know what it means to be transparent? Where does she get these buzzwords?

"Aurora told me no thanks," Alice says. "I told Aurora that was OK and to let things calm down."

"Then Aurora just says, 'Nope,'" Alice continues. "So I backed off. Then I wanted to make her feel safe and valued, so I told her about our little dog not eating his food and asked for her advice."

No, talking about a dog makes people feel safe.

"I also asked about my Christmas cactus," Alice says. "Aurora gave me some good ideas. I'll keep plugging away at her. I'll also reach out to Tim and Momma. Tim needs to know we're not against him."

Plug away, plug away. But what about Bill? What's happening with him?

20 April
Where Do Ashes Go?

Morning brings four inches of fresh snow on the hyacinths, coyotes running through the distant plains, quail pecking around the bird feeder, and South Mountain blanketed in snow. Alice calls early.

"We're making a plan for Bill's ashes," Alice reports.

Oh dear, another plan.

"Momma and Aurora have found an urn, but it is two hundred twenty-five dollars. Aurora thinks this is too expensive."

Such a steward, Aurora thinks it's too expensive. Alice doesn't pause or ask what I think about the price.

"Momma wants a military funeral at Fort Richardson, where they have a veteran's cemetery, but they don't have a permanent installation for funeral urns."

"Is a funeral urn different from a regular urn?" I ask.

"Dunno how, but they just are," Alice says. "I talked to the people at Fort Richardson."

Does anyone know Bill at Ft. Richardson?

"What do people do with the urn after the funeral?"

"Momma could keep it or could scatter the ashes," Alice says. "I had a brief exchange with Momma about the ashes. I told Momma I had Daddy's ashes in a box in my living room. She said, 'Well, don't put me there.' I asked her where she wanted to go. She said next to Bill."

It takes me a second to do the mind jump to realize Alice is talking about JB. It always amazes me that both Alice and Aurora still refer to JB as Daddy.

Up to the end, I never called him Daddy—even while he was dying in Alice's living room. I didn't talk to JB for twenty years and finally reconciled with him for Alice and Aurora. It hurt them that I hated him. Alice brought JB to her house when he got sick. Palmer called me and said, "Come quick." We stood vigil over JB as his tongue swelled, so he couldn't talk and his liver swelled, refusing to produce albumen, so he couldn't breathe, and the pain swelled, so he needed more and more morphine.

I took the midnight shift and sat next to JB, the man I hated so long. I comforted him as his appetite disappeared, urine turned dark, hands and feet mottled then turned blue black and then finally ice cold. When the Cheyne-Stokes breathing started, JB opened his eyes, bolted up in the bed, stared at me, and looked around.

"Where am I?" JB asked.

On your way to hell, I wanted to say. "Go back to sleep. We can talk in the morning," I said instead.

The Cheyne-Stokes continued with each breath growing farther apart from the last breath until there was no breath—a soft chest shudder and it was done.

Good riddance.

Alice gave us herbs and flowers from her garden to place on JB's chest. We stood around JB with ritual beauty and said good-bye and wished him safe journey. One by one, we placed the herbs on his chest and a kiss on his forehead. He laid there serene and majestic, in death finally loveable.

I called Mother and Bill to tell them JB had died. Bill was proud we had stood by JB until the end. Bill's own adult children had disowned him when Bill divorced their mother and, years later, married my mother. I remember that pride and sensed the longing for his own children lurking behind it. When it was Bill's turn, I promised myself to be there to the end.

I remember my fear when they took JB away. What if he wasn't dead when they cremated him? The hospice nurse took my hand and said it was her job to confirm the death. He would not suffer anymore, she said.

Let him suffer

"So I was thinking if Momma wants to be next to Bill, she's thinking more about burial plots," Alice says.

I'm jolted back to the present. What is Alice talking about?

"So I contacted the City of Homer and asked about their cemetery," Alice says. "We can buy a plot in the Homer Cemetery for two hundred dollars from the city clerk. The cemetery is up on Diamond Ridge Road. It'd be great to have that nice view."

What a grand plan. Sometimes it's a relief when Alice is off running with a new plan. I don't have to talk. But Bill won't be there to enjoy the view. He's going across the Inlet.

"I haven't scattered Daddy's ashes because I want a place where I can come visit him. You can't do that if there's no final resting place," Alice continues.

Scattering the ashes? I like it.

"The Homer Cemetery accepts cremated remains," Alice says. "There's no rule against having more than one person's remains interred in one plot. I could have my ashes put there. It'd be like having our own piece of Homer forever. What do you think?"

I'd prefer to scatter Bill's ashes, this last dust of leftover bones, this evidence of one man's existence, to the wind or over the sea or, better yet, over the Inlet.

"Excuse me, what's happening with Bill? Is he about to die?"

21 April
Relapse II

"Bill had a stroke last night. He can only speak in garbled, slurred sounds, and he can't swallow," Aurora calls to report what's happening in Wasilla. "It's a definite relapse. His feet and hands are cold but not blue or dark.".

"Mama was there, but she didn't do anything. She was just sleeping on the couch."

I feel the venom in Aurora's voice even over the telephone. My head is full of chatter, and it's difficult to focus. What's Aurora is saying?

"Mama doesn't give Bill enough fluids," Aurora says.

"I want to go back to Wasilla," I tell Matt.

"You just got back home," Matt says.

I understand that Matt doesn't understand death. Just a few months ago, Matt's stepmother called to tell us that Matt's four-month-old nephew had died in the night. The family was devastated, especially Matt's stepbrother.

"What should I say?" Matt asked me.

"Just say you're sorry," I suggested.

So Matt left a message on the stepbrother's answering machine.

I returned to New Mexico mostly because of Matt's voice, with the strain, crankiness, and irritation clearly evident. For Matt it was manageable that I was gone for one or two weeks, but over a month up in Wasilla was too much.

"Mama won't cook," Aurora says. "She just gives Bill yogurt."

I hear the contradiction. Bill can't swallow. Mother won't feed him. Aurora's lying.

"Mama just sits there," Aurora keeps saying.

"Where's your mother," Bill always asks.

How his eyes light up when Mother appears and sits on the couch.

The chatter in my head roars, and my mind goes to old images of bad days with JB. Mother had sat there, hardly talking, barely moving all day for days, for weeks. I remember cooking the meals, making spaghetti with hot dogs for supper or peanut butter sandwiches for breakfast. JB would come home drunk, if he did come home, sometimes crawling to the door. We helped him to the couch and made him tea and something to eat. Mother sat there, not speaking, not moving, and imperceptibly rocking herself. Most of the time, she was in her pajamas, all day in her pajamas.

I remember Alice and Aurora as children, trying to get a response from her.

"Momma, Daddy helps help," Alice would say.

"Mama, Daddy's sick," Aurora would say.

In those moments Mother might glance in our direction, but there'd be no hint of recognition. If she glanced at JB, she might recognize him, and her eyes would unglaze and then fire up before the fire went out and they glazed over again.

"Mama, Daddy's sick." Aurora would tug at Mother.

Alice would hide in her hobby room to study star maps and rearrange her spaceship models by size and color.

"Mama, Daddy's sick," Aurora would insist.

"So?" Mother would push Aurora away.

Once I asked Mother why she stayed with JB. "Please leave him," I had begged her.

"Father Francis says this is my cross to bear," she told me.

"That can't be right," I tried to object. I hope that priest rots in hell.

"Besides what would I do?" Mother had asked me.

Her words knocked reality into me, and there stood a great truth right before me. Yes, what would she do? In that crystalline moment, at eleven years old, I vowed I would never be dependent on a husband.

"Mother won't take care of Bill," Aurora says.

My mind comes back to Aurora. I sense Aurora's manipulation. She wants Mother to be helpless or demented or incapacitated or some other thing that might give Aurora some legal or medical premise to control Mother's money.

"Mother is doing the best she can and doing what Bill wants her to do," I say.

What if this relapse is the final one? What if the funeral is in a few days? What if I need to fly back to Wasilla?

"You don't need to be there right now," Alice tells me later. "Palmer and I are returning to Wasilla in less than two weeks, and we can go up sooner if need be."

"What would I do?" Mother's words haunted me.

"Go to school," I kept telling Mother.

"No, you go to school," she said.

Through the years she did go to school, between teaching me to drive, to sew, to train dogs, to bake, to love music, and to manage money in white envelopes. She earned a business degree by the time JB abandoned her and left her to deal with the IRS taking her house, her bank account, and her every last dime. I have watched her collapses; relapses; on the couch; catatonic-like; often rocking herself; and saying her prayers, a rosary, with special prayers to St. Jude, the patron saint of desperate cases and lost causes. And I watched her give JB twenty-five dollars each month to pay on the annuity in my white envelope.

"Go to school," she told me over and over. Stalwart. Never giving up.

What would I have done without her?

Later, Mother got her first job, as a volunteer with a crisis line for abused women.

"I am well qualified to help these women," Mother told us.

"Mama won't do anything," Aurora calls again.

I ignore Aurora because I don't believe her. Perhaps I should fly back up to Wasilla.

"I told you that you don't need to be there. Palmer and I will be up there soon enough. We'll check on Momma for you," Alice says. "It's one of our main reasons for going back up. Even if Bill died tomorrow, the funeral won't be right away. We haven't finished planning it."

I don't need to be there. It's what I needed to hear for my husband's sake. Matt will understand later, another time. Perhaps I don't need to be there, but the idea of Mother ignored and alone disturbs me.

"Momma will be OK," Alice says. "She's not always alone. The priest visits. She prays a lot, too. She told me once that it gives her solace. Momma's a tough cookie. She's survived before."

I hate priests.

Yes, Mother survived. I remember the bruises, the excuses, the first time I saw JB hit Mother. It was an accident. It had to be. But it wasn't.

"You give me the money," JB had yelled the last time he hit her.

"It's for the girls," Mother had insisted.

"Hell with the girls," JB yelled and slammed Mother's face into the wall, blood spurting from her mouth, her teeth broken.

She yelped and then was quiet when she saw me. I yelled at him to stop, but he kept slamming her face into the wall. She kept refusing to give him the money. There was only that one yelp. I grabbed his shirt and tried to pull him away.

"Dumb-ass girl," he said as his fist came down on my face.

"Here's the money," Mother said immediately and gave him all the money she had saved in several white envelopes. "Don't hurt the girls."

That was my second crystalline moment. I vowed never to have children, never to be that vulnerable. At school the next day, my teacher asked me about the bruises on my face and my broken nose.

"My father hit me," I said to my teacher, the school nurse, and the police officer.

"Do you want to talk about it?" they all asked me.

"No, he won't do it again," I told them. "We have an understanding now."

"If it happens again, will you tell us?" they asked.

"Yes," I said. "But don't worry, it won't happen again."

That night, after school, after homework, after Alice and Aurora were asleep, I cleaned the kitchen. I was twelve years old, tall for my age, and strong from living in Alaska with few rules and minimal convention or supervision. And I raged and hated. I washed the dishes, cleaned the flour dust off the counters from where we had rolled out pizza, and wiped the flour off the old solid-wood rolling pin. I heard the car, saw the headlights, and went out to greet him.

Beer smell reached me before he did.

"You're up late," JB said.

I shrugged.

"Are you baking?" He pointed at the rolling pin.

"You will never hit Mother again." I took one step toward him and waited.

"What?" JB started to say something.

"You will never hit or hurt Mother again." I took another step toward him.

He was so much taller, heavier, and stronger than I wasme, but I doubted he could rage more than I could. He was drunk, clumsy, and not expecting this.

"If you ever hurt Mother again, I'll kill you." I took another step toward him, close enough for him to strike me, dared him to. "Do you understand what I'm saying?"

"You dumb-ass girl." JB started to strike, but he was too drunk and too confused, and I was faster, younger, and raging. I beat him with that solid-wood rolling pin on the face, on the head, on the back, on every surface I could reach while he tried to grab at me, grab at the rolling pin, until he was covered in blood and blood gushed all over. The rage I felt transferred into that rolling pin, and I continued to beat him until he fell on the ground screaming for me to stop, screaming I was a dumb-ass girl. I continued to pound on him until Mother pulled me away.

"Do we have an understanding?" I yelled at JB.

He didn't answer.

"Do we have an understanding?" I growled as he struggled to stand up.

He still didn't answer.

I pushed Mother aside and ran at JB again. "I won't stop until we have an understanding." I struck JB on the side of his face, the hardest blow I had yet delivered, so powerful I was amazed at its force. JB reeled backward. "Do we have an understanding?" I roared and stood poised to hit him again.

JB nodded.

"Is that a yes?"

"Yes, it's a goddamned yes," JB said.

"All right, now, you understand that if you ever hurt Mother or us girls again—" I looked straight at him. "I'll kill you."

I turned around to go back into the house. In the window there were Aurora and Alice watching me, their eyes big and wide. Go back to sleep, little ones. You're safe now.

"We're talking about a woman who ran away from home at age nineteen to join the army because her dad wouldn't let her go to college," Alice was saying.

What is Alice talking about now?

"Momma has backbone. Where do you think we got ours from?" Alice adds.

Many years later, Bill told Mother, "Let's get those pretty teeth fixed."

22 April
Stand By

Aurora calls to report that Bill babbled incoherently all night, so she and Mother stood vigil, thinking it was time, with Aurora taking first shift and Mother taking second shift.

"I fed him strawberries blended with a little water, "Aurora says. "That's all he's eaten in two days. Our lawyer filed a motion to dismiss the child abuse charges against Tim," Aurora says. "The lawyer also heard the deposition with Tim's daughter. The poor little girl could only say she didn't remember or she didn't know. Tim's wife would feed the daughter answers and try to trick the daughter into giving the answers the wife wanted. It's clearly a scam."

Scam? You should know. That soon-to-be ex-wife must be very angry. So angry, she's willing to subject her child to these trumped-up charges.

"We have a new caregiver. Mike, a retired veteran—navy," Aurora says. "He starts on Friday. All my begonias have sprouted," Aurora says. "It's getting warm. We're going to have to shave Bear-Bear's winter coat off early."

Aurora continues to cheerfully report about Tim and her begonias and Bear-Bear and other important things in her life. My mind's still with Bill. Should I go back?

I finish our overdue taxes, drive into town, and deliver the tax packet to our accountant. I don't say much, go home, go out into the garden, and hose down the rocks to wash off the dust.

"Talk to me." Matt sits on the nearby park bench. "What's going on?"

"Aurora and Mother stood vigil with Bill last night." I sit next to Matt. He knows that standing vigil is our code for death is near.

"Do you want to go back?" Matt asks.

"I don't know. I'm not sure I believe her. What if it's another scam?"

"It might be," Matt says.

"I'm not handling this well," I say. "Not being there, not knowing what's really happening."

"When you think about it, you didn't know what was happening when you were up there," Matt says.

His comment cuts, and I suppress the urge to retort back harshly. But it's true and it's the part that eats at me.

"I know, I know."

"If you want to go back, it's OK," Matt says.

There it is. It's OK. I need him to say it's OK, though needing him at all isn't easy. I don't like it, but the act of needing is what makes our marriage.

Back on our wedding day in Homer, Bill hobbled shakily on his walker, just three months after a hip replacement. He remained downstairs on the patio watching the eagles so he wouldn't have to navigate the steps up to where dinner was being served. I offered to bring plates and eat with him.

"No, you go back upstairs," Bill had said. "You belong to Matt now."

"But I don't want you to be down here all alone."

"Where's your mother? She's going to join me."

We hugged, and I went upstairs to join my new husband.

"Sweetie," Bill called after me. "Don't be afraid to need him."

Needing has plagued me all my life.

"You don't need me," my first fiancé had told me.

You're right.

"I don't feel needed," my second fiancé told me.

No, you're not.

"You don't need me or anyone else," my first husband told me.

I can take care of myself, even the divorce.

"Do you ever need anyone?" my first serious boyfriend asked me years after that divorce.

"You only need your dog," my fourth serious boyfriend told me.

Yes, I went home every night to the marvelous white dog named Spot.

"I don't need a husband," I told the therapist. "I have built my life on this premise."

"How's that premise working for you?" the therapist asked.

"It's not. It seems people need to be needed."

"Tell me more," the therapist had said.

For fifteen months, every Monday morning, I told the therapist more. Each time, I relived the fear of what it meant to need. Each time, I told less of JB and more of Bill, until the day came when it was OK to need. And when Spot died of old age, I held his furry dog body, sang him a lullaby, and, later, sprinkled his ashes over the Inlet and let him go and didn't need him anymore.

Dust on the birdbath becomes visible in the afternoon sun. Dust on the brick walkway and the sedum also becomes visible. I pick up the hose and spray the bricks within reach of the park bench.

"I don't know what to do."

Matt puts his arm around me. I can't fly back to Wasilla and not think of Matt, can't stay here in Edgewood and not think of Bill.

"You can go back up whenever you want," Matt says.

"Can I be on standby? Go back when the time is right?"

"How will you know?" Matt asks.

"I'm not sure, but I think I'll know."

23 April
Thank You for the Memories

While on standby I update my scrapbook and linger over the photographs and mementos related to Bill. The first time I saw Bill was at the Homer Senior Center where Mother was working as a bookkeeper. I went to the center to see Mother's new office. A happy man came to the office and greeted Mother. They exchanged pleasantries.

"This is Bill," Mother said.

"May I cook for you?" Bill asked Mother.

"Why, yes." Mother blushed and glanced at me. "Yes, of course."

Bill presented in a short haircut, khaki jacket, conservative navy pants, and pressed shirt, hat in hand. Retired military, perhaps air force. His confident manner said officer.

He cooked for her for several years, and one day, surprised her with an engagement ring featuring the biggest diamond I'd ever seen, and they were married in the Homer house. Bill's first two priorities were to fix her teeth and set up a retirement account for her.

The first time I gave Bill a Father's Day card, tears welled up in his eyes. His own three children, two sons and a daughter, had disowned him for divorcing their mother, even though they were adults when Bill filed for divorce. Those kids should've understood why the divorce happened. To this day these adult children of Bill have not spoken to him. Every Christmas, we detect a melancholy note in. Aurora told me Bill would think of those children from his first marriage, perhaps remembering Christmases gone by or Christmases that would never be. Aurora would ensure Bill had lots of gifts under the tree and that Bill got extra hugs. She even counted the gifts as they appeared under the tree to be sure that Bill got the same amount of gifts as everyone else.

At first I loved Bill for loving Mother. He was more than devoted to her. His life became a mission to protect her. He was nine years older than Mother, and he knew he would die first. He tolerated no debt and grew Mother's retirement account until he felt safe Mother would be financially comfortable if Bill were to die. Then I loved him because he helped me love others.

"You should make peace with your real father," Bill told me.

"He's my biological father, not my real father," I replied, perhaps too curt, too sharp.

I saw the Christmas melancholy come into Bill's eyes and understood that to respect Bill was to somehow respect JB.

"I know, but I'm not ready yet," I said and softened my voice and let him imagine that someday his own children would make peace with him.

"Well, get ready," Bill said. "And before he dies."

"You need a husband," Bill told me another time.

"I don't need a—"

"Don't fool yourself," Bill said.

Alice calls and interrupts my reverie with the scrapbook.

"I'm sending you the cremation paper work," Alice tells me. "As executor you need to read it, sign it, and return it. Be sure to initial each page."

"Can't you look it over?"

"Momma wants you to do it," Alice says. "You're just granting permission for the funeral home to perform the cremation."

I look at the paper work. It includes a detailed description of the cremation process, and I note a sentence that says the ashes are not ashes. They are pulverized bones.

I start at the top and dutifully read.

We humans are about 60 percent water, so we require a huge amount of heat, 850 degrees centigrade, to reduce the body to ashes.

Wouldn't it be more accurate to say pulverized bones?

Cremation times are between forty-five and ninety minutes.

The detailed description immediately disturbs me as I start to initial the pages.

All clothes and jewelry will be removed. The body will burn outside to inside in a cycle of dehydration and ignition. The heat dries out the skin, and the skin ignites.

I feel queasy.

The cycle continues until the fire consumes the entire body, until the evidence of our existence is a pile of powdery flecks; flakes; bits and chunks of bones; and metal parts, such as Bill's titanium hip joint.

The body continues to burn in layers in this dehydration-ignition cycle. In the guts, steam and gases form, expand, and escape, drying out the torso and then igniting into flames. Slowly, all the skin burns off, starting at the ends of the limbs where there is not much muscle or fat. The bones appear, and the skeleton becomes visible.

I feel nauseous.

Once the body is reduced to fatty bits, cremation proceeds more rapidly and intensely, more inferno–like—wild and consuming the flesh as it dries out. Bones glow white in the flames, and the skeleton falls apart. Some of the bones fall into pieces while other bones remain whole.

Some body parts resist, especially the chest contents and the brain. Even after the heat cracks the skull into pieces, the brain hangs on, a darkening clump, surviving until almost the last moments of cremation.

Oh God! Why are they describing it this way? I hope Mother hasn't read this.

In the end most of the body goes up in smoke.

I imagine a trail of white and gray smoke curls appearing above the chimney and wonder if the neighbors wonder about this smoke. Do they ask, "Who is that smoke?"

The body has now been reduced to about six pounds of powdery bone clumps and pieces. These bone fragments are pounded or pressed, and the bones are pulverized into small fine pieces. Metal parts are removed. Then the pulverized bones are pressed through a sieve to achieve an even finer consistency.

I stop reading because I know how it ends. The resulting powdered bones resemble pure white sand, which is transferred into a pristine plastic bag and labeled "Bill." When they hand us the bag, it is done quietly with heads bowed.

And the pulverized bones are called ashes because we are afraid of bones. So we call them ashes, receive the bag reverently, and are not afraid.

I sign the last page, go into the bathroom, bend down, lean into the toilet, and vomit. What did I just read? I shake violently and continue to vomit, flushing it away, trying to make the cremation images go away as the sound of running toilet water soothes me.

I don't want to touch or think about that document again and ask Matt to send it to the funeral home. Above all, I don't want Mother to touch it.

24 April
Time

> My name is Father's Joy. I listen for the time. Moose hears it. Snow goose hears it. The Inlet hears it. I listen on the winds of spring chinook and winter williwaw. I ask crow. I call across mud flats and sea grass. But there is no time. There are no calendars here to tell the seasons. Rivers break up in spring. Reds run north in summer. Caribou migrate in fall. Eagles return in winter. There are no clocks here to tell us time. At daybreak, go out. At low tide, dig clams. At high tide, sail. When fish fever hits, go fish. Only immeasurable metrics are here that tell us we will not escape the tsunami, we will live only three minutes in open water, and we will die after the fireweed blooms.
>
> —Abby l Miller, morning pages

Time is different now for Bill. He counts time in extraordinary beats of breaths and bowel movements and brief moments of awareness when he recognizes the sound of our voices. Or time is told with a wave of his big gnarly hand when he's content for one of us to sit there next to him, silent, watching cowboy movies, and life is still good. I want to be there and be with him to welcome the spring, to take him out on the terrace. Let him feel the breezes and watch the mother moose and her baby munching on birches. I envision the Inlet and the ice chunks breaking up in it.

Aurora calls to report Bill is better, but grumpy. He ate ice cream for supper. Bill's speech is better, and Aurora can now understand him when he talks.

"Why is he grumpy?" I ask.

"He wants to go somewhere," Aurora says. "Mother won't let him go."

"Let me talk to him."

"Hi, Billiam, this is your favorite daughter in New Mexico," I say.

"Oh, it's the Roadrunner," Bill says. He talks slow and hesitant, but the words are clear and lucid.

"What's happening?"

"They won't let me go," Bill says.

"Where do you want to go?"

"Across the Inlet," Bill says.

I sense his lucidity drift, and it's truly more of a sensing for there are no cues or slurred speech or inarticulate ramblings to signal what's real or unreal as he drifts in and out of his worlds. I readjust my mind to listen beyond the words, to the essence of the words.

"When do you want to go?" I ask again.

"Now," Bill says.

"What's stopping you?"

"The Malibu needs a tune-up," Bill says, the grumpiness and fatigue in his voice coming across the telephone.

"Bill, did you forget you need a plane or a boat to get across the Inlet?"

"That's all good, but I want to take the Malibu," Bill says. "Can you get the Malibu ready?"

Ah, he has unfinished business here. What business?

"Yes, I'll make an appointment to get it tuned up."

"Good," Bill says. "Tell your mother I'm going."

Unfinished business about Mother.

"You know, we can take Aurora's truck."

"Aurora needs her truck," Bill says.

Something about Aurora, too.

"Aurora can use Tim's car," I say. He doesn't need a car while he's in jail. "When you're ready, we can go anytime you want."

"Time is running out," Bill says.

His time is indeed limited and cannot be contrived into neat blocks or tidy checklists or a logical routine. Time is not an orderly procedure like his preflight. He no longer has earthly methods to measure his time. Thus he doesn't know when his time will be done, and he still has unfinished business. No wonder he's grumpy.

"I didn't say we, Roadrunner. You can't go with me."

"Well, how else can I help you get there?" I ask.

"Just fix the Malibu," Bill says. "My feet hurt. Where did you put my new shoes? I hope you didn't give them away. They cost me seventy-five dollars."

"Mother normally puts them under your bed."

"Give me the phone," I hear Aurora say to Bill.

"Gotta go," Aurora's voice comes over the phone. "Bill just pooped himself. Please call when you're alone," she adds. "No emergency."

25 April
Don't Worry

"I'm alone now."

"We had to clean up Bill three times yesterday," Aurora says.

You mean Mike, the new home health aide, or Mother cleaned him up.

"My begonias are doing so well," Aurora adds.

"That's great."

Aurora describes how the dog barked, and chats on. "I'm going to plant a fantastic vegetable garden this year," Aurora says.

"OK, so what's happening that is not an emergency?" I ask.

"Oh, don't worry about it," Aurora says.

I flinch at the words.

"Don't worry." JB had said it first.

Mother would ask if he had paid the rent. What about the taxes? What about the annuities for the girls? JB always had the same answer.

"Don't worry about it," JB said. "Don't worry so much."

Mother would tell JB about the propane tank that needed filling for the winter or the roof that needed the leak patched or the washing machine that needed the belts replaced.

"Don't worry," JB said.

Mother would say Aurora was flirting with the boys and I was skipping school and Alice was too withdrawn.

"Don't worry," JB said.

Most of the time, she didn't worry about things. She mostly worried abput us girls and getting us to college.

Over the phone Aurora happily chats on about whatever it is that's not an emergency.

"It's so funny—Mama puts Bill's shoes at the corner of the bed so he can see them," Aurora says.

I'm tired and don't want to play this chitchat game. In fact, I don't want to talk to her at all. "So what am I not supposed to worry about?" I ask.

"Nothing," Aurora says. "Don't worry about it. We'll manage."

It's the first part of her passive-aggressive strategy. She'll hint at an emergency until we pump her for the information. If pushed too much, Aurora might add with a fierce, growling tone, "Why are you worrying so much?"

Finally, we might think something's so wrong, especially Mother, that we might insist on giving Aurora money for good measure and without asking any more questions.

"OK," I say and make a mental note to log into Mother's accounts and check the balance and recent activity.

26 April
Reality

> My name is Father's Joy. When I was a child, we left our mother at home making oatmeal cookies and went to play by the Inlet in the soft gray sand near an overgrown graveyard gazing across the Inlet. One grave was marked, OUR MOTHER.

We thought she was ours. So we gathered fireweed, lupine, and squaw lilies for her. An old rusted pickup truck nearby leaned to one side. We made it a limo to visit and bring the flowers to her grave. We told stories of how she gathered wood, dug clams, or smoked fish. Later we guessed her to be the virgin and the grave was some little memorial for her, not understanding the reality of a grave.

—Abby Miller, morning pages

What's happening up in Wasilla? I think about how the snow glares in the spring sun, too bright too look at. In the birches that surround the Wasilla house, moose strain their necks to nosh on the higher branches. Piles of firewood cozily are stacked against the lower level of the house and promise warmth and shelter inside. In the yard there is Aurora's big truck and, of course, Bill's Malibu. Rickety deck stairs lead up to the sun-filled deck where the begonias will be relocated come summer. A rim of mountaintops is visible above the trees. Ah, there is the Inlet.

I go online and log in to Mother's accounts. I scan the expenditures but do not see any unusual activity except for large amounts of fuel for Aurora's vehicles. Something's happening with Aurora, but I can't see or feel exactly what. She's worried, more so than usual. I think back to Wasilla, back to Aurora's house, and examine in my mind what is going on in Aurora's world.

It's clear her world is upside down—parents moving in, sisters taking over, hospice people and volunteers and nurses and VA people all coming and going. Inside the house there is Bear-Bear, the many refrigerators, the baskets of medications, the big fireplace in the living room, the piles of papers and receipts in the game room, the twenty-four begonias sprouting under lights, the special exercise machines for Aurora's new knees, the piles of dirty laundry all separated into whites and darks, and piles of fresh laundry waiting to be ironed.

I try to sense Aurora's pain as she recovers from knee surgery, sense her determination as she exercises every day, sense her worrying about Tim and all the legal problems and the divorce. Aurora hasn't worked in six months, and Tim obviously can't work while he's in jail. I remember snippets of conversations I overheard back in Wasilla.

"I have a houseful of company, and my utilities have skyrocketed," Aurora told someone on the phone.

"The second mortgage on the house was denied," Aurora told us. She wanted the second mortgage to pay for Tim's lawyer.

"It'll be OK. We'll manage," I heard her tell Tim.

Images come forward in my mind: those piles of bills, again Aurora hobbling on a cane for six months, Mother's drained Wells Fargo account, monthly payments for the truck, the lawyer fees, the recent activity in Mother's account for fuel for Aurora's vehicles. Again, those piles of bills. Aurora knows we are watching Mother's money. Aurora knows getting access to more of Mother's money is not as easy as it used to be.

Yes, it's money. Aurora's worried about money, not the usual money worry, more desperate. My jaw clenches. How much will it cost this time? I know how it works. Aurora will remain quiet until the crisis is untenable, unretractable, unrepairable except with large chunks of cash, which she traditionally receives from Mother because the crisis will be unbearable for Mother.

Oh, Aurora, perhaps Mother did not want another child. But perhaps it was not about you. Perhaps it was more JB. Perhaps Mother confused love for you with love for JB. She distanced herself from you because she had to distance herself from JB. So you did the same, distancing yourself and coming to actually hate her, yet longing to love her and hating her even more because of that longing. No wonder you're confused. And now Mother tries to buy your love and fund your crises. And now, oh, Aurora, how I hate you.

What will the cost be this time: house note, car payments, utilities, copayments on medical fees for the knee surgeries, house and vehicle insurance, lawyer fee, the damn lawyer fee? If she is far enough behind, the crisis will be acute. Immediate action will be needed to prevent foreclosure proceedings on the house, repossession of the vehicles, termination of insurance coverage, and shutoff of the utilities. I feel her desperation strong and pulsing.

How would it be? Bill in the living room in a house with no heat or electricity. That alone would be too unbearable for Mother.

The phone rings. It's probably Aurora again.

"Abby Miller?" a somewhat familiar male voice asks.

"Yes?"

"This is Josh Terrino, from the Wasilla Funeral Home," he says.

"Yes, I remember meeting you," I say. "Is everything all right?"

"Yes, well, almost," Josh says. "Everything is in order except for one small detail."

"What would that be?"

"Yes, ma'am. Do you remember the cremation paper work you sent us?" he asks.

How well I remember. How well I don't want to.

"Is there something wrong? Did I forget to sign or initial a page?"

"No, ma'am, you did everything right," he says. "It is just that we need your mother to sign it. You're the executor of the will, not the power of attorney. Your sister Aurora is the POA. We need your mother or your sister to sign it."

"I see."

I hear the opening sentences: humans are about 60 percent water...a huge amount of heat...850 Celsius.

"Is this really necessary?" I say. "The description of the cremation process is rather, uh, graphic."

"I know, ma'am," Josh says. "Most people don't actually read it. But we have to fully disclose all the details to avoid misunderstanding."

Misunderstanding? How could anyone misunderstand? The body will burn outside to inside in a cycle of dehydration and ignition.

"Couldn't you describe it in a more gentle way?"

"Then people might not understand the reality of what happens," Josh says.

The reality? How could anyone misunderstand? Bones glow white in the flames, and the skeleton falls apart. Some of the bones fall into pieces while other bones remain whole.

"I'm very sorry that the description of the cremation disturbed you," Josh says. "That was certainly not our intention."

I vow never to be cremated, never to have to read cremation paper work again, never to put a family member in a position to have to read it for me.

"I'll see to it that my mother or my sister signs the paper work," I say.

What is Mother doing? Sitting by Bill? Talking to Bill? Cleaning up Bill? Will she sit next to him when she reads about the cremation process? Will she say, "Let me sit here beside you, Bill, and tell you about your final fire"?

Will she go into her bedroom or the computer room or someplace more private to read it?

Will Bill look around and ask, "Where is your mother?"

Will someone say to him, "In her bedroom reading about cremating you?"

Aurora is about to go into her next crisis. Do I care?

What's happening up there? Has the ice broken up on the Knik? Have the moose moved on? Have the clouds cleared around Denali for an afternoon? Has the Inlet opened up so the big barges can get through? Are the days long enough to kayak all of Resurrection Bay by daylight? Is Six Mile Creek raging with snowmelt, churning and foaming with class-five and class-six white water?

I print out the cremation documentation and see the words: some body parts resist, especially the chest contents. I rush into the bathroom, bend over the toilet, and vomit. I brush my teeth and rinse my mouth. My mouth still feels foul. I rinse my mouth again and wash my face. I lean on the sink, see the reflection in the mirror, and see Mother.

Returning to the cremation paper work, I carefully sign Mother's name and put her initials on each page. I think of Mother. Sh, you're safe now.

I think about Josh and the funeral home. I'll deal with them later.

27 April
Blah, Blah, Blah

It's Easter Sunday, and Aurora arranges a conference call for us.

"It turns out that Fort Richardson National Cemetery has a place for urns after all," Aurora begins. "Mike brought Bill to the table for Easter dinner. Bill wanted ice cream. Bill was too funny. He said he was going to die soon and could darn well eat whatever he wanted."

"It sounds like Bill is holding his own," Alice says.

"Ladies, I don't think I can live with Mama," Aurora blurts out. "Every time I turn around she is nagging me about money, how I need to save money and manage money better and blah, blah, blah."

"And I hate the way she treats my brand-new carpet," Aurora continues.

The carpet again.

"I thought, of all days, on Easter, a day of new beginnings, we could have peace," Aurora says. "But, sure enough, Mama starts nagging me about money again, about the fifty K we need for Tim's lawyer, blah, blah, blah."

Peace. Hmm. I guess peace is now Mother's responsibility.

"Then she nags about how much money I'm making and how much money I'm spending, blah, blah, blah," Aurora says.

"Are you having financial problems?" Alice asks.

What world does Alice live on?

"Yes, but don't worry about it," Aurora snips at Alice. "The point is that older people don't change. Mama is never going to change. She'll never let me be an adult. It was so beautiful here today. It got up to fifty degrees."

Why should Mother change? Because Aurora has moved Mother and Bill into the Wasilla house, because Aurora is costing Mother a fortune, because Aurora is having a crisis or having knee replacement surgery or ignoring Mother or whatever else the hell Aurora is doing. Perhaps Mother should change to accommodate Aurora better. It's Easter, and I hold my tongue and wait for Alice to chime in with a solution or, better yet, a plan.

"Aurora-Pooh, every adult child has trouble developing a mature relationship with his or her parents," Alice says. "Momma once told me she disliked going back home to visit her parents because she was treated like a child."

Aurora makes a snort-humph sound on the other end of the phone.

"Also, about money. Momma has given you a lot of money over the years. This means she has a vested interest in your financial status. Don't want Momma to bug you about money? Then don't take her money."

Alice probably thinks Aurora is listening.

"I've had hard times in the past when I pawned my engagement ring to pay bills," Alice says. "But I never asked Mother or Bill for money. If you want to establish your independence, you've got to be truly independent and stop depending on them to bail you out. This isn't a judgment or a criticism. It's a fact of life."

Not a judgment. How quaint.

I realize it's my turn to say something. "Well, Aurora, I don't think Mother can live with you."

I think I hear Alice muffle an objection, probably worried that Aurora's response will be ugly and unfriendly, which Alice wouldn't like and wouldn't have an immediate plan for. But

I'm tired of talking carefully around Aurora, tired of tiptoeing around her to avoid a violent outburst.

"I know you moved Mother and Bill up to your house with all intentions of Mother living with you after Bill's gone," I say. "If I'd known you were moving them, I would have stopped you. But it's not going to work. In truth I don't want Mother living with you." I let the words sting.

"Perhaps we could view this as a temporary situation," Alice offers.

"Anyway, how do you want Mother to change? Pray to your carpet?" Oh, let the words sting some more. Easter Sunday. To hell with Easter. "Aurora, I believe Mother has no clue what you need, and you have no clue what Mother needs. I believe you and Mother are emotional time bombs."

I wait for either Alice or Aurora to say something, but they don't.

"Remember when we were up in Wasilla, when you told me and Alice to have faith and told us about precious moments with Bill?" I ask. "Perhaps the time has come to have faith. Unless that faith talk was just crap talk."

There is more silence.

"Happy Easter, ladies," Aurora says and hangs up.

28 April
Head Doctor

I wake up early and tired from nightmares that have plagued me for several nights. The sun breaks out over the east horizon in brilliant orange streaks that light up the high plains. The morning then becomes a blur, and I don't know where it goes, and it's the white light of the noon sun that follows me to the computer. Aurora sends us an e-mail update, which surprises me since she hung up on us last night.

"Mike came by for two hours this morning. Cleaned up Bill and fed him. Mike is a twenty-six-year navy veteran, a brother Mason, and he knows people Bill knows in Homer. Bill really likes Mike," Aurora writes. "It's fifty-two degrees today. My knee doctor said I'm his star patient and doing better than most of his patients. I can go back to work next Monday if I want. I can't get in to see my medication doctor for two more days. Then my head doctor said if I don't improve soon, she will be forced to put me in the hospital. Mother is nagging me about a budget," Aurora says.

What's a head doctor? A psychiatrist or a neurologist? Put her in the hospital? It's the same old game. Aurora wants us to probe her for information.

"Congratulations on your knee!" I write back and resist the urge to ask questions and probe about the many doctors. "I'm delighted about Mike. It must be a relief for you. Hope things work out with the head doctor."

"So what's wrong with you?" Alice writes back.

"We don't know, which is why there are so many doctors" Aurora quickly responds.

"Momma isn't nagging. She's providing guidance," Alice writes. "Momma is a bookkeeper, for God's sake. She knows how to manage money. Besides, a budget is a good idea. That's why it bothers you. Get over it."

"I'm flying back up to Wasilla this coming weekend," Alice writes me privately. "I hope Aurora can hold off having a nervous breakdown until I get there."

29 April
Let Her Go

> My name is Father's Joy. Once a crystal sword called my name. I hung it over a delicate and lovely swan. Then I let her go to Eagle Island to sing soprano bel canto at dawn with a loon on tenor, an owl on tone, and a meadowlark on trill. To this day caribou herds migrate down to hear her breathy arias against the aurora borealis, her soaring soprano cavatina like translucent seamless-glass fishing

floats glimmering on the Inlet. Breathe with her,
like wave after wave gliding onto beach sands. Yes,
I let her go across the Inlet to Eagle Island. Sh. She
sings now.

　　　　　　　　　—Abby Miller, morning pages

How could I be pregnant? But here it is. My stomach bulges. The proof is here in that unused condom wrapped in foil; the black suede boot, mink lined and high heeled; and the telephone number on my fingertip. And here's the most damaging proof of all: a picture of me eating an entire chocolate cake.

I remain calm, sit in the waiting room, and look out over the Inlet. There's Mt. Redoubt. St. Augustine is about to erupt. Always volcanoes. Always ash. I fidget with my cameo ring from WWII France, a gift from Bill when he flew into France.

"Don't be nervous," the nurse says.

The nurse is a mother moose. Her new spring calves play in the corner. She removes a bunch of birch and alder branches from her ragged violin case that is decorated with Air France stickers. At least we have France in common.

The doctor finally comes in. He wears a police badge with the serial numbers filed off. He checks the watermark on the collar of my wet suit, the sure sign of a tired goldfish inside. He shakes his well-worn doctor's bag and looks inside it. His bag is decorated with Air France stickers, another France commonality.

"This ought to do it." He gives me a brass door knocker shaped like a grizzly bear head.

"Go sit on this door knocker while you're on that Royal Delft chamber pot." He points to a large beautiful blue and white vase. He hands me a coin. "Bite down on this if it hurts."

Mother Moose–Nurse leads me to the vase/chamber pot.

"It shouldn't hurt much," she says. She glances over at the calves, now sleeping in the corner, tangled in each other's spindly legs, one calf's long fuzzy nose resting on the back of the other's. "Put the coin between your teeth, just in case. If it hurts, bite down."

The doctor taps a syringe. He sees my interest in the syringe.

"Truth serum," he says. "This is a free clinic, only as long as you tell the truth." He eyes my camouflage-patterned daypack. "Who are you hiding from?" He gestures toward my daypack.

"Nobody."

"Then you're a hunter?" he asks.

Mother Moose–Nurse looks startled, gives me a concerned look, and moves between me and the sleeping calves. The radio blares another warning about St. Augustine. If there is too much ash, planes will be grounded.

"No, no, no, not a hunter," I say and begin to feel the pain from the door knocker.

"Bear down on that knocker, sweetie. That's why there is a bear on it," the doctor says. "Now, tell us the truth."

"I don't have anything to tell."

The doctor and Mother Moose–Nurse exchange looks. The doctor goes to the refrigerator and takes out a musty sachet ball adorned with a delicate grayish mildew. I gasp.

"Good grief, girl, stop being so squeamish. What do you think penicillin is?" he says. He scrapes off some mildew into a tube filled with clear solution. Then he injects the mildew-infused solution into a second syringe.

"I really need you to tell us the truth," he says. "Nurse."

Mother Moose–Nurse holds me down while the doctor injects my arm with the truth serum. I feel the prick of the needle and the wave of nausea that immediately ensues. Where is that matchbook with only one match left and the message, "Save this for last"?

The nausea passes and leaves me in a world with no hard edges or straight lines. The pain from the door knocker intensifies, and I bite on the coin. There is dust on the floor by my feet and speckles of dust floating around me.

"It'll take a few minutes," the doctor says. "Meanwhile, how's that knocker doing? I've unknocked a lot of knocked-up girls with that particular knocker. Thatta girl—bite down."

"So tell us now," the doctor says.

"Just tell us the truth." Mother Moose–Nurse flicks her big ears.

Dust swirls around me. The door knocker pain grows, and I bite harder on the coin.

"That's right. Bite down. Bear down. We're almost done, but, first, tell us the truth," the doctor says. He reaches over, gently takes the coin out of my mouth, and strokes my head. "Go ahead and tell us. Then it'll all be over, and you'll feel so much better."

The door knocker pain appears in short waves. The swirling dust is more problematic, distorting the room so it's difficult to see and filling the room so it's difficult to breathe. I can't see the Inlet. Did Augustine blow? I struggle to breathe and see what's happening.

"That's right, my girl, tell us," the doctor says.

I look toward where the Inlet should be, and though I can't see it, I sense its presence—the miles of beach and cliff; the masses of red salmon gathering and waiting for their signal to go up the Kenai; the fisherman leaning forward, ready, dip nets poised, waiting for the signal that the reds are running.

"Fish fever," I say. "Fish fever, fish fever, fish fever." I feel the relief of finally telling. "Fish fever, fish fever," I continue to mumble. "Fish fever."

The doctor and Mother Moose–Nurse come closer to me. The calves wake up and stumble over to me. One calf stares up into my face and sniffs the salt on my skin.

"No, dear, don't do that." Mother Moose–Nurse scoots the calf away.

"Fish fever," I begin to rock back and forth on the lovely Royal Delft chamber pot.

"It's OK now. We all know fish fever." The doctor takes my hand. He holds it gently, soothingly. "It's OK."

"Yes, we all know," Mother Moose–Nurse says so gently that I believe she does know.

"This is to protect you." The doctor injects the second syringe into my arm and hands me a scrap piece of paper scrawled in red ink: "No more numbers in nirvana, baby."

I wake to Matt shaking me. Did I scream? My pillow is wet with sweat.

"It's just a bad dream," Matt says.

"I know, I know," I say.

It's not fair. I haven't had this dream in twenty years. Why has it returned? I get out of bed, brush my teeth, and do breathing exercises to relax. My mouth feels foul, and I brush my teeth again. Why has the dream returned?

I was a still naïve twenty-seven-year-old when the dream first appeared. For weeks the dream came and left me in night sweats and shakes. I didn't plan to be pregnant. It just happened in a meaningless hormonal frenzy. I'd planned to keep the pregnancy secret and terminate it. Then my life could go on, but the dream continued, and my life couldn't go on. And the dream continued every night until I stood before the Sisters of Mercy.

"I'm pregnant," I said to Sister Mary Elaine.

She put her arm around me, and the dream disappeared. Except for Aurora, I kept it a secret, telling everyone else I'd had a job in Europe for a year.

"Your job now is to bear this child," Sister Mary Elaine told me. "We'll take care of everything else."

The adoption would be closed. The child would never know me. Never told the father, never told my family, not even Matt.

I gave the child, a beautiful baby girl, to the adopted family myself. The child cried out a piercing baby cry when the nurse handed the child to me.

Hush, little one, I thought. You're safe now.

The adopted parents came into the room, and I handed the crying, wrinkled bundle to the woman. The woman embraced the child, rocked it, cooed to it, and the crying stopped. Indeed the child was safe. The Sisters had screened the families well. The woman held the child for the man to see. When the man touched the child's nose, she instinctively made funny little honking sounds like a swan.

"Are you sure?" the woman asked me.

I nodded yes.

She held the bundle closer. "She is ours?"

I nodded yes again.

So why has the dream returned? Didn't I do the right thing? My mouth still feels foul, and I rinse it out. What has changed? I am forty-seven years old now. I have no regrets, no phantoms to haunt me, yet here is this phantom. Did I make a mistake twenty years ago? No, no mistake. It's something else.

30 April
The Manipulator

"I'm worried about Aurora," Alice calls and tells me. "Sounds like things are pretty bad between her and Momma."

"Be careful. Aurora is a master manipulator," I say. "She's saying all this stuff about Mother for a reason. Any idea what Aurora means by head doctor? Is that a therapist or a neurologist?"

"No idea," Alice says.

"Any idea what she meant about the head doctor might put her in the hospital if she didn't improve soon?"

"Not a clue," Alice says.

"Oh well. She's just trying to manipulate us," I say. "Notice how she throws out the dramatic statement about the head doctor and then stops. That's how she gets us to probe her for answers; get involved; and, ultimately, offer our help in some way. Probably with money."

"That's pure speculation," Alice says.

"You'd like to think so. Remember a month ago, when Aurora told us that Bill was going to die in two or three weeks?"

"Yeah, yeah," Alice says.

"We rushed up there, wanting to be there to say good-bye, to have no regrets. Heck, we even witnessed end-of-life signs. Aurora knew all along that Bill would not die in two or three weeks."

"And?" Alice says.

"We rushed up there, helped out with Bill, and Aurora did nothing. She never even came upstairs. She totally ignored Bill, totally ignored Mother, and totally ignored us. Do you realize that I only shared one meal with Aurora the entire month I was up there?" I open a jumbo bag of pistachios.

"The bottom line is that Aurora lied to us." I crack a pistachio between my teeth. "That bitch didn't want us to rush up there for Bill. She wanted us to be her nurse after she got her knee surgery. Aurora doesn't give a damn about Bill, alive or dead or dying."

The methodical splitting and cracking of pistachio shells.

"That's total conjecture," Alice says. "Give Aurora a break."

"Give her a break? The bitch used us and continues to manipulate us every time she has a crisis. Now she's trying to drain Mother of every penny, ignoring Mother, accusing Mother of nagging, and on and on. The bitch doesn't even have the sense to pretend to be nice to Mother."

Salt. Sucking the salt off the pistachio shells before discarding them into a growing heap of shells. Salt lingering on my lips.

"I'm more aware of Aurora's manipulation now. And I agree it's possible Aurora got us to fly up there for her own needs," Alice says. "But I'm not going up there for Aurora anymore. I'm going for Momma and Bill. I want to get Momma and Bill out of there safely, one way or another."

"I hope you're not hoping to relocate Bill," I say. "Mother panicked when someone simply mentioned this before."

"No, but I want a backup plan," Alice says.

"After the funeral I hope to get Mother to come to New Mexico," I say. "I think she could use some time and space to figure things out."

"Momma needs a plan," Alice says. So like Alice.

I reach for more pistachios, cracking them open one by one in a smooth, soothing nonstop rhythm. I'm not aware of their taste.

"What are you thinking?"

"Not sure yet, but we need a plan," Alice says.

As we're talking, an e-mail from Aurora arrives.

"I made a coconut pie. Bill loved it. Made mushroom soup. Bill loved it, too. I had my knee therapy, and now my knee hurts," Aurora writes in her e-mail. "It's fifty-three degrees."

Later that night I gather papers, sweep up heaps of pistachio shells, crumple the empty pistachio bag, and push the bag down into the trash. The wind rattles the weather vane on the roof and vibrates through the chimney baffles. Sleep is restless.

"Don't be nervous. Go sit on this door knocker and tell us the truth," the doctor says.

"Tell us the truth." Mother Moose–Nurse looms over me, flicking those big ears.

I wake, trembling and sweating. I get up, brush my teeth, rinse my mouth, and wander the house in the dark. I stare out the big windows across the high plains and listen, but there's only the wind, no coyotes tonight. "Why has the dream returned?" I ask the wind.

But the wind only howls, and there are no answers tonight.

1 May
Taking Stock

Right now Alice is about to board a plane in Seattle to fly back to Alaska. I'll stay here in New Mexico and stand by.

I log into Mother's Wells Fargo account for my daily monitoring, scan the numbers and columns and names of merchants and notice more fuel purchases for Aurora's truck. I make a mental note to start monitoring Mother's other accounts and make another note to find the paper work for Bill's stock portfolio. The thought of Bill's stock strategy makes me smile.

"What's in Seattle?" Bill asked when Alice moved to Seattle. Then he bought Microsoft stock.

"What's in New Mexico?" Bill asked when I moved to New Mexico, and he bought Intel stock.

Knowing Aurora liked dogs, Bill bought Purina stock. Bill liked ice cream, so he bought what he called a "double scoop" of Dairy Queen stock.

"You're my sweetie-pie," Bill told Mother, and so he bought stock in Mrs. Smith's Pies.

Through the years the stock portfolio became a fun little story of our lives with each new milestone celebrated with a few shares of stock: more Purina stock for each new dog of Aurora's, Boeing to celebrate my marriage to a pilot, EMC to celebrate Alice's graduation from law school, McDonalds to commemorate Bill's meeting place where he and his buddies gathered to drink coffee and tell stories, stock in a silver mine to celebrate his and Mother's silver anniversary. It was so charming. Mother would surely want to save the portfolio for her scrapbook.

I watch the evening news and become nervous when a story comes on about a volcano in Alaska, St Augustine, rumbling, possibly about to erupt. St. Augustine stands guard on a tiny island, created by the volcano itself, at the entrance to Cook Inlet. From Homer, Augustine looks like it is floating in the Inlet.

Volcanoes are real to me as well as earthquakes and tsunamis. I've seen the plume of St. Augustine, its dark smoke trail against fiery skies and a smoking red sunset. I've felt my bed shake in the night from tremors coming across the Inlet. I've gone out to the Homer Spit to watch the boats, and I knew if a tsunami came, there was no safe harbor.

The TV reporter announces it is Code Yellow for aviation. The plane with Alice will approach from the southeast, heading north along the panhandle up through the Gulf of Alaska. Traditionally, the ash plume will stream northeast toward Anchorage.

I send Alice a text: "Call when you arrive in Anchorage."

Alice is on the plane now, so I'll have to wait for a response. It'll take four hours for Alice to reach Anchorage. Any ash plume from St. Augustine will be slower.

When Alice flies over, the Cook Inlet belugas may already be in the Gulf of Alaska, making their way to the Inlet. What will they do when they feel Augustine's rumbling? Warn other creatures as they are known to do? Will all three hundred belugas wait at the entrance to the Inlet and stand guard?

Once when we went halibut fishing, a lone beluga came close to our boat and squeaked and clucked at us. We reeled in our lines and squeaked back, clucked, and tried to teach the beluga to whistle. We squealed in delight when the beluga whistled back at us. We clucked and whistled with the beluga for an hour, pulling up the anchor and carefully following the pure whiteness of its blunt little head and smiling face. We soon noticed the beluga was leading us back toward Homer and knew the beluga wanted us to go home. We clucked and squeaked farewell and headed back. When we got home, Mother was relieved to see us. There was a tsunami warning out. St Augustine was about to erupt, and the tremors had already started.

Four hours go by and no word from Alice.

I send another text: "Are you there?"

No response. I go to my computer and search for recent news about Augustine. Increased activity. May be upgraded soon to Code Orange for aviation. I should call Aurora and see if she picked up Alice at the airport. No, I don't want to talk to Aurora. The witch.

Eight hours go by and still no word from Alice. It's silly to worry so much. But where's Alice? When will Aurora announce the new crisis? What's happening up in Alaska now? Where are the moose? I search on the computer and find no new news about

Augustine. Minitremors must have started by now. Childhood memories float by: lying there in the shaking bed pretending it was a roller coaster or watching TV as the couch shook or pretending the house was haunted. Why hasn't Alice called? I make strong, hot coffee to help quiet my mind.

I resist the urge to send another text to Alice. She'll think I'm nagging. I resist the urge to call Aurora. She'll think I care.

2 May
Life Is a Bear

> My name is Father's Joy. I learned life is worth a pancake from a yearling bear cub at our cabin across the Inlet in Chinitna Bay. He rattled our tin roof come mornings, smelling coffee and bacon, and grumbled until I gave him pancakes. Another time, he ate all our razor clams and watched me catch salmon with a gill net. One day, I slept on the sand in the sun. Felt a fly by my head and swatted it. Swatted his bear whiskers instead. After that we called him Whiskers. The next summer, Whiskers tore off the tin roof; clawed our dinghy; tore the fabric off our plane; and, finally, lunged at us. Resolute, I shot him. We sent the meat to a family, the rug to a friend. Whiskers wouldn't be wasted. But I knew what the universe was thinking: for pancakes.
>
> —Abby Miller, morning pages

A plane trip from Seattle to Anchorage usually follows the panhandle, over the permanently snow-topped Coast Range, over open water often accented with iceberg chunks. At thirty thousand feet, no accident involving a fall to the mountains or the ice fields or the open water is survivable.

Twenty-four hours and still no word from Alice. No news is good news, but I need to know. I wipe away nightmare images of Mother Moose–Nurse and the doctor and go to my computer.

"What are you doing?" Matt enters the room.

"I am checking on Alice. I don't know if she made it to Anchorage."

She'll fly over the largest temperate-latitude ice fields in the world. Glaciers fill every valley. To survive a plane crash in those ice fields is to experience hell before death, before freezing and becoming part of the ice itself.

"When was she supposed to arrive?" Matt asks.

"Yesterday, about noon our time."

"Do you have any reason to think she didn't get there?" Matt sits in the chair next to the computer desk.

"Augustine is erupting. The last I heard, it was Code Yellow and about to go Orange."

"You're worried about an ash plume?" Matt says.

He is a pilot. He understands the significance of ash plume and airplane. Those moments before impact. The thought of Alice hitting the ice fields or hitting the water, engulfed in the water or engulfed in ice. Will the belugas be there to save her? We get on a plane, and we believe the plane will take us there. We don't truly grasp there is no escape, that we may not get to Anchorage, that we may go across the Inlet instead.

"I'm sure she's OK." Matt pulls his chair close to me and takes my hand. "You're overreacting as usual."

"I don't understand why she hasn't called. We always call." I frantically search the Internet for news of a plane gone missing in the Coast Range or over the Gulf of Alaska. Those moments before impact. I feel them. I feel the fear surge, the survival instinct kick in, the momentary struggle before release to the water or the realization before crashing into the ice fields of hell that death would come slow and without feeling.

"Stop, sweetie," Matt says. "You're obsessing."

"I know, I know. I can't help it."

"Sweetie, you can't protect your sisters and mother every second of their or your life."

"I have to. It's what I do. It's my job."

126

"No, it's not your job," Matt says.

"I'll call up there, talk to Bill," I say. All my life, I have tried to keep them safe.

"Sweetie, stop it. Stop it right now," Matt insists.

"I can't. I have to do something."

I have to know where she is. To know where people are located is paramount and can make the difference between life and death. Alaskans know this. I remember our summer camping place up in the Denali, a ten-hour car ride from Homer.

Then it was a three-mile hike to the little lake, which was connected by a narrow channel to the big lake. It took an hour's ride in the dinghy to get across the big lake to where we camped. We named the big lake Bottomless Lake because we couldn't see the bottom. We named one mountain Bear Mountain because we saw bears there. We named another mountain Bug Mountain because there were so many mosquitoes there. We named the little lake simply Little Lake.

JB would ferry us back to the campsite in the dinghy. Then he would make a second trip to bring the camping gear and supplies. One day he ferried us to the campsite, dropped us off as usual, and motored back to the little lake to get the supplies. We expected him to return in about two hours. Only the weather out on the lake became nasty with the wind turning the normally smooth lake into a sea of waves and whitecaps and driving rain. We knew JB would not be able to make the return trip in that storm. We watched the storm rage all day and well into the next day. We understood how dangerous it would be for JB to cross the lake and knew he would wait it out. We would wait it out, too, in the relative calm of our little cove at the back of the lake.

A beaver dam was nearby, so we borrowed wood and sticks from the beavers to build a fire. Alice always insisted we have an emergency plan, so we typically carried daypacks filled with emergency supplies. We had matches, fish hooks, and some basic survival gear. We built a lean-to shelter from branches, leaves, and tundra moss. We created fishing poles from long sticks and twine and discovered that fish liked cheese, and we actually caught fish, which we boiled in lake water in a coffee can or roasted on an old piece of grate. We waited for the weather to turn, swatting mosquitoes and big-bite-no-see-ums, watching beavers do maintenance on their dam and bears lumber down from Bear Mountain to drink and fish in the lake. Once, we spotted a sheep on a far mountain ledge.

Mother told us to keep fishing and to watch for bears and bury the fish guts far from camp so bears wouldn't smell the guts near us.

Aurora carried a .45-caliber pistol and twelve-gauge shotgun, loaded with slugs, that JB instructed her to carry at all times. She was the only one of us girls strong enough to handle the recoil. She carried the .45 under her arm in a shoulder holster and the shotgun in a sling. Aurora was in charge of close range.

"Don't shoot the bear unless the bear has Abby's head in its mouth," JB always told Aurora. We all knew JB really didn't mean this. We understood that he meant, *Don't shoot the bear unless we have no choice or someone's life is in danger.*

I carried a .338 Mag rifle. In camp I carried the rifle in a sling across my back. When hiking I carried the rifle out front like a soldier. I was in charge of long range.

Alice wore a coffee can attached to twine and looped around her neck. Her job was to bang and clang on the coffee can with an old pair of scissors and make enough noise to scare bears away. Alice was in charge of early warning.

When the weather turned, it drove the storm into our camp, and we hunkered down in the wind and drizzling rain, and we challenged each other to gather wood, fish, or pick blueberries. We were unafraid, doing our parts and taking care of business. Unafraid until the biggest bear in the world came to camp.

"Freeze," Aurora whispered.

I didn't see the bear at first. I smelled it: a combination of dead fish and excrement.

"Where's Alice?" Mother whispered.

In slow motion I turned so I could see the bear. The giant brown bear sniffed around the edge of our camp. I saw Aurora. Where was Alice? Aurora touched her .45 in slow motion. I shook my head and patted the sling to my rifle to signal her to use the shotgun. It was too easy to miss the shot with the pistol. And if she needed to shoot, she couldn't miss. I watched her move inch by inch, getting the shotgun, with those deadly slugs, in position.

I slowly got my rifle in position. I would give the warning shot and try to scare the bear away. The big bear moved in closer toward our fire site. Where was Alice? The bear was getting too close now, sniffing around, and moving closer to the fire site only ten feet from the lean-to. It was time for the warning shot. I nodded to Aurora. She nodded back. Where was Alice? I fired straight up in the air, didn't hold the rifle tight enough, and felt the recoil slam through my entire upper body, ignored it, and moved back fast as I could, back far enough to possibly get a shot at the bear with the rifle. The warning shot echoed off the mountains. The bear didn't seem even a little startled and continued to lumber toward the lean-to.

Mother sat in the lean-to, motionless except for her eyes that were wildly searching the area. I knew she was looking for Alice. Our daypacks with any leftover snacks and food items were in the lean-to with Mother. The bear sniffed around the fire site and lumbered toward Mother.

Alice appeared on the little ridge that led to the beaver dam, running, breathless. She must have heard the warning shot and came running, the coffee can bumping against her chest. She froze when she saw the bear, unknowingly right between Aurora and the bear, directly in Aurora's line of fire to the bear. The bear continued toward the lean-to.

I saw Alice see me as I moved back. I saw her notice Aurora ready to fire the shotgun and Mother in the lean-to with the bear lumbering toward it. Then Alice started yelling at the bear, and she clanged and banged on her coffee can.

"Here bear, here bear—come get me," Alice yelled at the bear. She reached down and picked up a rock and threw it at the bear. The rock hit the bear in the rear haunch. The bear turned and seemed to look at Alice.

"Over here, bear. Don't eat Momma." Alice clanged on her coffee can and threw another rock at the bear.

Usually bears will run away with enough noise. The yelling, clanging, and warning shot should have scared him off, but the bear turned and moved toward Alice.

"Good bear, good bear." Alice tried to encourage the bear.

I was still too close for a rifle shot and kept stepping back. I signaled Aurora to be ready. Alice continued to yell and clang as the bear continued to move toward her. I memorized everyone's location so I could give the right signal to the right person.

"Drop," I signaled to Alice.

"Freeze," I signaled to Mother.

The bear continued toward Alice to the point of no return, the tipping point, the point when the bear would have Alice's head in its mouth.

"Now," I signaled Aurora.

She fired the shotgun, sending a solid slug into the bear's shoulder. The bear seemed only somewhat startled, paused, and resumed its movement toward Alice. The bear was a few feet from Alice, who lay flat as she could on the ground.

"No!" Mother unfroze and screamed at the bear. "Over here."

The bear seemed to take notice and took our breath and heartbeats away as it stood up on its giant hind legs, sniffed, and looked around, exposing its underside and underarm. Aurora sucked in her breath, exhaled purposively, and I heard another crack of the shotgun, sending the slug to the bear's underarm area. The bear twitched its nose and eyeballed Alice.

"God, don't take my child." Mother jumped out of the lean-to, stood, and yelled.

I could see Aurora shaking, the panic starting to overcome her. I tried to get a bead on the bear with the rifle, though I knew I was too close.

"Sometimes," JB had said. "You have to feel the shot. Just aim, breathe, and fire."

So I tried to feel the shot, aimed, breathed, and fired. This time the bear stopped, looked confused, and dropped dead about a foot from Alice.

We didn't move until we were certain the bear was dead, and then we approached.

"I'm sure Alice is OK." Matt puts his arm around me.

Mother raced to Alice, and she and Alice held each other, both of them shaking. Aurora ran to me, and we, too, stood there trembling, almost convulsing, our faces contorted with leftover fear and panic. It was such a big, beautiful bear.

"You can't be obsessing like this," Matt says. "It's tearing you apart."

It seemed like JB returned while we were still shaking. He was gaunt and pale, and seemed to be shaking, too. I think he saw the whole thing from the dinghy out in the lake. He and Aurora gutted and skinned the bear. He would give the bear meat to friends and the bear skin to another friend who owned a hunting lodge.

It took several trips in the dingy to get us, all our gear, and the bear back across the lake. I can still see that beautiful, big bear.

"Abby, listen to me," Matt shakes me ever so lightly.

How could he know about the bear and the ice fields and open water and what might happen to Alice if the plane crashed? How could he understand that life here on this earth was as fine and delicate as a solitary whisker on a bear's nose and knowing where everyone was?

Where in the hell is Alice?

3 May
Rituals

> My name is Father's Joy. I send you my name from
> water on a mountaintop flowing down to the Inlet.
> Glorious with one precious pebble at low tide, one
> purplish shell, one weathered chunk of driftwood,
> one kayak slipping into a soft wave ripple full of
> grace. Or I send it with gulls gliding over clam
> beaches; with belugas poking their heads up in the
> Inlet; with the low rumble of bore tide running
> back to shore, descending over mud flats, pulling
> in kelp and more driftwood and a lump of coal to
> heat our house. Thus go the rituals of the Inlet.
> Alleluia.
>
> —Abby Miller, morning pages

It's still early in Wasilla, and the morning routine has barely start-ed. Mother will still be sleeping. So will Aurora and Tim. Alice may still be sleeping, if she ever got there.

"Hello," an unfamiliar voice answers, probably a new care-giver. It's confusing to know who is who or what—who is from hospice and who is from the VA and who is from the church.

The television plays in the background with the morning news, which means Bill is awake and watching the electronic ticker tape with the stock market reports.

"Hi, I'm Abby, Bill's daughter."

"Oh, hello. I'm Sherrie, one of the new home health aides. Today's my first day."

"Nice to meet you, Sherrie," I say. "Is Alice up yet?"

"Alice? I don't know. All the bedroom doors are closed, and I haven't actually met Alice yet, but nobody seems to be moving around. I don't think anyone's awake except for Bill," Sherrie says.

"May I talk to Bill?"

"Bill?"

"Sure. Turn the phone on speaker, and set it on his shoulder."

"You have a phone call," Sherrie says in the background.

There's static and a change in the sound as the phone is switched to speaker. I put my own phone on speaker so I can check my e-mail and see if Alice sent a message.

"Who, me?" I hear Bill say.

"Hi, Billiam."

"Why, it's the Roadrunner." The delight in his voice warms me.

"How are you doing?"

"You know, we can't get the Malibu fixed," Bill says.

"Hmm. I thought we had that figured out."

"Your mother and Aurora think there's nothing wrong with it," Bill says.

"Do you really need the Malibu?"

"Yep."

"Where are you going with the Malibu anyway?" It is our private question. He talks about the Malibu, and I ask where he's going. I know the answer.

"Across the Inlet," Bill answers.

"You should take a plane," I give the expected response.

"Yep."

An e-mail report comes in from Alice. Finally!

"I arrived at the Anchorage airport," Alice begins her e-mail.

She's probably typing down the hall from Bill, in the guestroom with the door closed.

"Yep, but the only plane I've got is *Belle of the Ball*," Bill says. "A C-130 is kinda big for just one person. Perhaps I could put it in stealth mode so nobody would know it's only me onboard." Bill chuckles.

"Aurora was not at the airport to meet me," Alice writes. "I e-mailed her a plan before I left Seattle, but when I arrived in Anchorage, Aurora was nowhere to be seen. I was so angry. Why didn't she just stick to the plan? I almost got on the next plane back to Seattle. I called her house, and someone named Linda answered the phone. She said Aurora was downstairs sleeping. Linda said she'd wake up Aurora and they'd come to the airport right away, which means an hour at best. So I cooled my heels at the airport. It turned out to be a good thing because I made some important business calls and had calmed down by the time Aurora and Linda arrived."

"I've got to get going," Bill's voice crackles.

"What's the hurry?" I ask.

"They're talking about Saint Augustine on the news."

"I know. I read about it," I say.

"Even so, I'm running out of time, and nothing is working right," Bill says.

"Aurora was pretty much unresponsive when she got to the airport," Alice continues her report. "All the way home, I chatted amicably with Linda, who's apparently a good friend of Aurora's, pretending that I didn't notice anything unusual about Aurora. The house was a shambles. There were dishes all over the kitchen, some clean, some dirty. I tried to put the clean dishes away, but I didn't know where to put stuff. The kitchen arrangement had changed. The spice jars were out of order, and I was looking around trying to find places for things when Aurora snarled at me. So I stopped."

"Everything takes so long," Bill adds.

"What takes so long?"

"Getting ready to go."

"I know, Billiam. I know." I'm not sure what to say. I am not sensing him like I usually do. It is not as easy over the telephone. "Is Alice talking your leg off?"

"I saw her in the fireplace."

"Alice?"

"No, Ruth. Pay attention. She was talking to Slim," Bill says.

Slim was Bill's buddy and had died a year ago. Ruth was Bill's sister and had died several years ago. Bill respected Ruth but was not close to her.

"What were they talking about?"

"Oh, they were fussing. Slim told Ruth to go away. Ruth told Slim that she was family, not Slim. Then Slim told Ruth to go suck eggs and that he'd take me across the Inlet, not Ruth." Bill's voice became more serious. "That's why it's critical to get the Malibu ready."

"Bill, sweetie," I say. "Forget the Malibu. Take the plane. Get the preflight done, and go whenever you want."

"Yep." Bill sighs. "But Augustine is about to go. There's always something."

I begin to sense him more. He's waiting for something.

"There were dirty clothes scattered all around," Alice reports in her e-mail. "Garbage everywhere, empty boxes, dirty paper towels, soda cans, crumpled-up chip bags. I went around and picked up the garbage. I folded clothes and put them away. I learned later that Jessica, Aurora's little teenager-helper-friend, was on vacation."

"Time is running out," Bill says. "Your mother should be getting up soon. She wants to go to church today."

"As I was cleaning up, Aurora made lunch for people—bacon and eggs—and created more dirty dishes, bacon grease spattered all over the stove and a panful of burned scrambled eggs," Alice writes. "Aurora snaps at Momma all the time. Only Linda seems to escape Aurora's bad temper. It was a ghastly welcome."

"When are you coming back up?" Bill asks me.

Matt appears and stands in the doorway to my office, listening to Bill's voice on the speakerphone.

"Don't know yet," I say. "Soon."

Matt shakes his head.

"What's the matter, Roadrunner?" Bill asks.

Three meadowlarks appear in the crabapple tree outside my window. I feel Matt watching me. The meadowlarks sing their lilting morning song. The neighborhood quail covey skitters by. The neighbor walks her dog. The irrigation for the roses kicks on with a whish. The morning sun lingers over the plains and lights up my garden in lovely, shadowy morning light before beginning its daily journey to the mountains in the west. These are the morning rituals of my world.

I sense Matt in the doorway, watching me, listening to Bill talk, and I look around for the bag of popcorn usually kept near the computer.

"Nothing. Why?"

I think of the morning rituals up at the Wasilla house. The television comes on with the news, the weather report, and the stock reports. Some juice for Bill. Warm towels on his face. A hot breakfast. Help Bill eat breakfast. The daily hygiene. Go back to sleep.

"After lunch it was a warm, sunny day," Alice writes. "I sat out on the deck and chatted with Linda, who told me that Aurora is supposed to go back to work tomorrow for half days. She doesn't think Aurora is emotionally ready to go back to work. At first I was empathetic about Aurora going back to work after all the surgery and six months of not working. I talked to Aurora about her anxiety. Aurora said she was worried about Bear-Bear being lonely. Give me a break. She's worried about the damn dog. I stopped being empathetic."

"Forget about the Malibu," Bill tells me.

"Oh?"

"That's the crew chief's job," Bill says.

"I know, Billiam. But I wish I could be there to help."

"You worry too much. Take care of your husband."

I glance at Matt standing in the doorway."

"Don't take chances, Roadrunner," Bill says.

"Momma came out to the deck later," Alice writes. "Momma and I gossiped and chitchatted about the birds, nothing really significant. But it broke the ice for later conversation about a plan I hope."

"Ah, here comes your mother," Bill says.

I envision Mother padding down the hall bundled up in her flannel robe and sitting on the stool next to Bill. She might discreetly sniff the air to check for poop smells.

"Who are you talking to?" Mother asks Bill.

"It's the Roadrunner," Bill whispers to Mother. His voice is muffled as if he is holding his hand over the telephone. "She's checking to see if Alice made it here OK."

"Hey, how do you make holy water?" Bill asks.

"I dunno. How?" I give the traditional response.

"You boil the hell out of it." Bill laughs, and the laugh trails off into a cough.

"Did you give him some juice?" Mother says in the background.

"Bill seems slightly weaker," Alice writes. "I gave him some water, and he sipped through the straw. Later I gave him juice, and he couldn't use the straw. He didn't eat much today. He was lucid, held my hand and responded to me, but didn't talk much. Momma said his legs hurt, and he often needs pain pills."

Matt still stands in the doorway. He adjusts his tie and continues to listen to me and Bill.

"Aurora is limping badly. She walks as slowly now as she did a few weeks ago," Alice says. "Tim's still in jail and constantly calling Aurora. Linda said that Aurora thinks God is testing her. This is one dysfunctional household right now. The stress is so thick, you can cut it with a knife." Alice concludes her e-mail.

"Gotta go, Roadrunner. I was just informed that I'm tired," Bill says.

"Soon?" Matt raises one eyebrow.

"What else could I say?"

"You know, you're here, but you're still up there." Matt sighs. "I'm going to work."

"I can't help it." I look out to my garden. "What would you have me say? I'll come up for the funeral?"

But it's not my garden anymore. It's Aurora's backyard. The neighbor dog is a moose, and the crabapple trees are birches.

4 May
Is It Safe?

> My name is Father's Joy. Don't say my name when
> the tide ebbs and holds it breath for a moment in
> time after the Inlet drains out to expose the tidal
> flats where truth is found in a razor clam. Touch it
> if you dare. It will not move then, and you can pull
> it out of the mud and rejoice in a clam sandwich
> or fritter sprinkled with salt. Don't say my name in
> this one place in space before the Inlet calls the
> tide back, pushes me back to shore, and returns
> all as it was.
>
> —Abby Miller, morning pages

The new morning comes with leftover dream images of Mother
Moose–Nurse and news of Augustine smoking and sending more
ash toward Anchorage. News of Augustine is familiar. Volcanoes,
earthquakes, and tsunamis were among the things we considered dangerous, but expected, especially where the land ends
out on the Homer Spit. There's no escape there, but we go there
anyway to admire the towering, surrounding mountains and
the Harding ice fields. Tourists go there and stay long enough
to marvel at the warning sign, "In the event of tsunami, seek
shelter."

Those of us who live here go out to the Spit, stay there,
and linger. We look out to where Kachemak Bay meets the
Inlet and Augustine stands guard. Or we watch the eagles. Or
we gaze up to where the mountain peaks touch the sky and
wonder if that's where heaven begins. Perhaps we hear a giant
C-130 rumble by, practicing touch-and-goes at the Homer airport. Perhaps we peer at otters bobbing on top of the tide or
at an orca cutting through the waves. Or we watch the ferry
come into dock. Perhaps we contemplate the bay and breathe
in the briny, slightly fishy sea smells. If the wind comes from
the north and the tide is out, we can smell the rich, heady

fragrance of exposed mud flats. Sometimes we stand on the land's end and take in the immensity and know we are not safe, yet we crave this for it tells us there is a possibility that God exists.

"You look tired," Matt enters. He's fresh, spicy, and ready to go to work. His aftershave lotion reminds me of…My head swims with everything reminding me of something.

"More nightmares?"

"I didn't sleep well."

Outside my window the morning birds gather.

"What's on your schedule today?" Matt asks.

"I don't remember exactly. Clients," I say. "I keep thinking about Bill."

"Try not to." Matt kisses me lightly. "Don't forget we are going to the birthday dinner for my father tonight."

In that moment I don't like Matt. His father is alive and mobile and lives here. My stepfather, who should've been my real father, lies bedridden in Alaska, in hospice world, wandering between lucidity and some unknown world. Meanwhile Mother wanders the Wasilla house and fears Aurora is the new JB. I resent Matt for not understanding this, for not feeling it, for expecting me to live now freely and gaily. Is Mother safe? Are we safe? Is anybody safe? Go to work, Matt.

I turn on my computer intending to work. What is safe now? I've stood out on the Spit, faced that immensity, and imagined the danger. I've stood out on the Ninilchik cliffs and looked out at the combined beauty and terror of miles of exposed mud flats during a minus-four tide. I've watched the tide return later, sometimes as a bore tide six feet high rolling and roaring back to shore at ten miles per hour. I've known not to stand on uncharted mud flats where the mud may be unstable and might suck a person down into the ooze.

I learned what is safe on the clam beds across the Inlet. We had camped in the small cabin that JB had built. I was up at dawn to greet the minus tide and left Alice, Aurora, and JR sleeping in the cabin. I donned a packboard and headed out for the clam beds with my dog, Spot. It was a treat to be across the Inlet. There would be no other clam diggers stomping the mud. We were going after the prized, succulent Cook Inlet razor clam. Ah, to sauté up one razor clam for a clam sandwich or fry up a batch of clam fritters.

My packboard was custom fitted for clam digging. JB had cut the top off an old five-gallon Blazo can, punched holes along the sides of the can, and laced the Blazo can to the packboard with old tent straps, which gave us an easy way to carry the heavy razor clams.

I am startled when the computer makes the chirp-like signal that a new e-mail has arrived. It's from Alice.

"Hello," Alice writes. "I got up this morning and was sort of disappointed that Bill is still alive. I feel terrible thinking that. I walk around quietly so as not to wake him. As soon as he wakes, the TV goes on and the morning duties start."

It took an hour to reach the prime clam beds. The mud flats shone with the soft sheen of wet mud and were fragrant with the smell of salt and dead seaweed. It was a minus-4.2 tide, a huge sprawling low tide that uncovered miles of mud flats, along with new clam beds that are not often dug. These beds have clams by the hundreds in one small area or clams that had grown to six to eight inches in length. We were headed for those beds. Spot walked softly ahead of me, padding gently against the mud. His white fur was already covered in mud and silt, but even so, the silver tips of his fur sent off small sparkles in the morning light. He was a big square Samoyed from championship lineage but was too shy for dog shows and preferred to be alone with me.

"Yesterday Momma told me Aurora is going to lose the Wasilla house," Alice continues in her e-mail. "Momma said this in a matter-of-fact way. I fear this is true. As you know, they weren't approved for a second mortgage, and they continue to spend money on questionable items. There's new exercise equipment in the basement, new laptops in the computer room, a new chair in the living room, and new white towels in the hall bathroom. I don't understand why Aurora needs more white towels. I did the laundry and folded all the towels, thinking I had done it right this time, but Aurora fussed at me for folding them wrong."

I was eighteen years old when we walked out on those miles of mud flats and clam beds. Each new clam bed was dotted with clam holes, and at each new location, I stopped and saw another bed up ahead that was more promising, so we pushed on.

"I expressed my concern about all the expenses," Alice writes. "I offered to help with the paralegal stuff to minimize the attorney fees, but apparently it's a lump-sum price and can't be lowered."

My mind wanders between Alice's e-mail, the birds outside singing, and the mud flats.

We continued to chase the most perfect, most promising clam bed for another hour, possibly two hours, maybe three hours. I lost time. At one point I lost my sense of place and could only see the shore as a faint line along the beach. In the other direction, out into the Inlet, I couldn't see where the tide ended. The shiny expanse of exposed mud flat and clam bed reflected the gray blue of the sky. I couldn't discern land from sky. It was difficult to tell up from down, near from far, back to shore from out to Inlet. This could quickly turn to vertigo, and vertigo eats you, clutches at you, and causes a panic that trumps all other fears. My Blazo can was now full and heavy with clams, and my pack probably weighed sixty pounds. It was time to return. It would take at least an hour to walk back, just ahead of the turning tide, to reach high ground.

"I wish I could take Momma away," Alice writes. "Momma spends an hour every night saying her rosary. I asked her if she thought a nursing home might be better for Bill. Well, you guessed it. She was adamantly against it."

I scanned the mountain ranges that rimmed the horizon all around me. The cabin was at the base of Mt. Redoubt, to the west. I turned toward Mt. Redoubt. It was an active volcano, but quiet this year. Sometimes it sent up smoke or steam, but it had not erupted in several years, and it always served as a good landmark.

The phone rings. It's Alice.

We continued to walk toward Redoubt. Though I knew to retrace my steps exactly as we had come out, I didn't remember exactly how we came. As I took the next step, my weight shifted into it, and I sank waist-deep into the ooze.

"What the fuck," Alice says. "A guy from the electric company just came by and said he was going to shut off the electricity unless the bill was paid right now. Momma wrote the guy a check for eleven hundred dollars."

"Damn," I say.

The ooze. It's the Inlet's version of quicksand. Ooze. It's why we fear the mud. More dangerous than quicksand because of the suction that clamps down on its victims, holds the victims there until panic sets in, high tide rolls back, and the victim drowns. Ooze. It's what we take every precaution to avoid. Ooze. To get caught in the ooze is to have ignored what is safe.

"Then after the electric guy left, Aurora came back upstairs and for some reason gave Momma a check for five hundred dollars. That check is not worth the paper it's written on," Alice continues.

The ooze held fast, and I couldn't wriggle free. It held with such suction and pressure that it actually hurt. I figured it was ebb tide, and the tide would rest briefly before returning back to shore. I managed to twist and turn enough to remove the pack board with the Blazo can full of prize clams. Spot came close to investigate and whined.

"All this is happening this morning?" I ask Alice.

I know it's a benign comment, but I can't think along one plane. My mind flits between thoughts of Bill, the memory of that day in the mud, Alice's e-mail, and my own physical presence here next to the computer.

Stay calm. The mud pressure will release when the tide returns, providing a possible opportunity to get out of the ooze. I didn't expect a swift, rushing bore tide, but I knew the incoming tide would be fast, possibly faster than I could walk to shore, and it was at least one mile back. My legs and feet tingled, though I couldn't move them, probably because of the ooze suction.

"Go. Go to shore," I directed Spot.

He wouldn't go. I commanded him several times, but he still wouldn't go. The mud flat sprawled out before me like a lake of mud with no beginning or end. Vertigo again. I tried to move, but the ooze held tight. Where was the shore? Yes, straight toward the Kenai Mountain Range to the east.

"If the guy was here to shut off the power," Alice continues, "then the bill hasn't been paid for months."

"Back when I was in Wasilla last month," I tell Alice, "I remember hearing Aurora telling someone on the phone that she had a houseful of company and that her utilities had skyrocketed."

"And there are so many damn white towels." Alice says. "I can't keep track which ones go in the bathroom and which ones go in the kitchen. They all get folded differently."

The ooze continued to hold tight. My legs went numb, and Spot refused to go to shore.

"Whatever happens, have a plan. Gather the facts, and make a plan," Alice had always said. So what were the facts? The incoming tide would release the ooze pressure. I needed help. There was no help except for this stubborn dog who wouldn't go get help. There probably wasn't time to get help anyway. Focus. What were the facts? I had a packboard, a Blazo can full of razor clams, and a big white husky that wouldn't go to shore without me. Bingo. A plan.

I unlaced the straps that fastened the Blazo can to the packboard and pushed the can aside. It fell over and several clams spilled out. I then looped two straps through the straps of the packboard. With the other straps, I created a strange harness for Spot and slipped it over him. Then we waited for the tide.

Alice talks on about the electric bill and white towels.

"What was Momma supposed to do? Allow the electricity to be turned off? Bundle up Bill in blankets? Cook him breakfast in the fireplace. I think Bill's losing it. He keeps talking about people in the fireplace," Alice says.

Up in Wasilla, the moose will drop their new calves soon. Bill likes to see the new red calves. The Chinooks, the warm snow-eater winds, will soon blow down from the mountains to evaporate and melt away any last snow. Here in Edgewood, different Chinooks will blow down from the Rockies onto the high plains and blow for months.

"Gotta go now. Something's happening," Alice says and hangs up.

The phone rings again. It's Palmer, calling from Seattle.

"I just spoke to Alice, and I'm worried," Palmer begins. "I'd like to ask you a question."

"Sure."

"Do you think Alice is safe up there?" Palmer asks. "Alice can deal with clutter and Bill's worsening condition, but it seems pretty desperate up there, and I don't want Alice in a situation that's so tenuous. What do you think?"

Tenuous. It's curious how Palmer can't say anything specific.

"Do you think she's safe?" Palmer asks. The mud flats are never fully safe, even around the known clam beds.

Then the tide came and the ooze pressure changed with it.

"Pull!" I commanded Spot. "Pull!"

The dog knew the command and knew how to pull. He could play tug games and pull a wagon and even a sled, though the sled commands were different.

"Pull!" I commanded again.

Spot barked with glee, dug in, and pulled, slow and steady and careful as a Samoyed's instinct tells him to, never fast, but steady and steadfast and, always, stubborn.

The first fingers of tide waves lapped at me, the ooze pressure lessened, and Spot pulled me free.

Still tingling and very unsteady, but ahead of the main part of incoming tide, we tried to trace our way back to shore, exactly as we had hiked out. At times, I wasn't sure we were headed in the right direction, so I kept my eyes on Redoubt. Each time I slipped or sunk even a little in the mud, there was momentary panic before I completed the step. My skin itched from the ooze mud drying on my skin. Focus. Stick to the plan. Keep walking.

When I got back to shore, I washed off the mud and silt in the icy glacier-melt creek near the cabin. How would I explain? Why did I leave the clams behind? JB would no doubt call me a dumb-ass girl. Oh, the hell with him.

I didn't bother to explain. Much later, I told Mother and watched the fear come into her eyes and, after, the look of incredulity.

"You did good," Mother had said, and I knew she was proud of me. Then she asked her traditional next question, "What did you learn?"

I learned thank you, Alice. Safe is having a plan. Safe is to fear the mud.

"The universe has dumped a lot on Aurora right now and, yes, everything seems very scary up in Wasilla," I tell Palmer. "In truth there's potential for violence in all of us. In Aurora's case I think it's temporary."

"You think so?" Palmer says.

"Aurora has been through worse," I say. "This time she knows there's light at the end of the tunnel, but she may need to be reminded. Tim's divorce will be finalized. Aurora and Tim will be married. Aurora's knees will heal. Aurora will go back to work, and the paychecks will return. Bill will die, and the Wasilla house will return to normal."

"I hope so," Palmer says. "I still wish Alice was back home with me."

"Plus, to my knowledge, I've never known Aurora to be violent toward anyone, except herself," I continue. "Aurora is simply in crisis, and her solution to crisis has traditionally been a solution of manipulation."

"What do you mean?"

"An entire range of response is possible. Attempted suicide, passive-aggressiveness, withdrawal, temper tantrums, and so on. It all depends how desperate she gets."

"How disturbing," Palmer says. "But no violence?"

"So far none toward others."

The day continues with e-mails and phone calls from Alice, Aurora, and Palmer. Each e-mail and phone call features Aurora's need for money. The water bill has not been paid. The house note is in arrears. Tim's lawyer is demanding money before he files divorce papers for Tim or files papers to dismiss the child molestation charges against Tim. Aurora's handyman has not been paid. Aurora and Tim don't have the money for medications. The Child Services Department has garnered Tim's wages for child support, but there aren't any wages as long as Tim is in jail. The payments on Aurora's vehicles, insurance for the vehicles, gas bill, and cable TV bill and copayments for Aurora's knee surgeries are unpaid and behind several months.

I've seen all this before. The crisis is close. Try to work. Schedule appointments with clients. I'm happy when Matt gets home.

"There's nothing you can do," Matt says.

"That's my Mother we're talking about," I retort. "That's my stepdad dying in the living room."

"They have an entire hospice team helping them," Matt says.

At night the dream returns. The old doctor hands me the brass door knocker.

"Just tell the truth, and everything will be OK," Mother Moose–Nurse says.

Then it changes, and a new dream scene appears. Mother Moose–Nurse is on fire.

5 May
Regret

Alice sends her morning e-mail. "I'd really like to get Momma and Bill out of Aurora's house. I deeply regret helping Aurora bring them up here. I wish we could convince Momma to move Bill to a nursing home."

Right now, I hate my sisters—myself, too—and want to run away. Crisis and chaos has become our world.

"Yes, let's send Bill to a nursing home," I write back. "Or even better, let's send Bill and Mother back to Homer."

"We need a plan for alleviating the stress," Alice writes back quickly and ignores my sarcasm. "And the major source of stress is Aurora's money situation. Perhaps we can help Aurora figure out how to manage her money. Maybe we could get her to divulge her financial situation and help negotiate an arrangement."

Oh, let's make a darn plan.

"Perhaps Momma could pay off Aurora's outstanding bills. We could ask Aurora to provide collateral, and maybe Momma could become the beneficiary to the Wasilla house. Or Momma puts a lien on Aurora's house. Or Aurora agrees to turn over her paychecks to Momma. It doesn't matter how, we just need a plan," Alice writes.

"Your need for a plan is what *you* need, not necessarily what Mother or Bill needs," I write and instantly regret it when I click the send button.

Alice doesn't respond back.

6 May
The Plan

To my surprise Alice sends her regular morning e-mail report.

"Mike, the lead health aide, is here today from ten in the morning until four in the afternoon to provide respite for us. We're supposed to go out and have fun. I'll see if Momma wants to go for ice cream.

"Mike is a very nice guy. He has a seventeen-year-old son with autism. Yesterday, the son had an episode, and Mike spent most of the day in and out of the hospital with the son. Plus Mike's ex-wife is a druggie and highly emotional. Poor Mike had to deal with the ex-wife, too," Alice writes. "I'm telling you this because Mike told me this in a very matter-of-fact way. His attitude seems to be this is life, and it may be a challenge, but it has to be dealt with. I find this approach to life to be calming and inspirational."

Of course it's calming. Whatever feels logical or matter-of-fact would be calming.

"My plan now is to take a matter-of-fact approach," she begins. "In reality we have a win-win situation here in Wasilla. We need to recognize it and formalize it by creating a cost-sharing arrangement between Aurora and Tim and Momma and Bill."

Oh no. Alice is in planning mode. I don't see any win-win.

"First, Momma is keenly aware that moving Bill to a nursing home would be very expensive; inconvenient; and, obviously, very traumatic. Besides, Momma likes being in a home environment," Alice writes.

"How's Bill doing?" I write back.

"That should be worth something to Momma," Alice continues. "Second, Aurora and Tim need money. I know they've taken a lot of money from Momma and Bill already, but that's not the point now. We need to create stability and a safe place for Bill to die."

I don't respond. The plan will change.

At night the dream comes again. Mother Moose–Nurse stands serene while the fire-breathing doctor sets fire to her and watches the flames burn away her fur then burn through the layer of skin then a layer of fat, sizzling.

"It's OK. It's just a dream," Matt reassures me.

But I know different. It's something else. Recurring dreams happen for a reason, but the reason for this dream isn't apparent yet.

7 May
The Right Direction

The morning e-mail report from Alice arrives.

"While Aurora may not deserve any more money, she definitely needs help because there are expenses to having Momma and Bill living at the Wasilla house," Alice begins.

Here we go again.

"My thought is that Momma and Bill pay $3,000 to $4,000 per month in rent," Alice writes. "This is their part of the food, power, and so on. This allows Aurora to accept the funds with dignity and allows Momma the opportunity to pay for a place for Bill that is affordable and comfortable."

The Homer house would've been affordable and comfortable. Aurora and Alice should not have moved Mother and Bill to Wasilla, but I don't say it. I wasn't there when it happened.

"The weak point in the plan is that Aurora can't manage a dime, let alone thousands. But I think it's the right direction. Thoughts?"

"What's on your agenda today?" Matt comes in.

"Funny, I don't remember. Have to check my calendar," I tell him.

"You never remember anymore. And you haven't been out of the house in days." Matt hesitates as if he's expecting me to interrupt, object, make an argument, or say something. I turn to look at him, but I don't know what to say.

"I haven't seen you out in the garden since you got back from Alaska," Matt adds.

"What are you trying to say?"

Matt glances at my once-pristine desk strewn with empty chip bags, coffee cups, and newspapers turned to the crossword puzzle. "I'm not sure. I'm just concerned."

"There's no reason to be," I say.

Moments later, just after our morning off-to-work kiss, I hear the crash and feel my nerve ends tingle. I jump up to the window and see Matt drive away. Another crash, more of huge clang, and then I realize it's just the wind clanging the fireplace flue. It's only the high plains Chinooks blowing down from the Rocky Mountains. Back to Alice.

"That's too much money for Mother and Bill to pay to live at the Wasilla house. It didn't cost that much for them to live back in Homer. It shouldn't cost them two to three times more to live in Wasilla," I reply.

The Chinooks up in Wasilla must be screaming down from the Chugiak Mountains about now, fierce but relatively warm, melting away any last bits of snow.

An e-mail from Palmer comes in. I hadn't noticed he'd been included.

"I think this is the right direction. There are legitimate expenses that are incurred by Momma and Bill, and Aurora desperately needs the money," Palmer writes.

I snap to attention and quickly fire off another e-mail, "What legitimate expenses?"

"It's not so much about expenses and Momma paying rent. It's about funneling money to Aurora in a dignified manner," Alice writes back quickly.

"Aurora's dignity is of no concern to me," I write.

"My thought is that Momma doesn't really care what the amount is, as long as she knows what the amount is," Palmer writes.

"Having Momma pay rent will ensure that Aurora can pay the bills," Alice responds. "I just want to make sure Momma and Bill have a stable place to live."

"If we want them to have a stable place, the mortgage has to be paid also. The house note is in arrears by many months," Palmer adds.

Didn't we just say all this? I try to reply to each e-mail, but the e-mails come in so fast it makes me frantic. Soon I feel numb, stop replying, and just read. It doesn't matter what the plan is, only that there's a plan. Anyway, the plan will change.

"We probably don't have to worry about the mortgage," Alice continues. "It takes at least three to four months to get a house into foreclosure. I don't see Bill lasting that long. He's getting weaker with each passing day. He's only awake a few hours. I've seen a definite deterioration in his stamina."

So Alice is a doctor now.

"I'll snoop around when Aurora and Tim are asleep or gone and see what I can find out about the bills," Alice writes.

"Aurora told me once that the light bill is running $400 to $500 month," Palmer writes.

"Momma told me she usually pays the grocery bill," Alice continues.

"They need to get rid of that monster of a truck," Palmer writes.

"Yes, a big issue is Aurora's commuting costs. She drives that big truck back and forth to Anchorage every day. It costs over $125 for a tank of fuel," Alice writes.

The flurry of e-mails continues more frenzied to the point that I can't keep up.

"They can do without Internet," Alice writes.

"Why do they need a handyman and a teenage girl to help with chores?" Palmer writes.

"They need to make menus."

"Tim's lawyer costs too much."

"Why does Aurora have such a big house anyway?"

I notice a bluebird checking out the birdhouse in the garden. An unseasonably early hummingbird zooms by and checks to see if the feeders are out yet. Bill is weaker, Alice says. What are you doing now, Bill?

"Thoughts?" Alice writes, and the e-mail traffic pauses.

Enough. My fingers fly to the keyboard, bang on the keys with violent clacking noises.

"Hear me loud and clear," I write. "Not the right direction. Stop trying to control everything. Stop looking for a damn easy answer that makes you feel all good and fuzzy." Send. Alice and Palmer don't respond.

At night I stay up late to avoid the sleep that brings the dream.

"Come to bed." Matt trudges into the living room where I sit on the couch and peer out the big window.

There is a bright moon over the plains tonight. Maybe there'll be coyotes.

"I'm not tired," I say.

Matt gives me a quizzical look and shrugs.

But the dream doesn't care how late it is, and when sleep finally comes, the dream comes, too, with the fire-breathing doctor setting the clinic and Mother Moose–Nurse on fire, the calves napping in the corner.

"It's a dream—it's a dream," Matt says, shaking me.

It has become our night ritual.

8 May
Silence

There are no morning e-mail reports from Alice.

I research recurring dreams. When did the dream first start? Over twenty years ago when I stupidly got pregnant. I'm still embarrassed. When did the dream first go away? When I went to the Sisters of Mercy in lieu of terminating the pregnancy. When did the dream return? I can't pinpoint it yet.

9 May
Silence Hangs On

Again, there are no morning e-mail reports from Alice, and there's no peaceful sleep. The dream continues. Each night Mother Moose–Nurse goes up in flames, and the fire eats at her a little more until bits of skeleton begin to appear through the flames.

"Sweetie, sweetie, it's OK." Matt wakes me.

When the dream first came those many years ago, I'd kept it a secret from everyone except Aurora. I needed someone to talk to, someone who'd understand, someone earthy and real. She simply hugged me when I told her about the dream and the pregnancy and knew she understood.

At night I wander the house, sometimes stare out the windows and try to see coyotes in the dark. I hear coyotes singing in the distance. No, it's just the farm dogs across the prairie.

10 May
Electricity

I go to the computer, bleary-eyed. There's an e-mail from Alice.

"Aurora just told me the $1,100 check Momma wrote to the electric company last week was only enough to pay what was past due," Alice writes. "The electric company now wants another $1,500 for a deposit or they'll turn off the electricity."

"Try to get some rest," Matt tells me before he leaves for work.

"Palmer and I will pay the electric bill. I'm not going to have Momma worry about the power being turned off," Alice writes.

I send a quick response. "Matt and I'll split the electric bill with you."

An e-mail from Palmer arrives. "I don't understand why we should feel compelled to pay the electric bill for Aurora."

Alice writes back. "We don't have another solution right now."

11 May
The Exact Situation

"Well, hello, Roadrunner," Bill's voice crackles, and the twinkle in his eye is evident even over the phone. "How do you make holy water?"

"You boil the hell out of it," I say.

"No, silly, you scare the devil out of it," Bill says, and we chuckle.

"How's it going?" I ask.

"You know that Slim keeps pestering me about..." Bill's voice trails off.

"He's getting weak. He can only handle a minute or so." A different male voice comes over the phone, probably Mike, the new home health aide. "But he's smiling. Thanks for calling him. You made his day."

Why doesn't Alice or Aurora tell me what's happening with Bill? It seems the only thing that merits attention is Aurora's money problems.

I send Aurora an e-mail. "How's Bill doing?"

"Abby-Pooh, for the last few days," Aurora replies quickly, "I've just wanted to curl up in a corner and die. Yesterday, the electric company sent me a letter saying that since my bills have been so high and are always so late that they're requiring me to make a deposit of $1,500. I'll go talk to them today. I hate going to them and begging, but for the greater good of the family and my Tim, I will."

I pull out a bag of pistachios from my desk drawer and prepare myself for the monologue that's about to come.

"Alice and Mama went to the Fuzzy Moose Greenhouse and the commissary," Aurora continues. "And Bill wants me to go across the Inlet with him. I don't know if God wants me to die the same time Bill dies, but I agreed to go with him."

I recognize the tactic. It's one of her best. She moves quickly from subject to subject, interspersing the trivial with the dramatic, the mundane with the shocking, clarity with confusion— mixing, masking, intertwining the real issue in between the frivolous and overlapping the truth with the nontruth. I'm not sure what to believe.

"I lost another four pounds last week. Total is twenty-one pounds in four weeks," Aurora says. "I exercised too much yesterday and paid for it last night. Both knees are hurting real bad. I had to take six Percocets. I almost went for Bill's morphine. I don't feel good today."

I send another e-mail. "Aurora, what is your exact financial situation?"

"Bill is tired but doing well today. He's looking forward to a turkey dinner tonight. Bear-Bear is such a good dog. He's out in his yard watching the cow moose and her baby. He's not even barking. Gas is $4.22 a gallon, and diesel is $4.55 a gallon. Are you coming up when Bill dies? Jessica is here today helping me with my spring chores."

This goes on all day, and I'm startled when the room glows in orange sunset light and Matt walks in.

"Hi, sweetie." Matt gives me a hug. "Get some work done?" The smell of Old Spice shaving cologne still lingers faintly on him. It's a classic, old-fashioned cologne that reminds me of Bill.

"Aurora is having a bad time up there."

"That's how she lives," Matt says. "How much money did you give her?"

"Well, yesterday, I told Alice we would split the electric bill for the Wasilla house with her and Palmer," I say. "I'm sorry I didn't talk to you about it first."

"That part doesn't matter. But let me use the words I've heard you use," Matt says. "Aren't you enabling Aurora?"

"What else can we do?"

"I know," Matt says. "Now, go brush your hair, you look like the wreck of the Hesperus."

12 May
What If?

I send Aurora an e-mail first thing in the morning. "Aurora, what's your exact financial situation?"

Aurora replies almost instantaneously. "Terrible. With me not working yet and Tim in jail because of his damn wife, we don't have any income. My vacation and sick leave are all used up. I don't know how I'm going to pay the mortgage this month or next month. I'm already getting nasty letters from the bank. Having Mama and Bill here has caused the utilities to jump up, and the gas bill has also jumped up, about $400 a month. I have already pawned my pistol, rings, and rifle."

She's lying about the numbers. For one thing the only gas usage they have is the kitchen stove, and that certainly would not eat up $400 a month.

"What's the minimum amount of money you need to survive until you start working again? Don't get your hopes up. I am not saying I can give you the money. But I have an idea."

The e-mail traffic goes quiet, another one of her more effective tactics.

After about twenty minutes, Aurora's e-mail appears. "I'm not going to tell you. We'll manage."

She wants me to beg her to tell me. After I beg enough, she'll tell me, and by then I'll feel emotionally committed to give her money. Brilliant tactic.

"I can respect that," I respond. "However, what if we could create a peace treaty that included the entire family working as a united front? What if your financial situation is the universe giving you an opportunity?"

Aurora writes back in what seems an instant. "Here is my situation right now. For the next two to three months, I need $9,945 for the mortgage, $166.20 for gas, $310.33 for cable TV, $266.75 for the home phone, $160 for the cell phone, $930 for the truck payment, $3,800 to bring the credit cards up to date, and $130 for an extra credit account that we have."

A truck payment? Mother and Bill paid off the truck last year.

"I also need $233 for my knee doctor," Aurora continues. "And $844 for my handyman, $1,200 for my little Jessica, $196 to make a payment on the big blue chair, $5,000 for Tim's psychiatrist, $2,500 for Tim's shoulder doctor, $750 for car and house insurance, $600 to repay my 401K, $1,200 for groceries, $175 for dog food, $2,500 for fuel for my truck. What do you mean—a peace treaty?"

I sit at the keyboard and ask myself the same question. What do I mean—a peace treaty? Focus. Bag of chips. Think of something. I write back to Aurora.

"A peace treaty is different for all people and situations. For the sake of explaining it, let's say the primary people in the peace treaty are you and Tim *and* Mother and Bill. The secondary people are Alice and Palmer *and* me and Matt."

So far so good.

"With that in mind, a peace treaty often looks like this: The primary people each say what they need or want. Sometimes, the needs of the primary people turn out to be exactly the same," I write.

Now suggest compromise.

"The primary people agree to give each other what the other person needs. Sometimes they have to debate a little. Sometimes things are added or deleted. Almost always, there is a little give and take."

Hmm, let's deal with Alice.

"The secondary people agree to support the primary people and not interfere."

What if Alice doesn't like whatever plan Mother and Aurora agree on?

"All people agree not to judge the other people. Sometimes, folks agree on what should happen if the peace treaty is broken."

Aurora writes back. "I forgot; the attorney is $2,000 a month."

"Good," I reply. "What are your thoughts about a peace treaty?"

"This is your idea? A peace treaty?" Aurora writes. The e-mail goes quiet for a short time before Aurora responds. "Mama is not going to change. She nags me all the time about money. She says she is enabling me, that I need to be independent. I really don't want her money. We'll manage."

I feel her desperation. She's trying to hide it, but I realize she's in survival mode, and her desperation won't abide peace treaties or fluffiness. This is the desperation that will drive us do and say things we'd never consider in better times. Survival. Food. Sleep. Shelter. Her house. Dog food. Heat. Get Tim out of jail.

"OK, I'll back off. I apologize if I sound pushy," I write back.

The day goes by, and I hear news of Augustine's escalating activity, with the ash advisory upgraded to Watch and the aviation Code Yellow upgraded to Orange.

I receive a late-night e-mail from Aurora. "We can try a peace treaty," she writes.

The dream returns, but I expect it now. Mother Moose–Nurse never complains as the flames take her and burn through her until I see her brain through a crack in her skull. I yell.

Matt shakes me, wakes me, and reassures me, and I wander the house.

13 May
Her Father's Daughter

I send Alice an e-mail describing the peace treaty concept. "Could you talk to Mother? Perhaps we could negotiate a financial peace treaty. Would you be comfortable asking Mother if she would be willing to help Aurora one last time? Then talk to Mother about what she'd like in return?"

"Oh man! At first I was inclined to sympathize with Aurora," Alice writes back. "Then, in my snooping around, I found her bankruptcy file, one dated 1996. There were two loans listed from Momma for $5,000 and $7,000."

So Alice is really snooping around.

"I realized with great sadness that Aurora's life has been a train wreck for as long as I can remember. I can't remember a time when Aurora's life was stable," Alice continues. "There is never one last time for Aurora."

We all know this.

"I talked with Buddy last night. He is the person who will be renting the Homer house," Alice writes. "He told Aurora he'd pay $1,500 a month in rent. Aurora told Momma and me that Buddy agreed to pay $1,000 a month. Maybe it's an honest mistake. Who knows?"

It's not a mistake. It's desperation.

"Charlie told me he gave Aurora one hundred dollars for an old exercise bike that Momma had in the house. Momma never saw the money and never authorized the sale of the bike. When I asked Aurora about the discrepancies, she just snapped at me."

Survival. That one hundred dollars buys groceries.

"I've tried to help Aurora over the years. But she has snapped at me for the last time. I'm not inclined anymore to help her extort more money out of Momma, which is what we'd be doing. Call it a peace treaty if you like, but it's extortion all over again."

I sense Alice's mounting anger, the same anger I felt when I thought about having Aurora arrested for abusing a vulnerable adult.

"Tim can't control his spending any more than Aurora can. Plus, he has two kids he's paying child support for and a vindictive soon-to-be ex-wife. There's absolutely no evidence whatsoever of fiscal responsibility anywhere."

This inability to help, to make a plan and save the world debilitates Alice. I feel her powerlessness.

"Alice, I know and struggle with this, too," I write back. "I know there'll never be one last time with Aurora. It was the same with JB. Aurora is his daughter, JB incarnate."

And I hated JB, ignored his existence for over twenty years, and only made peace with him because it brought solace to Alice and Aurora. But, and most of all, to show respect for JB was to do the same for Bill. With time I accepted JB for what he was—a train wreck.

"You never gave up on JB the train wreck. How is Aurora the train wreck any different than JB the train wreck?" I ask.

As expected, there's no response from Alice.

At night the dream returns, and dark circles appear under my eyes from lack of sleep.

14 May
It Happens Again

There are no morning e-mail reports from Alice. It's OK. She's miffed about the train wreck language, but she'll get over it. She's been miffed before, and she'll be miffed again.

I go to bed later each night, wake up earlier and earlier in the remnants of the dream, and then wander into the living room. Perhaps I should get sleeping pills.

15 May
The Dream

> My name is Father's Joy. Who will sing my name in a lullaby, in a tender tenor duet with the wind while I sing soprano with coyote, and mourning dove coos chorus? Who will watch me sleep when Augustine erupts while aftershocks shake my head and floods float me across the Inlet. Or in the Inlet. Or by the Inlet. Always returning to the Inlet to find who I am in the tides. Always the tides. To become new again. To find grace again.
>
> —Abby Miller, morning pages

"That's right. Just tell us the truth, and everything will be OK," Mother Moose–Nurse and the old doctor keep saying.

"Who are you running from?" the old doctor asks.

When the Mother Moose–Nurse dream first appeared so long ago, the dream left me trembling and wondering about truth.

"I'm pregnant," I said to Sister Mary Elaine.

"How wonderful," she said and put her arm around me, and the dream went away.

We rejoiced together when we put the baby girl into the hands of the adoptive parents, who rejoiced and could not believe the truth of the child they held.

I go to the study and stare out at the high plains of Edgewood with pinkish streaks of sunrise beginning to appear in the east. We have spectacular sunrises and sunsets here.

The streaks across the eastern sky deepen and redden, spectacular, although I look out over the plains and wish I were looking out over the Inlet. I search for coyotes and look for the morning birds and rabbits. Except for the intensifying sunrise light, there's no movement on the plains. Even the wind is still. There's no Sister Mary Elaine to put her arm around me and rejoice. There's nothing out there to soothe me, to rock me back to sleep. I yearn for the Inlet.

16 May
The Carpet

"What do you mean? You want to go back to Alaska?" Matt says. "I thought we'd agreed that you would be on standby."

"That's true, but I need to go back."

"Dammit, Abby, what is going on?" The hazel in Matt's eyes flares to green. "You've been strange ever since you returned, and now you want to go back?"

"I'm sorry, honey."

I want tell him about being twenty-seven years old and Mother Moose–Nurse and the Inlet. But I can't. I'm too ashamed. Only the Inlet, with its soothing tides, can take away the shame and remind me I'm human, I'm alive, I can be forgiven, and that life is beautiful.

"I have to go to work." Matt puts on his hat and takes his lunch bag. "Can we talk about this tonight?"

"Of course," I say and think of Bill.

My job is here, Bill would say.

"You belong with Matt now," Bill had said.

Out in my garden, the crabapple and plum trees are starting to bloom. If the Chinooks don't blow in too hard, the trees will bloom fully and produce fruit. However, the winds usually come in too hard and relentless. How did I end up living so far from the Inlet? Yes, I ran way. It's what I do.

I log in to my computer and notice two e-mails from Aurora.

"Abby-Pooh, I think Mama should sell the Homer house, now, instead of renting it. Then she wouldn't have to pay property tax—no utility bills, no snow plowing, no mowing the lawn. She could move into the Homer Senior Center. She'd be with her friends and her church and near Bill after he's buried in the Homer Cemetery. This would be cheaper for her than living with me. It would also be cheaper for Tim and me."

Yes, I run away. I am the lost child. Alice is the overachiever, and Aurora is the rebel. We are the children of JB. What else could be expected?

Aurora writes a second e-mail. "Here are my needs. Guests, including family, don't pay attention when I post signs. Mama does not respect my new carpet. Guests won't leave my laundry alone. Guests wash my clothes and shrink the clothes. I try to tell guests that if they don't know where something goes in the kitchen, leave it on the counter."

I sense her anger and can actually understand it. She probably feels that an entire village is traversing through the her house, doing business in her house: home health aides, visitors, nurses, the chaplains, the teenage helpers, the handyman, the social workers, Mother, Bill, us sisters—all coming and going, all lumped into the category of guests.

"Guests don't turn the lights off, forget to turn the gas stove off, forget to put water in Bear-Bear's bowl, forget to put stuff away. It's like having children around. I always have to repeat myself over and over. But guests don't hear me. I want my house back to normal," Aurora continues. "For the good of the family, we moved Bill and Mother to my house. I realize now this is probably a mistake. But Mama will never respect my carpet. I can tell Mama isn't happy here. But I really don't know what to do about it."

Should Mother put down her rosary and worship the carpet?

17 May
Forgiveness

I wonder will happen after Bill dies. The Homer house is about to be rented, so Mother can't go home. Mother won't be able to sit in her own living room and be surrounded by memories and mementos and familiarity and look at Bill's chair and remember him sitting there looking out the window and watching the boats and barges and the ferry coming into Kachemak Bay and saying, "Look, the Tustemena is coming in."

Mother won't have familiar rituals to help her grieve. I wish Bill would die so I can take Mother away from the Wasilla house. No, I don't mean that. Yes, I mean that.

It may have been a mistake. Aurora should've thought first instead of flying off in an impulsive fit. Or perhaps that is your genetics for you are JB's daughter and his entire life was one impulsive fit, even as he truly loved you. JB never complained about your weight or your grades or your ways with boys.

"If you like the boy, you can sleep with him," JB had told us.

But he didn't think that way when it happened. Aurora was only eleven years old when I learned the two college boys who were fishing the beach that summer were having sex with her. Perhaps the boys didn't know Aurora's age, for she was a tall, chubby-curvy, good-looking girl. She could have easily passed for eighteen. Alice had told me to make a plan before I told the boys. So I did.

"She may be eleven, but she's sure eighteen when she takes her clothes off." The boys laughed. "Besides, she likes it."

"Stay away from her," I said.

"She wants it and likes it," they insisted. "She comes around here begging for it. Hell, she can't get enough."

"Stay away from her."

"And, if we don't?" One of the boys leered into my face.

They were big strong college boys, not afraid of hard work and not afraid of me. I was tall and strong but not as strong as they were. If they were drunk, I might have an advantage. But they were sober, and I wasn't threatening to them. Focus. The boys were here for the summer. They lived in the fishing shack on the beach and fished for the Johnsons. The boys made good money, enough for college, for a car, for parties. They were almost men, full of machismo, swaggering, preening, posturing—almost men. Perhaps I had a little advantage.

"Well, let's see." I paused. "I can think of several choices you can make, mostly about who you'd rather to talk to. And you'd better choose fairly quickly. Oh, say, in about ten minutes. First choice is you could tell your story to the state troopers after I report you for statutory rape of an eleven-year-old child."

"That's crazy. Your sister will never press charges," one of the boys said, grinning.

"She doesn't have to. She's a minor. Besides, sorting through it could take forever, maybe even all summer." I blinked slowly. "By the time it gets sorted out, all the fish will be gone."

"You're probably just jealous. You're probably a whore just like your little sister," one of the boys said, jeering. "Do you want some, too?"

"What's another so-called choice?" the second boy asked.

"You could talk to my father." I blinked again.

"He doesn't care." The second boy laughed.

"We are talking about a man's eleven-year-old daughter," I said and paused long enough for their machismo to emerge. "What would you do if we were talking about your eleven-year-old little sister, or maybe one day your eleven-year-old daughter?"

"She's bluffing," the boys said to each other. But doubt appeared in their eyes. They knew what they'd do.

"You're bluffing," one boy said.

"I say you're blowing smoke," the second boy said.

"Or you could talk to the Johnsons after I complain about the noise, the harassment, the questionable fishing practices, the parties, the booze bottles littered all over the beach," I said. "They'd fire you in a heartbeat."

Fear finally emerged in their faces.

"Maybe you'll get to fish somewhere," I said. "But not here. How long would it take you to find another fishing job? Maybe, you wouldn't."

"Or you could talk to your families, maybe your girlfriends, after I tell them what's been going on here," I said.

"You're all talk and nothing but a stupid bitch." The taller boy stood up straighter and squared his shoulders.

"So what's it going to be, fellows?" I ask.

"Go to hell," the taller, straighter, squared-off boy said.

"That's what I figured you'd say, so I went and chose for you." I looked at my watch. Ten minutes were up. I saw JB and Spot walking down the little gravel road to the beach. JB carried a shotgun. Spot barked when he recognized me and ran to my side.

"Aurora, come out of there," JB shouted toward the fishing shack.

Aurora appeared in the doorway. I didn't know she was in the shack. How did JB know? Aurora stood there for a moment, disheveled, then smoothed her clothes and tried to wipe the tears off her face, and I knew she'd heard everything the boys had said about her. Give me that shotgun, I thought. Give me a rusty fishhook to rip off their testicles.

"Take your sister back to the house," JB told me. His blue eyes blazed.

Back at the house, Aurora cried, and I held her and rocked her in my arms.

"I thought they liked me," Aurora said.

I heard the shotgun once and then twice. Then I heard the boys' truck start up, the tires dig into the sand, the roar of the engine up the gravel road, the tires screeching onto the hardtop, and the growling acceleration down the main road. I never saw those boys again. About a week later, two new boys appeared, fresh and beaming.

As for Aurora's e-mail full of rambling complaints, I understand JB was there for her. Mother was not.

165

"Will you ever forgive Mother?" I write back.

"Why do I need to forgive Mama?" Aurora replies.

18 May
A Little House in Mexico

An e-mail arrives from Aurora. "Abby, will you and Matt lend Tim and me $9,620?"

I feel her expectation and resent it. JB had the same expectation. Not long after I reconciled with JB, I asked Matt for $5,000 to give to JB because JB suddenly wanted to buy a little house in Mexico. I did it more to make Alice and Aurora happy. They wanted him to have a home. They were troubled that JB wandered the countryside in a broken-down camper. The little house in Mexico was the only sign of stability JB ever exhibited.

Another time we gave JB $600 because his truck broke down. And another time it was $6,000 so JB could buy a new camper. And every month for the last two years of his life, I sent JB care packages with coffee, books, and cash. I hadn't done this for JB. I hadn't reallly done it so Alice and Aurora would feel good about JB. I had done it to honor Bill.

So Aurora wants $9,620? Matt left for work as usual this morning. Not remarkable, except Matt reports to work each day and brings home a good salary that allows us to live well and debt-free and allows me to freelance as a therapist. It's Matt who earned his PhD and put it toward fiscal responsibility. And it's Matt who continually pays for JB and Aurora. I can't keep asking Matt to do this. I still resent JB.

That afternoon another e-mail from Aurora arrives. "Abby, I took the first step this morning at 11:48 a.m. Alaska time. I asked Mama to forgive me, and I told her I forgive her. Mama busted out crying. Alice was there, and she busted out crying, too."

I send Aurora an e-mail. "Wonderful about you and Mother."

"What about the $9,620?" Aurora writes back

19 May
The Good Lawyer

I don't talk to Matt about the $9,620.

Several e-mails arrive from Aurora. "Ladies, my new diet is working. Lost two more pounds," Aurora writes in the first e-mail.

I don't have the patience for this today.

"Our attorney is so good! The paper work for Tim's divorce is at the judge's office, and the judge will be signing it this week. Tim and I can get married right after that."

Hello, Tim's in jail.

"Our attorney has been arguing with Child Support Services," Aurora writes in the second e-mail. "Remember, several months ago, they increased Tim's monthly child support from $600 a month to $1,300 a month without authorization from the court. Well, now, they have to reimburse Tim. Isn't this wonderful? I sure hope we get the reimbursement by May 30. Our attorney is so very good."

Your attorney is a sleazy leech. Tim should be out of jail by now.

Outside, the late spring winds, the last of the Chinooks, howl down from the Sandia Mountains and blow giant tumbleweeds across the brown treeless plains. The tumbleweeds roll in the winds, scattering tumbleweed seeds everywhere ultimately resulting in more weeds to pull and more debris to pick up. I resent the eternal, infernal wind. I resent the lawyer. I resent JB. I resent Aurora. I resent Tim. I resent this place, this ugly, wind-infested Edgewood place.

"Ladies, I asked human resources for the names of the people who donated annual leave to me when I had my knee surgeries so I could thank them," Aurora writes in the third e-mail. "I was told that all donations are done anonymously. Then the HR lady told me that a lot of people like me. Guess what? People like me!"

I'm glad someone does.

20 May
Mornings

My mornings are about hot, strong coffee, morning birds and critters, the garden lighting up with morning shadows, and the chance to see a coyote trotting across the plains. Mornings continue with typing up notes and answering e-mails.

I wonder if Bill can see Wasilla's morning birds or the moose out in the yard or the last icicles melting and dripping off the eaves. Does the morning news and stock report still provoke him? What is morning for Bill now? Does he tell the time and the day by who is there? *Carol is here. It must be Sunday.*

There is no schedule at the Wasilla house for the nighttime. That's Bill's time. It's when he talks to the people in the fireplace, gives his preflight briefings, and debates with Slim about where to go fishing. It's the time for old movies and ice cream. I wish I was there.

Matt comes home, and our evening rituals begin.

"It must be morning." Matt eyes me. "I see you're still in your pajamas."

21 May
Relapse III

"No. For the last time, no," Matt says. The hazel of his eyes turns green. They always turn green when he is upset or angry.

"Just one week," I insist.

"That's what you said last time, and you stayed a month," Matt says.

"That's because we thought Bill was going to die any minute."

"The fact is, Abby, he is going to linger. It could be weeks or months. For all we know, Bill could linger for years." Matt shakes his head.

"I need to go to the Inlet," I say.

"Why?" Matt turns to look at me, the question more in his eyes than the words, the green in his eyes fading to gray.

"To make the nightmares go away," I say.

"Abby, you have clients who need you, a husband who needs you, and you're ignoring us all. Hell, you're ignoring yourself." Matt's eyes return to hazel brown rimmed in green. I love those changeable eyes.

"I need to go to the Inlet."

Matt watches me as if analyzing me, looking for a solution. "Do you have to go all the way to Alaska to make a bad dream go away?"

"I know it doesn't make sense."

"No, Abby, it doesn't," Matt says. "I have trouble believing that you can't figure out how to deal with a bad dream."

"Sweetie, just a week," I say.

"This is silly," Matt says.

"Just a week?"

I don't really need his permission. I hear Bill's words from my wedding day: "Go to Matt. You belong with him now."

"Abby." Matt's tone becomes serious. "I'm going to have to put my foot down."

He doesn't have to say more, and I won't be going to the Inlet.

Instead I go to my computer to check e-mails and listen to music. There is an e-mail report from Alice. It's been a while, and I welcome her report.

"Hello, family. Bill had bad day yesterday. We had to clean him up twice just in one morning. He gets weak during the cleanup, but he still has enough energy to announce that he's spreading the love every time he poops," Alice writes. "His legs hurt a lot. Momma gave him morphine. He vomited during the evening, and Momma had to clean him up yet again.

"Bill sleeps most of the time," Alice continues. "He barely eats. I doubt if he eats a few hundred calories a day. They won't do a feeding tube because he's a hospice patient. His urine is dark red as if blood is in it, and he has a urinary tract infection to boot, which won't be treated. Tad, the hospice nurse, says all this is part of the process.

169

"Turning Bill every two hours is problematic," Alice writes. "We sometimes forget, and when we remember, we end up hurting him. He's so fragile that all movement hurts him. We now have a timer to remind us. Momma's exhausted. That's all for now."

Another e-mail from Alice arrives.

"News flash. The state troopers just came and confiscated Tim and Aurora's computer, their laptops, and even their cell phones. Apparently, Tim's about-to-be ex-wife has made some new charges about Tim engaging in some sort of child pornography over the Internet. Don't know the details. Troopers aren't talking. Aurora's in hysterics. She's cursing and going ballistic. It's awful. So humiliating. Gotta go."

22 May
All-Night Vigil

Both Aurora and Alice don't answer my e-mails, and nobody answers the telephone at the Wasilla house. Come nighttime, I still don't know any more about what's happening up in Wasilla. I try to sleep.

Mother Moose–Nurse appears in flames, calm and serene, and I wake to my own shouts while Matt calls my name to lead me back to the nondream world.

I wander the house again and wait for the dawn. Tonight the great high plains shine with a full moon so bright I can easily see any coyotes. Moonlight bounces off the metal roofs of neighbor houses, and the world glows, but it is not the glow of the Inlet. I scan for coyotes again. It's almost dawn, and coyotes often hunt just before dawn.

I find my favorite music, Rachmaninoff's *Vespers*, to keep me company while I wait for the dawn and coyotes. It's my favorite piece because it's Bill's favorite piece. I put on headphones so I don't disturb Matt. The tenor chant opens, followed by the call to prayer. I sense movement behind me, and Matt touches my shoulder. I remove the headphones.

"You should go back to Wasilla." Matt sits next to me and pulls me to him, and I lean into his chest, causing the headphones to come loose from the computer, and music swells around us with the alternating soprano and alto choruses of the Anchorage Arctic Ensemble. The ensemble came to Homer once and they sang on Bishop's Beach. That day, they sang "The Flying Dutchman," and before us the phantom ship emerged in the voice of the ensemble, and years later, I've only to think it to hear it again.

The first streaks of pinkish light appear to the east as the tenor begins the lovely hymn of the "Gladsome Light." In my mind I see the Inlet shimmering. Across the Inlet I visualize the horizon of snowcapped volcanoes lining the western coast, first Augustine standing guard and smoking and then Redoubt then Illiamna then Spurr. Even more, I feel the Inlet. I feel its loveliness and infinite danger. The tenors sing, "Lord lettest thou thy servant depart in peace." The sopranos enter. I feel their voices lift and soothe me, renew me. The lower notes of the tenors balance the high sweet sopranos. For me this is the voice of the universe with its exquisite balance, like the coming and going of the tide, like the Inlet itself. And for one moment in time, I am transformed and become one with that universe.

Part 3

SEWARD

---

23 May
Home Again

> My name is Father's Joy. Welcome me home again by Knik Glacier. Gaze on Lake George. Drink, drink, drink with me that unsalted water that quenches no thirst; that sea of ice so endless; that face of hell with ice chunks shaded turquoise, ready to break to send down spring floods. Now they're no longer massive because the Good Friday earthquake changed all that. Now see the moose gathered there. Welcome me home again after breakup. Come kayak with me in Seward on Resurrection Bay, that ice-free port of call. Paddle slow, stroke smooth, be still. Otter approaches. Orca breaches. Oyster pearlizes. Now look up and see the herons return.
>
> —Abby Miller, morning pages

The thump of touchdown thrills me because I know I am home. It's midnight—planes always arrive in Anchorage at midnight—and as the plane taxis up to the gate, the nearly full moon glows on the dark glistening Inlet water.

Alice and Mother pick me up at the airport. Alice drives, and Mother sits in the back. I get in beside her, surprised she's come to the airport, which means being away from Bill for several hours. Mother looks thinner and tired, but her eyes energize when she sees me. I'm also surprised Alice is driving and not Aurora. Driving is a mundane detail, and Alice doesn't like mundane details. We greet and give each other car-hugs.

"So what's happening?" I ask after we are settled in the car.

The night is clear, and the mountains are still snowcapped with pools of moonglow on the northwest faces and more pools of glow on the snowy peaks themselves. The night sky is brilliantly clear, and I strain and look to the north to see if Denali is visible, but, no, she's not out tonight. We drive into Anchorage.

I smell the humidity in the air and the salty fishiness of the Inlet. The tide must be out. The old familiar sights appear: the twinkling white Christmas lights kept lit year round, murals of orca and beluga on the sides of buildings. We drive by Merrill Field, and there's Peggy's Airport Café where Bill used to like to have pie. I look at the small airplanes tied down on the field just as I have done a thousand times. It never gets old.

"I've been coordinating with Buddy about renting the Homer house. He gets rental assistance from Alaska Housing Authority, so it would require a one-year lease. Buddy said if Momma didn't want to rent her house for a year, he'd make other arrangements."

I glance at Mother and notice that her lips are pursed.

We turn onto the Glenallen Highway, and we drive by more familiar things. There's Carr's Grocery Store, the espresso wagons, and ice cream shops. There's the Ice Palace Saloon, the Northern Lights Barber Shop, and the remains of melting snow dumps.

"How's Bill?" I turn to look at Mother.

Her eyes seem stoic and calm. Her lips unpurse. "He sleeps most of the time now. He barely eats," Mother says.

"Momma, do you see yourself moving back to Homer after Bill passes away," Alice asks. "I know Abby says you aren't supposed to be making decisions right now, but I need to know because of the deal with the Housing Authority."

"No, my life will never be the same," Mother says to Alice. "I can't go back."

"That's what I figured," Alice continues. "So I told Buddy that we could do a one-year lease. I'm proceeding with the paper work. The rental arrangement will commence in June."

"Is he lucid?" I ask.

"Not really," Mother says. "Actually, it's hard to tell." Mother lowers her voice. "Why did you come up so suddenly? Do you know something?"

"I figure we should lower the rent in exchange for Buddy handling some of the maintenance," Alice says.

"No, I don't know anything," I say. "Just felt the need to come back."

"I bought a new kayak," Alice says. "This guy outside of Eagle River makes them out of wood. It's supposed to be good in the ocean and rivers, but not white water. I did a quick paddle to see how it performs. So smooth and zippy and, voilà, I bought it. Probably won't have time to go out and test it proper."

"Did you leave Bill alone?" I ask Mother.

"No, Aurora's with him," Mother says.

"Fair amount of storage can be put in the hold." Alice goes on.

"Sometimes I think we are about to lose him, so we stay up all night," Mother says. "Then in the morning he wants ice cream, and everything's back to normal."

Ah, that new normal. We drive into Eagle River. I look down as we go over the bridge. It's too dark to see the river, but I look down anyway.

Long ago, we got Spot from a well-known breeder of Samoyeds in Eagle River. Fifteen years later, I came back with Spot's ashes, and Aurora had helped me wade out and steadied me in the fast current as I threw the ashes out into the river to be carried out over the Inlet.

I look down and remember a dog who loved me through every adventure and every misfortune and every joy. I never got another dog.

"He's hurting more," Mother says. "But I only give him morphine when I have to."

"I know, Mother. I know. "I put my hand on hers.

"Right down that road is the place where the man makes the wooden kayaks," Alice says. "Apparently, he gets the kits from a place in Washington State. Anyway, back to the Homer house, we really need to get the place painted."

"All I can do is be there for him," Mother says.

"It's going to be a long haul," Alice says. "Tad, the hospice nurse, says Bill's vitals are fairly strong. Could be a while before Bill starts actively dying. Tad says Bill's only in the preactive phase."

Mother and I don't respond to Alice. Her technical tone irritates me. We drive past Eklutna with its little cemetery of brightly painted spirit houses used for graves, the old railroad buildings, and the centuries-old Russian Orthodox Church. Should we build Bill a spirit house?

"Momma, what do you think about getting the Homer house painted?" Alice asks.

We keep driving and cross the Knik and Matanuska bridges. The special moose lights shine amber onto the Knik hay fields. I see two moose. Mother sees another moose. There's a moose up ahead in the road. Alice slows the car and stops. We sit and watch. It's a cow moose. Two calves come into view, barely able to stand on their thin wobbly legs. Their fur is the rusty-red color of newborn moose calves. It's Mother Moose–Nurse! Cars stop behind us, and cars stop in the opposite direction. We all wait for the moose to cross. By the time we reach Wasilla, it's almost three in the morning and we've counted eighteen moose.

"We're here," Alice announces. "Momma, let's take care of the Homer house details in the morning."

I notice that Aurora's truck is not in the driveway and run upstairs to the living room to see Bill. His face is thinner, much thinner. He is crumpled into a sideways position, pressed against the safety rails. His large bony hands shake the safety rail as he clutches it. The smell is so overwhelming that I nearly gag.

"Howdy, Billiam." I go to him immediately. "It's your favorite daughter from New Mexico."

"Why, it's the Roadrunner," he says and grins and reaches toward me with one of those long bony hands.

"How are you d

oing?" I ask.

"Where's your mother?" Bill asks.

I kiss Bill on the cheek.

"I knew you'd come back," Bill whispers. "I told Slim you'd be back."

"You've been talking about me again?"

"You betcha." Bill chuckles. "Hey, can we get the Malibu fixed?"

"I need to get my suitcase first. I'll be right back," I say, but really need to get away from the smell.

Bill waves that bony hand at me. "Come back soon."

I start to go downstairs, and halfway down, Alice turns the corner and starts bounding up the stairs.

"He needs to be cleaned," I say. "What's that smell?"

"He's developed bedsores." Alice turns and looks at me. "Why are you here?"

"Where's Aurora? How long has Bill been left alone?" I ask.

"Don't you dare interrogate me." Alice goes upstairs.

I go downstairs and see Mother start to make her way up the stairs carefully, solidly. Her lips are pursed again.

"How is he?" Mother asks me.

"Mischievous and in need of cleaning," I say.

"He's not scared?" Mother asks.

Ah, Mother also noticed that Aurora's truck isn't here, which means Mother realizes that Bill has been left alone. I know that scares her.

"No, not scared." I see the relief on her face. "I'll get my suitcase, and I'll be right back."

Mother nods and continues her careful, solid ascent up the stairs to the living room.

The lower level is cold. The downstairs gas fireplace is turned off, and the two portable electric heaters are turned off. The game room section of the lower level is still a bedroom for Aurora, Tim, and Bear-Bear. The bed is unmade. The pool table is heaped with piles of laundry, papers, and stacks of clean dishes. The bar area is littered with dirty dishes, pizza boxes, and soda cans. In one corner heaps of clothes are piled around a wicker laundry basket. The couch is stacked with papers and receipts. I've never seen this room in such disarray. The baskets of medications are still stacked by the bed. Oddly, the only smell is a trace of bleach. The bathroom is even colder. There's another portable heater, but it's not turned on.

I hear Aurora's diesel truck out in the driveway, the truck door slam, and Aurora yell at Bear-Bear. She comes in to the garage with the aid of a cane but walking strong and steady. She sees me.

"Oh, damn. That's all I need," Aurora says when she sees me and then hustles past me into the game room and throws her purse at a chair. "Why in the hell are you here?"

"Why in the hell did you leave Bill all alone?" I say.

"I've got more important things to worry about. Besides who are you to question me?" Aurora rubs her face. Her makeup is beautiful and accentuates her naturally long lashes and almond-shaped eyes, and even though she is plus size, she looks elegant in her orange dress and matching jacket, until she faces me and the wildness in her eyes belies elegance.

"Those damn people at the jail." Aurora shakes her head and her hair clips fall out, causing her hair to fly out. "They're messing with Tim for pure spite. Now, they won't let him have his meds. They say Tim whines too much and if he doesn't stop whining, they're going to strip him naked and put him in solitary confinement."

They can't do that. Palmer Jail is an American jail after all. Aurora's anger touches me, and I relate to it. But I recognize it's only one of her strategies, the elicitation of emotion.

"It's cold in here," I say.

"It's cold in here." Aurora mimics me, and I watch her upper lip curl into a sneer. "It's going to get a lot colder. The furnace is not working, and I can't afford to fix it."

"Always something," I say.

"Always something." Aurora mimics me again with even more of a sneer.

Aurora goes to the other side of the bed and sits down, winces as she bends her new knees, her back to me. Bear-Bear jumps on the bed and lies next to her.

"Don't know why you're here," Aurora says without turning around. "Don't really care."

"I'm sorry that Tim's still in jail," I say.

"What do you know about sorry? You, with your perfect little life," Aurora snarls. "I don't care what it takes or what I have to do, I'll get the money to get Tim out of jail and to pay his lawyer."

I recognize this tactic, too—the ferocity, the underdog's call to battle against the odds, the noble fight, the veiled summons for us to come to her assistance and offer her aid.

"What are you going to do?" I say to Aurora's back.

"Whatever I have to." Aurora turns her head and looks at me. "Now, come on, Abby. Why are you really here?"

"I'm really here to see Bill," I say.

Aurora's eyes narrow. She rubs her knees in a slow rocking motion. After a few moments, she swings her legs in one smooth motion up onto the bed, reaches down, feels for the edge of the quilt, and pulls the quilt over her. Bear-Bear adjusts his position next to her, and Aurora puts her arm around the dog. "Good night," she says.

There it is. Welcome home, Abby.

24 May
The Peace Treaty

I wake to the smell of coffee, noises of people talking, and Bear-Bear barking in the yard. I look out the window and see a cow moose and her new calf, still unsure on its legs and still blinking in the unfamiliar light. Feeling bleary, I walk down the hall and peek into the computer room. Alice busily types on her laptop. Mother and Aurora sit at Aurora's computer desk, going over what looks like e-mails.

"So that's a peace treaty," Aurora says to Mother.

Mother nods.

"Let's figure out the terms of this peace treaty," Alice says.

"How about we start with the budget?" Mother says.

In the living room, Bill sleeps with his head hanging to one side, his mouth open, softly snoring. I get coffee and go sit next to Bill. He sometimes wakes to look at me or to look around as if looking for someone else, before his eyes roll up under his lids and he sleeps again. Foot check: warm, but swollen and blotchy.

Mother comes into the living room, takes her purse from the credenza by the hall, and sits on the couch. She's still in her pajamas. She takes out her checkbook, writes a check, records the check in the check log, and double checks what she wrote.

"I'm going to pay some of Aurora's immediate expenses, house expenses, utilities—get the furnace repaired." Mother comes over to me.

I glance at the check Mother just wrote for Aurora. The check is for $9,620.

"Don't you say a word. You're not supposed to interfere," Mother says.

25 May
Potatoes

"Please don't do this!" I've been trying convince Mother all day.

"Why? Because she's made mistakes in the past?" Mother asks.

"No, because she's exploiting you," I say.

"Only in your opinion," Mother replies. "You don't have all the facts."

"I have facts enough," I insist. "I'm going to call the police."

"Why? Is it a crime for me to help my daughter?" Mother seems to be smiling at me.

"What kind of immediate expenses cost almost ten thousand dollars?"

"It doesn't matter," Mother says. "Aurora and I are talking now. The money is small potatoes compared to that."

"Mother, she's manipulating you," I protest again.

"Abby, by your own description of a peace treaty, you are a second party, and you can't interfere," Mother says. "According to the peace treaty, you aren't supposed to judge either."

This is the first I've heard that Aurora is actually pursuing the peace treaty idea. Why didn't she tell me? It turned out so wrong.

"Mother, she's using the peace treaty to get more money out of you," I object.

"You're judging." her voice takes on a stubborn quality, and I know this debate is over.

I stay with Bill and watch him sleep his morphine sleep. I touch his hands: cold. Feet: warm. Toenails: blue. The kitchen timer goes off, and I start to reposition him.

"Not again," Bill gurgles. He's awake after all. "Don't move me."

I carefully place a pillow behind his back to change the pressure, trying not to hurt him.

"Are we alone?" Bill whispers.

"Yes," I say.

"I've got to go to Seward," Bill says, his voice low. "Slim reminded me it's an ice-free port. I can navigate around to Homer and then across the Inlet."

"How can I help?"

"By not telling the others." Bill looks around the room. "They won't let me go."

"OK."

"It's not OK," Bill says. "Where's your mother?"

"She's in her room."

"Music," Bill says.

I see the CD for "The Flying Dutchman" on top of stereo where I left it months ago, so I play it. The song of the weary helmsman begins. "Think no more of it. Sleep sound, Captain." Bill's head sinks deep into the pillow. He sighs and falls asleep.

Alice comes into the living room with a laundry basket. She sits in the recliner and folds towels, by color and function, into thirds. All the folded edges go in the same direction. We listen to the familiar music until the last words: "Here I am, true to you till death!"

Those last words seem to somehow affect Alice, and she looks at Bill. "I've said good-bye to him. He's no longer lucid and is pretty much gone now."

Alice's cold, brutal statements don't usually bother me, but this does. No, he's not gone, and I'm sure he can hear you.

"I feel better now that the tension is reduced between Momma and Aurora. I'm helping them with the terms of the peace treaty," Alice says.

Damn the peace treaty.

"I've got Palmer managing the Homer house, and we have established good communication with Buddy, the renter," Alice says. "I want to get the peace treaty figured out so we can have a real plan and I can go home. Palmer's been bugging me to come home."

"The peace treaty is a ruse, you know," I say.

"It was your idea," Alice says.

"I didn't think Aurora would abuse it, turn it into something ugly," I say.

"That's just it—you didn't think," Alice says. "I told you a while back that it was just another name for extortion." She gets up. "Now, we can't interfere, and Aurora has license to manipulate all she wants." Alice goes to the kitchen.

I spend the rest of the day with Bill, though mostly I just watch him sleep, and I worry about the outcome of the peace treaty.

Aurora seems radiant. "Don't the begonias look great?" She joins Alice in the kitchen, chatting, buzzing, putting dishes away, arranging pots and pans, and then the softer noises of peeling potatoes. "I want to plant potatoes in the tires, like you did last summer."

All bubbly and happiness…She must've pocketed the check for $9,620.

"Oh, yes, it works nicely," Alice encourages Aurora.

"How exactly do you do it?" Aurora asks.

"Well, you put a little dirt in the bottom of the tires. You set the seed potato on top of the dirt and cover it with little more dirt," Alice explains.

"I forgot to mention it. We just got approved for extra home health care for Bill. Two extra hours a day starting next week," Aurora says.

"That's great. Then as the potato plant starts growing, you add more dirt, a little at a time," Alice says. "The idea is to keep most of the potato plant buried in dirt."

"Oh, my knee check is tomorrow afternoon," Aurora says.

"Eventually, the plant will grow above the level of the tire," Alice says. "At this point, your dirt should reach the top of the tire."

I continue to catch snippets of conversation in the kitchen. But the cheery, buzzing, nonstop talk annoys me.

"Tim and I have to appear in court later this week," Aurora says.

"How many of these should we peel?" Alice asks.

"All of them," Aurora says. "Got carrots planted, and my green onions are doing good."

"I'm sorting stuff for the yard sale," Alice says.

"I borrowed fifteen tables from the office," Aurora says.

"What do you think about making coffee for the yard sale?"

"Do you have enough tires to plant potatoes?"

"Let's work on the peace treaty tonight."

"What does Bill want for dinner?"

"Mashed potatoes. Besides, it doesn't matter. He doesn't know what he's eating."

I check Bill's feet: Cold. Pink.

"Psst."

I look up and see Bill watching me.

"No potatoes. I want ice cream." Bill winks at me.

"Roger."

"Roadrunner," Bill hesitates. His thin face has become a sheet of translucent skin pulled taut over his skull. His eyes are starting to sink back into their sockets. He doesn't move much because every move hurts now. "Roadrunner, go get some rest. You look terrible."

26 May
Dinner and a Movie

I like serving ice cream to Bill because of the pure delight ice cream gives him. Besides he needs the calories. The rest of us need fewer calories and are in various stages of dieting. Alice follows a structured plan with prepackaged foods. She's lost thirty pounds, as she so often reminds us. Two years ago, I lost seventy pounds, but I didn't tell anyone, and nobody noticed or at least didn't say anything. I've gained all the weight back and, curiously, Mother and Alice often remind me of it. Aurora says she has lost weight but says she still has 150 pounds to lose. Mother's dieting and trying to undo the pounds gained through the years, especially these last years as Bill declined and enjoyment was limited more and more to food.

It was that way for JB. Food was enjoyment, security, and even a communal activity. He told us stories of his childhood, being the youngest of ten children growing up in the depression years when food was scarce or nonexistent. A pantry stocked with food signaled security for JB. A root cellar full of potatoes, carrots, canned goods, and smoked salmon signified the comfort of warm suppers. A cache laden with moose meant meat all winter. Suppertime was sacred time when we didn't argue or talk negative and Mother said the blessing. It was the only time JB allowed Mother to be religious. It was the only time we acted like a family.

Alice often helped JB order seeds for the garden. As she got older, she helped JB design methods for food preservation. She created a smokehouse out of an old refrigerator and built drying racks to sun-dry tomatoes and wild mushrooms. Once, she developed a method to improve the air circulation in the root cellar for storing onions.

Alice created many plans: a planting plan, garden maintenance plan, harvest plan, preservation plan, and what-to-plan-in-the-winter plan. On a big calendar, she and JB marked out the fishing, clamming, and moose seasons. These were supplemented by the blueberry, cranberry, and mushroom seasons. Alice calculated the cost and savings for chickens and fresh eggs. Then one day JB brought home laying hens. JB and I didn't do projects together. He resented me too much for being a girl. I was never his bundle of joy, but when Alice and Aurora were born, he somewhat accepted them as girls.

Now food is our bane. We're all overweight, except for Bill of course.

"Dinner's ready," Aurora announces.

Dinner is salad with grilled halibut. Aurora takes her plate downstairs. Bear-Bear pads after her. Alice and I take our plates to the sofa, and settled in, we begin to crunch on our salads.

An old favorite cowboy movie, *The Bravados*, plays on the movie channel, though muted. Mother takes a plate to Bill's side table. He's awake and watching the movie, reciting the dialogue along with the actors. Mother says the blessing, and Alice and I pause in our crunching.

"I'm going to Rio Arriba," Bill says.

"What's your business in Rio Arriba?" Mother says.

"I've come for the hanging." Bill waves his hands in the air.

Both Mother and Bill know the words to the entire movie.

"The Sheriff doesn't want any strangers in town for the hanging," Mother says.

"Then I've come for pie," Bill says, and we laugh.

"I think I'll hike around the Inlet tomorrow," I say to Alice.

"You know, we missed Mother's Day. We could celebrate Mother's Day," Alice says.

"What about a picnic? We have respite care tomorrow," Alice says. "Momma, would you like to go somewhere tomorrow?"

"I don't go to church anymore," Bill says, still saying the actor's lines.

"Oh, I'm so sorry," Mother says, right on cue.

"Go to Seward," Bill says.

"Why Seward?" Alice asks.

"It's ice-free," Bill says.

"Yes, of course, Seward," Alice approves. "Though it would be an all-day trip, mostly for the drive. I could test my new kayak. Momma?"

"Go to Seward." I see Bill silently mouth the words to Mother.

"OK, let's go to Seward," Mother says. "Besides I'd enjoy seeing you test the kayak."

A weather advisory banner skims across the bottom of the movie. It's a tsunami advisory: increased activity at the St. Augustine volcano island with undersea ground swelling, steam and smoke, and minitremors reaching the Kenai Peninsula coastline. Persons on Homer Spit are reminded they have sixty minutes to take cover once a tsunami warning is given.

27 May
Mother's Day

"You want me to drive to Seward while Tim is in jail?" Aurora accuses us.

"It might help soothe your nerves," I say.

"Not much you can do for Tim on a Sunday," Alice says between sneezes.

"I can visit him twice. Visiting hours are at six in the morning and in the evening," Aurora snarls.

"I'm nervous about leaving Bill," Mother says.

"Go to Seward," Bill says to Mother.

"Go to Seward," Bill then says to me.

Alice enters the room. "Will someone come help me load the kayak?"

The phone rings. It's a collect call from Tim at the jail.

"Yes, I'll be there. Yes, yes, it's only twenty minutes away," Aurora says.

"You're sure?" Mother says to Bill.

"Yup," Bill tells her.

"Damn, I've got to call the lawyer." Aurora slams down the phone. "They still won't let Tim have his meds."

"Mike will be here all day," Bill reassures Mother.

Bill waves his bony hand at me. "Be careful around the ice."

"I can't find the dry suits," Alice says and sneezes again.

"Sounds like you're catching a cold." Mother turns to Alice. "You can't test the kayak with a cold. You'll catch pneumonia."

"Well, I could do everything except the rolls."

"I'll test it for you," I say. "Don't forget a hood."

"Don't forget the ice." Bill seems agitated.

I go to Bill and watch his eyes, which seem lucid. His voice seems lucid. All seems lucid, though I'm not sure.

The phone rings, and it's another collect call from Tim. Will we ever get out of here?

"What do you mean?" Aurora says. "Yes, yes, I'm on my way."

Aurora slams down the phone and tries to brush the hair out of her face, but her fine hair crackles with static electricity and flies out from her head. Her eyes seem on fire.

"I've got to go. I've got to find money for the lawyer." Aurora heads downstairs. She pauses, her back to us. "Since my own family won't help me."

We hear the truck door slam, the diesel engine start, and the sound of the truck moving down the driveway.

"Are we alone now?" Bill asks.

"Yes, what's up?"

"When you get to Seward, check the ice," Bill says. "And send me a pilot report. I can't go unless I know the way is clear."

"OK," I say.

What's happening with him? I can't sense him today.

"Not OK," Bill says. "That's the problem. Go on to Seward," Bill says before I can say more.

Driving to Seward takes us first around the Knik Arm, through Anchorage, past Potter's March, and then to the winding Turnagain Arm created a millennia ago when ancient glaciers retreated. The road winds and turns and turns again with the mountain on one side and the Inlet in all its glory and power on the other side.

At Beluga Point, we see a bore tide rushing in. We stop and watch, listen to its force, its oncoming rush so like the sound of an oncoming train. No belugas.

I love these drives, these moments by the Inlet. Be at peace, the Inlet seems to tell me. Go in peace. We follow the road around the Inlet, past Portage with its stately ghost forest created by the tsunami sent by the Good Friday earthquake of 1964. We pass Girdwood and head inland, past the Hope turnoff and start climbing up to the summit.

We reach Tern Lake where the road forks. Go right to Homer. Go left to Seward. Tern Lake is a water-filled moraine, with a menagerie of birds, bird-people, and photographers. Alice stops the car so we can walk out on the viewing platform. This is a good time of the year to see birds. On several treetops bald eagles perch. A flock of Arctic terns swims out in the middle of the lake. A pair of swans glides far across the water, two pure-white specks against the dark. We see groups of goldeneyes and mergansers.

We reach Seward, and ahead lies Resurrection Bay, an immense fjord surrounded by snowcapped mountains that shelter the bay from harsh winters. In early spring gray whales stop here on their way to the Arctic, and flocks of herons stop and visit on their way to Homer. The humpback and killer whales also stop here. Sea lions, seals, and otters live here year round.

Everything is relatively new in Seward, all rebuilt after the Good Friday earthquake. With a magnitude of 9.2, the earthquake shook for nearly four minutes. The roads cracked, and fissures opened up. Large sections of land sank. Then the tsunami came and battered the city's oil-storage tanks so violently that oil spilled out, caught fire, and burnt the town down.

We drive into Miller's Landing. Alice gets a day pass at the office and arranges to rent a kayak so we'll have two kayaks. I'll use the rented kayak until it's time to test Alice's new one. We build a fire in the fire pit, prepare lunch, and get Mother settled in a camp chair with blankets and a pair of binoculars so she can watch us. When we return an hour later, she's asleep, and the fire is a cluster of glowing embers. We wake her to tell her we're back and we're going back out to test the kayak. Mother's immediately alert.

"What's your test plan?" I ask Alice.

"First, see how it accelerates and holds speed, how it slows down without losing control, how it leans and turns, and then turn it into the waves if you can find any," Alice says.

"So the usual?" I say.

"Pretty much," Alice says. "Then the rolls. Remember once you start the rolls and get wet, you only have five minutes to finish. Can't have you freezing to death."

The usual.

"Oh, one more thing," Alice says. "It's designed for layback rolls."

I nod and already appreciate the kayak because the layback rolls are easier for me.

"When you roll, lean into it as slow as possible so I can see how much lean it will take," Alice continues. "Do the paddle first. Then do a hand roll. When you're all done with that, roll it again, stop the momentum, and swim out."

It's the test or "checkout" routine we've done for years for all our kayaks. We'd never take a kayak out on a serious cruise without knowing how it handled or knowing we could recover if it capsized. Bill always says we're doing a preflight for kayaks.

"Remember, we stop and head back to shore five minutes after your head gets wet." Alice hands me a neoprene hood and gloves. "I'll be calling the time."

As we slip into our kayaks, I hear one of the kayak guides talking to Alice.

"Need any help?" the guide asks Alice.

"We're just testing out a new kayak," Alice says and sneezes. "You know, seeing what it can do."

"That's a cool kayak," the guide says. "Where did you get it?"

"I got it from a guy in Eagle River. He built it from a kit he got from a place in Washington," Alice says.

"Sweet," the guide says. "It looks fast. Do you folks kayak a lot?"

"I guess you could say that. We grew up in kayaks," Alice says. "I'm the technically savvy one, but my sister here is more intuitive."

"Well, if you need an extra hand, I'd be happy to give you one," the guide says. "Plus, it would be sweet to see what this kayak can do."

"It wouldn't hurt to have another safety," Alice says.

"Great, I'll get my stuff." I hear delight in the young man's voice.

I fasten the skirt over the hatch, put on the hood and goggles. Ahead of me the tide is coming in and the bay lies smooth and silky. Several sea otters float on their backs.

I push out into enough water where I can wait for Alice and the guide to gear up. I stroke the sides of the kayak. Alice says it's a Pygmy design, a Murrelet 4PD, which doesn't mean much to me. The kayak is entirely made of wood, shiny, earthy, and beautiful to look at, probably too beautiful to be functional. I lean back and feel the back support and note the ideal height of the deck for lying back.

Alice and the guide push off into the water with Alice on my right and the guide on my left. I turn and wave at Mother, who is watching us through binoculars; nod to Alice and the guide; and paddle out.

Magic. The Murrelet accelerates so fast I immediately leave Alice and the guide in the shallows, fly by the otters, and head out to the middle of the bay. After a minute I look back, see Alice and the guide are far behind, and slow down to let them catch up. When they catch up, I head out again, letting the kayak accelerate faster than I've ever known a kayak to go. Bay breezes whip by me. There are more otters, and there's a sea lion; the warm sun above; the soft, almost-silent paddle sounds, the rhythm of the paddle dipping and pulling and dipping and pulling. Yes, it feels magical and mystical here on Resurrection Bay, often called the second part of the trinity— the Inlet and Kachemak Bay down in Homer the other parts of the trinity.

I slow the pace to let Alice and the guide catch up again, then maintain an even speed so they can stay with me and observe how the kayak performs. The water taxi passes us on its return trip back to Miller's Landing. As it passes, I turn toward the wake; lean into the turn, almost touching my right side to the water;

lean even more into the paddle; complete the turn; and cruise straight into the frothy wake of the water taxi.

"Yahoo," the guide yells behind me.

Next, I lean left, almost touching my shoulder to the water, leaning more and more, feeling for its limits, doing a 360-degree turn, and race once again into the wake.

"Great balls of fire," Alice yells.

The Murrelet continues to track and turn and sprint with such grace and agility that it seems to be guiding me, not me paddling the kayak. Then I feel it. The belugas are close by! What are they doing here? They're supposed to be on their way to the Inlet. I push out farther into the bay until I'm nearly past Caines Head.

I hear Alice's safety whistle, one long blast, the signal to come back. I continue pushing forward toward the belugas, pulling the paddle deep in the water along the side of the kayak, sliding, gliding across the water.

I look back and see Alice and the guide pounding the water to catch up with me. I put the paddle far out in the water and lean my hip into a slow, steep, edgy 360-degree turn. Oh, beluga, where are you?

I let the kayak come to rest and bend forward on the front deck, putting my ear down against the wood of the kayak. I hear water making soft the sides of the kayak. Bay breezes seem to whisper around my head. Gulls laugh far away, a train whines back at the Port of Seward, and the paddle sounds of Alice and the guide become more distinct. I listen deeper and hear my own breathing, the gentle whoosh action of the surge, unknown slippery sounds, my toes moving, the folds of my dry suit rustling. I stroke the wood of the kayak and tap it several times with my fingers. The tapping sounds are probably too low, but taps against wood are boat sounds, and belugas will recognize boat sounds.

"What is it?" the guide asks.

"Shh, she's found something," Alice says.

I hear an eagle cry above, and all manner of slurping, swishing water sounds.

"What's up?" Alice asks, still panting.

"I could probably hear them if I were underwater. Let's sing to them," I say to Alice.

"Belugas?" Alice sounds excited.

I nod. The eyes of the guide widen.

"Any requests?" Alice asks.

"Well, this is Resurrection Bay. Why not *Vespers*, the tenth movement," I say. Alice has good range and can handle both the alto and the soprano, but she excels at the soprano.

"What are we doing?" the guide asks. "What can I do?

"We are calling them in," I say. "By the way, what's your name?"

"Bill," he says.

Another Bill? Somehow, this seems right to me.

"Well, Bill, if you could whistle while my sister sings, that would be nice. Just whistle any old way," I say. "I'll tap the wood. We'll give them a concert."

We paddle out quietly, dipping our paddles shallowly and delicately toward the mouth of the bay. Alice begins singing the alto part. Bill whistles. I tap the wood of kayak.

"And we hymn and glorify thy holy resurrection." Alice then changes to soprano, her voice high and reaching across the bay. Bill whistles along, not harmony, but synchronous. I tap the wood. We swoosh along the great bay—swoosh, tap, and whistle.

"Come, all you faithful," Alice sings higher and higher, then switches to alto. Tap. Swoosh. Whistle. Whoosh. Where are you? Swoosh. Tap. Swoosh.

I sense them first and then feel them rubbing the side of the kayak.

"Joy has come into all the world," Alice sings.

I signal to Alice that I'm going to start the rolls. Then, after the next paddle stroke, I put on my goggles and place the paddle behind my head and lean into the water, rolling the kayak upside down, my head slipping into the icy water just before seeing the belugas appear around us, smiling, their eyes seeming to twinkle.

The frigid water on my face and hands startles me for a moment, but the iciness on my scalp and the back of my neck, even with a hood, stuns me, and I almost panic. I know Alice has started the five-minute countdown. I sweep the paddle, just enough to gather momentum; grab the side of the Murrelet; and roll the kayak back up, lying all the way back on the deck, slowly sitting up as the kayak rights itself.

The belugas gather around us, clicking and squawking. I quickly count eleven or twelve pure-white adult belugas plus numerous gray juveniles. I take a few more paddle strokes and lean left and roll the Murrelet again, this time ready for the icy blast on my scalp. Under the water the blunt shapes of the whales appear with their melon heads, mouths open as if singing. One beluga comes close and rubs against the edge of Murrelet. I feel the warmth emanating from the beluga and hear a variety of high-pitched whistles and clucks accentuated by an occasional squeal. Several more belugas cluster around. I have only seconds before I must grab the side of the Murrelet and roll the kayak back up.

There are belugas all around, some sticking their noses and smiling faces up out of the water. Alice watches me, watches beluga, watches her watch, watches me, watches beluga. Bill remains speechless, mouth hanging open.

"Four minutes left," Alice says, almost a whisper. "Hello, beluga."

I take a few more paddle strokes, hold the paddle against the side of the kayak, and roll the kayak once more, briefly hanging underwater, reveling in the sight of these pure-white creatures. The icy water numbs my scalp, but I feel at ease. Each time I roll the kayak, one of the belugas approaches me and rubs the edge of the kayak with its bulbous white head. I want to reach out and touch the belugas, hug the belugas, listen to their whale song, swim with them.

These are the Cook Inlet belugas, the belugas we've grown up with. Several belugas seem to look at me—several others hang suspended vertically as if standing at whale attention. Several float close to each other, bumping and rubbing against other. Their chirps and clucks mesmerize me. Focus. I grab the side of the kayak and roll the Murrelet up, lying back on the high deck and then sitting up.

"Three minutes left," Alice says.

I take a few more paddle strokes and roll the kayak again. The belugas glow in the dark water, in ranges of creamy white to yellow white to white white. They are the true white whale, without malice or spite or reprisal. They are total purity, complete piety, and majestic simplicity. I roll the kayak up, lying back on the deck, and feel the blazing sun on my face as I look up.

"Two minutes," Alice says.

I bask in the sun for a moment before sitting up. The sun's heat on my face makes the rest of my body feel colder, and I nod to Alice to signal the swim-out to her. She paddles in close. My hands are numb, and my fingers feel clumsy when I pass my paddle to her. I roll the kayak one last time and let my weight go to deadweight. I lose any momentum left from rolling over and simply hang there upside down. A group of belugas bob their heads up and down in the water. Several are close enough to touch. I'm in the middle of their pod, the water around me swirls and undulates with belugas touching and rubbing and surfacing, and the space around me reverberates with beluga squawking and mewing.

Such glory, these beings. They renew me. How I savor this moment, this cup of life, this reminder that life is precious and beautiful and that life itself is sanctity. Then all of it comes to me in a flash of indescribable beauty and I understand why the Mother Moose dreams reappeared.

I see it. The dream was triggered by the cremation paper work for Bill, though not the concept of cremation. It was the description of cremation, a description that, for me, violates the spirit

194

of human existence, a description that reduces human spirit to a pile of bone dust and fragments and brains bubbling in cracked skulls. This description, like my initial desire to terminate a pregnancy so many years ago, is technically accurate and logical and efficient but violates what I feel inside—that life itself is sanctity. I know now what I need to do.

Three belugas hover close to me, smiling, as if agreeing, their melon heads changing shape as they chirp and start to whistle. I hang there and wish to stay, but finally bend upward to give the OK signal. I feel the fatigue and want to sleep.

I sense Alice and Bill's kayak approach close to the Murrelet. So tired. Focus. One beluga nudges the edge of the Murrelet. Another beluga joins in. Soon, the belugas have closed in around me, and I touch one.

The belugas whistle more than chirp now, which means they are alarmed. I sense they are worried about me and give the biggest beluga the OK sign then reach behind me to unfasten the skirt. The skirt is snug tight around the hatch, and my hands ache as I clumsily unfasten it.

I'd like to stay but can't hold my breath any longer. Right now, this is the longest I have ever held my breath. I blow out a tiny stream of air bubbles to relieve the carbon dioxide buildup in my lungs. The bubbles float up, sparkling and glinting like diamonds, and then dissipate. One of the belugas nudges me. A beluga behind me bumps me. Focus. I yank the skirt off the hatch and push myself away from the Murrelet and swim up to the surface.

"You're over five minutes," Alice announces.

I float on my back amid the belugas while Alice and Bill turn the Murrelet upright. The belugas start to squawk, which means they're happy again. Their white heads bob up next to me. Squawk. Then I hear a hundred honks and look up to see a flock of herons flying by.

Back at shore we sit around the fire and listen to waves lap the shore and gulls cry to the fishermen for more fish. I'm dry, my hair is almost dry, and I'm warming up slowly. Alice boils water in a small soup pot, removes the kettle from the fire, waits for the boiling action to subside, and then throws in several handfuls of dark ground coffee. We watch the coffee grounds slowly sink to the bottom of the pot. After the coffee grounds have mostly settled and the water transforms to a lush, dark espresso, Alice serves us cups of steaming coffee sweetened with a touch of raw sugar. The Resurrection Bay before us, otters floating on their backs not far from shore, our little fire—yes, life is good.

"I want to say something," Mother announces.

"Yes, of course," Alice says, poking the fire with a stick.

"I've made a decision." Mother pauses and looks at me long enough for me to see the stalwartness in her countenance and those pursed lips.

"I need your full attention," Mother adds.

Alice stops poking at the fire.

"I want to make a gift of an early inheritance to Aurora," Mother says. "I want to give her enough to pay all of her bills, get the house out of arrears, and pay Tim's lawyer. I want Aurora free and clear, moneywise."

"Are you insane?" I object.

"I want her to have a second chance."

"It won't help," Alice says. "It won't ever end."

"Never mind all that. Alice, I want you to calculate how much money this involves and figure out a plan to ensure the money goes directly to the debts. Abby, I want you to become my legal representative. Go to the lawyer and figure out the paper work," Mother says. "I charge you both to help me give your sister a second chance."

"Aurora is exploiting you again!" I continue objecting. I feel the ire, but the beauty of the beluga comes back and calms me.

"She doesn't know I'm doing this," Mother says.

"Momma, why on earth would you do this?" Alice asks.

"Hear me and hear me well," Mother says. "First, Bill will be gone soon. I don't know what my life will look like after that. But I want to be free to go live a new life or die in peace. I want to know I did all I could for Aurora. I want to have no regrets. I want to do this for me, not for her. I want your support in this. I want this as a Mother's Day gift."

"But—"

"Second, he that soweth sparingly shall reap sparingly also." Mother recites the passage we've heard her say many times. "And he that soweth bountifully shall reap also bountifully."

What could we say?

28 May
The Funeral Parlor

"You need a plan," Alice says. "You can't barge in there, make demands, and expect them to acquiesce. Let me help you."

So with the help of Alice, the master planner, I'm prepared, planned, and portfolio-ed when I enter reception room of the funeral parlor.

"Hello, I'm Josh Terrino," the young man says.

"Hi, I'm Abby. We spoke on the phone several weeks ago about the paper work for my stepfather's cremation," I say. "For Bill McCray."

"Yes, I remember," Josh says. "Please, sit down. How can I assist you today?"

"I'd like to speak with your manager."

I notice the awards on the walls: a Quality Service Award, a Certificate of Recognition from the city and a Certificate of Appreciation from a local church. An arrangement of fresh flowers sits on a low table, and the smell of tuberose delicately wafts through the room. Upholstery is done with a soft fabric in shades of brown. Fuzzy white pillows that resemble polar bears are scattered about. I'm struck by the soothing quality of the room. It's also a quiet room. No music. No water trickling over pebbles. No phones ringing.

"We don't have a manager," Josh says. "We have a director."

"Please don't play games with me," I say. "I want to speak to the person in charge, whoever that is and whatever you call that person."

"I'm sure I can handle your needs," Josh says and folds his hands on top of each other on his lap in the sign of respect and tranquility that he's been trained to do.

"Get your director."

I pick up one of the fuzzy pillows and read the tag: "A Pillow to Hug. Take me home. Made for you by the Hug an Alaskan Project."

Josh leaves the room and returns with an older man, Neal O'Brien, the director of the funeral home. We go to Neal's office, which features polished wood furniture and framed photographs of famous churches from around the world.

"How can I help you," Neal says after we settle into our chairs.

I open my portfolio and hand Neal a copy of the cremation paper work. "I want you to change this."

He takes the document and scans it enough to recognize it. "Of course," he says. "We can change anything you want. Did you want a burial option rather than the cremation option?"

"No," I say. "I want you to change the language pertaining to the description of the cremation."

Neal and Josh exchange puzzled looks.

"I feel the language is offensive and violates the sacredness of the human spirit."

"I spoke with Abby several weeks ago and explained this paper work was just a legal necessity, that nobody really reads it," Josh says.

"I read it," I say.

"I meant most people don't read it," Josh says.

"And I found it offensive.

"It was not our intention to offend you," Josh says.

The director watches me.

"But it did offend me," I say. "And I want the language changed."

"The language is standard in the business," Josh says. "We have to explain the process to avoid any misunderstanding, to avoid causing any undue trauma to families already in grief."

"I beg your pardon," I say. "But it's not the standard in the business."

"Here's a copy of the paper work for the North Star Mortuary." I reopen my portfolio and hand the director a document.

"And here's a copy of the paper work for the Life's Celebration Crematorium...And here's a copy of the paper work for Matanuska Mortuary Services...And here's one from the Neptune Society...And if you have any doubt at all, here's one from a pet cemetery."

The director flips through the documents and then leans toward me. "Ma'am, I don't see anything wrong with the documentation from our competitors."

"Exactly." I notice a little wood carving of a bear on the director's desk. A small engraved plate on the base of the carving reads, "To Neal, thank you for all you did for us, from the Clemmons family."

"Let me read your documentation," I say.

"We humans are about 60 percent water, so we require a huge amount of heat," I begin.

"This isn't necessary," Josh says.

"We know what our documentation says," the director says.

"Well, just listen for a minute," I continue reading. "The body will burn outside to inside in a cycle of dehydration and ignition. Sometimes, early in the cremation process, the heat causes the body's torso to violently flex forward."

The director looks startled.

"So you don't know what it says." I continue reading. "Slowly, all the skin burns off, starting at the ends of the limbs where there is not much muscle or fat. The bones appear, and the skeleton will become visible."

"These details are all technically accurate and necessary for legal reasons," Josh insists.

"Really? No other business has details like this," I say. "Bones glow white in the flames, and the skeleton falls apart. Some of the bones fall into pieces while other bones remain whole."

"We have to explain the process properly," Josh says. "Or we'd risk litigation."

"Tell me if this part is proper and protects you from litigation," I say. "Some body parts resist, especially the chest contents and the brain. Even after the heat cracks the skull into pieces, the brain hangs on, a darkening clump, surviving until—"

"Enough." The director turns pale and gives Josh a questioning look.

"Oh, but it's not enough," I say. "Bone fragments are then pounded or pressed and—"

"Enough, please!" the director shouts. "I'm sorry. I didn't mean to shout. It's just that I didn't realize how—"

"Ah, you feel it, too." I soften my voice. "I believe this language triggered recurring nightmares for me. I believe if people read this, they'll have a similar reaction to what you just experienced and to what I experienced," I say. "That's why I'm here. I can't stand by and let this happen to others."

"Neal, this paper work is necessary," Josh says.

"Yes, but you don't need this specific language," I say. "Your competitors don't."

"What, may I ask, is wrong with this language?" Josh asks. "Our business strategy is to be honest and authentic. You want us to craft some fluffy words so one overly sensitive customer doesn't have nightmares."

I look at the carving of the bear on the director's desk, this little token from one customer sitting in the director's personal space. Oh, I think the director cares about one overly sensitive customer.

"Yes, we want to be honest and authentic, but—" the director says.

"Many people might not read the paper work," I say. "But what if someone does?"

"Are you threatening us?" Josh says.

"Why would you feel threatened," I ask. "This so-called honest and authentic documentation might be completely accurate in technical terms, but it violates something central to the human spirit, something that's related to our hope for an afterlife, something related to the essence of the person who just died. And, in my opinion, it could cause more trauma to people who are already in trauma. Most of all, it's not necessary."

"That's just your opinion," Josh says. "Who are you to come here on a mission to save the world, spout your opinion, and demand we change our business?"

I'd like to say the belugas sent me, but instead I hand my business card to the director. "As you can probably tell from my card, I'm qualified to make such an opinion."

The director looks over my card. I pick up the carving of the bear. It's a handmade carving with fine details showing even the hairs of the bear fur and a superb hand-rubbed shine and that accompanying engraving: "To Neal, thank you for all you did for us, from the Clemmons family." The director sees me examining the little carving.

"A family member made that for me," the director says, and a faraway look comes over him for a brief moment. "It was an especially difficult time for that family."

I return the carving to its base. The director puts down my card.

"I agree with your assessment of the language. We will change it by Friday, close of business," the director says.

"But my plate's full. I don't have time to work on this," Josh adds.

"I know. Let's talk about that later," the director says and then walks with me to the front door. "I know there's nothing I can do to repair the damage already done, and I apologize for that. But going forward, if there's anything I can do, please allow me to.

Perhaps I could drive out to your house and bring you the new documentation."

"Thank you, but no. I'll stop by next week," I say. "You've done plenty. You allowed me to fulfill my mission, to prevent what happened to me from happening to others. Thank you."

"And I thank you for bringing this to my attention."

That night, the Mother Moose dream does not return.

29 May
The Flight Line

"We're going to have fifteen tables! This will be a humdinger of a yard sale!" Alice proclaims.

We've spent all day organizing and sorting Mother's household goods from Homer. Boxes and bags line the circular driveway. Sometimes Bear-Bear wanders over and pokes his nose into one of the boxes. Mother emerges from the shed with a blue coffee mug decorated with the air force insignia on one side and a C-130 named *Belle of the Ball* on the other side.

What are you doing with that mug?" Aurora asks.

"I'm going to keep it," Mother says.

"Didn't you approve everything in those boxes for the yard sale?"

"This was—is Bill's favorite mug." Mother turns the mug so she can look at it.

"What else have you taken out of the yard sale boxes?"

"For Pete's sake, she can take whatever she wants," I say. "It's her stuff."

"Did you or did you not approve everything in those boxes!" Aurora says accusingly.

"Yes, I did." Mother continues to look at the mug.

"Then put that damn cup back in the yard sale box," Aurora says.

"I want to keep it," Mother says. "Slim gave him this cup."

"She can change her mind," I say.

"Give me that," Aurora grabs the cup out of Mother's hand and moves toward the shed.

Mother seems too stunned to respond. And she wants to give Aurora a second chance. Why?

"I'll get it back for you," Alice whispers to Mother.

I step in front of Aurora and grab her wrist. "Give her back the cup."

"Go to hell," Aurora hisses. "You think you're so tough."

"Give her the cup," I repeat. Aurora is stronger than I am, and I can't hold onto her wrist much longer. Second chance, my ass. I kick her in the knee. I know it hurts, almost feel the hurt.

"You bitch!" Aurora howls, throws the coffee mug at Mother, and hobbles toward her truck. "I'm getting out of here." The mug lands in the grass on the side of the driveway.

"Here, Bear-Bear," Aurora calls. Aurora and the dog climb into the truck, and she revs the big engine and screeches off with gravel spitting out from behind the rear tires.

"You didn't have to hurt her knee," Mother tells me.

"I know, I'm sorry. My temper got the best of me," I say.

"Here's your cup, Momma." Alice stands there, holding out the cup.

That evening, we eat dinner without Aurora and watch the news on TV. One reporter stands on a beach and talks about St. Augustine, about seabed rumblings and potential ash clouds. Any time now, experts say, the volcano is expected to erupt. Residents along the southern beaches of Cook Inlet are urged to stay tuned for updates.

I stay up and watch old movies with Bill. It's past midnight, and Aurora's still not home.

"She's not back yet," Bill says.

"I know." I sigh.

"Can you move me?"

"Where to?"

"Off the flight line," Bill says. "They're doing touch-and-goes with *Belle*, testing hydraulics I think. They didn't tell me. And here I am in the middle of the flight line."

I look for the truth in his words. I scan the living room, the adjoining kitchen-dining area, and the hall. There it is: the blue night-lights shining along the hall, the yellow ones above the stove, the glow of the amber streetlights out in the yard, the many red pinpoint lights of the coffee maker, the digital clock on the stove, the stereo, Alice's laptop on the couch, the doorbell, the telephones, and the controls on Bill's air bed. The area is indeed lit up like a runway.

I unplug the night-lights, turn off the kitchen light, and close some of the curtains.

"Ah, just in time," Bill says. "Here she comes."

I hear an engine rumble and the crunch of snow under tires, and for a moment I think a plane is landing. I look out the big window and see a large tow truck, lights blinking, enter the driveway. Aurora sits slumped in the passenger seat.

A few minutes later, Aurora comes upstairs, slowly. Step, pull up a foot, step, pull up the other foot. I remember kicking her in the knee, her brand-new, still-healing knee. When she sees me, she straightens up and goes to the kitchen. Her face is red, blotchy, and puffed.

"You're up late." Aurora moves into the kitchen, not looking at me. She takes a glass from a cupboard and leans against the counter.

"What on earth happened?" I ask.

"I wrecked the truck." Aurora smashes the glass into the sink. Alice and Mother appear.

"What happened?" Alice inquires.

"I got into an accident." Aurora leans on the counter, her back to us. "The truck's all messed up. The tow truck driver gave me a ride home."

"Are you OK? Was anyone hurt?" Mother asks.

"Bear-Bear is," Aurora spits out. "He's hurt bad. He's at the emergency vet place."

"Were any people hurt?" Mother asks, with an emphasis on people.

"That dog means more to me than any person in this world." Aurora swings around and faces us, her eyes burning, almost sending sparks out to us.

"Well, at least the insurance will cover the truck," Alice offers.

"I don't have any damn insurance for the truck," Aurora growls. "I only have liability for the guy I hit. I cancelled the comprehensive because I couldn't afford it."

I hear our collective sucking in and the gasp. Aurora pushes past us.

"Good night, Bill," Aurora says softly to Bill, who has fallen asleep, sidled up to the safety rail. "Has anyone moved him in the last two hours?"

Yes, I moved him off the flight line.

30 May
Unmanageableness

> My name is Father's Joy. My father's name is Bill. He lies here, wings clipped, a snow goose hurting. Let us pray him a prayer to spare him agony. Grant him ecstasy or respite. Let swan and loon sing "Mi Sheberach" for him. To restore him, heal him, strengthen him, enliven him. Soon. Speedily. Without delay. Let him fly again. And let us say amen.
>
> —Abby Miller, morning pages

"The bedsores are getting worse," Alice says. "We need to call the hospice nurse and figure out how to manage them." She scurries down the hall with a bundle of dirty sheets and turns into the laundry room. In the living room, the bright early morning light streams through the big windows. The mother moose and her calf are munching grass in the front yard. Even with the sunlight pouring in, the room is cold. I'm surprised Aurora hasn't made a fire in the big stone fireplace. I hear banging and commotion from downstairs and notice there's a van from Northern Lights HVAC Services in the driveway.

"The furnace is broken." Mother startles me. She sits next to Bill on the little stool.

How long has she been there? Has her hair always been that white?

Aurora comes upstairs, followed by a man from Northern Nights HVAC Services. The embroidered name on his shirt says his name is Norm.

"The furnace is toast," Aurora announces. "I hate this house."

"Well, it is almost sixty years old." Alice enters the living room.

"How bad is it?" I ask.

"When was the last time the furnace was serviced?" Alice asks.

"It's never been serviced," Aurora jeers.

"Servicing is not the problem," Norm tells us. "I can clean out the ducts and change the filter and do some other things. The real problem is the furnace itself."

Aurora sits down. "Let's hear it."

"First, like the house, it's almost a sixty-year-old floor furnace," Norm explains. "The average life span of a furnace is about twenty years, depending on the type and maintenance. Second, it's the wrong size furnace for this house. Third, it's not installed correctly. It's not vented right and is overheating. That's why it keeps shutting off."

"How much will a new furnace cost?" Aurora asks.

"I'd have to do some checking, but I'd say about three grand fully installed," Norm says.

"I didn't expect to have to replace a furnace right now," Aurora says.

"It's not something we really think about," Norm adds. "I can leave you some information on different models, price points, how to get the right size furnace."

"Do you have furnaces in stock?" Alice asks.

"Depends on the model." Norm makes some notes on a clipboard.

"A whole new furnace." Aurora stares out the window closest to her.

"How long will it take to install," Alice asks.

"It depends on if we have the furnace you need in stock," Norm says. "If we have it, probably a week."

"Well, I really can't afford a new furnace," Aurora says.

"How much will it cost just to service it?" Alice asks. "Maybe we can get it to limp along until fall, when there's more money."

"You shouldn't use it at all," Norm says.

"Do you have any information on new furnaces?" Aurora leads Norm back downstairs.

"Psst." Bill signals to me. "Where's your mother?"

I look at Mother sitting on the stool next to Bill. She's so pale and sitting so still.

"Tell her to get dressed," Bill says. "Slim's coming."

"Mother?" I call softly. Mother doesn't respond.

"Where's your mother?" Bill's voice is weak but insistent. He needs cleaning up again.

"She's right over here, Billy," I say and walk around the bed to Mother.

"Mother." I touch Mother's shoulder. "Go get dressed. I'll stay with him."

When I clean up Bill, I notice the growing bedsores on his upper back, tailbone, and hip. I try to prop an extra pillow under his back to relieve the pressure. Bill flinches. I put the water glass with a straw to Bill's lips, but he doesn't drink. I dab his mouth with a little sponge like the hospice workers do.

"Where's your mother?" Bill asks hoarsely.

"She's getting dressed."

"There she is now." Bill cocks his head slightly to listen more intently.

I look down the hall, but Mother isn't there. I hear a big engine roar above that sounds exactly like a C-130, but it can't be.

"Tell your mother to be quick," Bill says.

"OK," I say.

"It's not OK." He falls back on the pillow.

"What's not OK?

"No, Slim, she's not ready yet," Bill mutters. "You know how women are. Here she is again," Bill continues to mutter.

I hear another big engine roar. I'm sure it's a C-130 and look out the window, but there's not a plane in sight.

"There's something wrong," Bill says between breaths. "Do you hear the pulsing of those engines? The propellers are out of sync."

The room is too cold, and I pull the blanket up around Bill.

"Where are my shoes...The new furnace needs to have the right BTU output...There's a formula for that...Is the Malibu ready...We gotta check on those props...Sit down, Slim. Maybe the Roadrunner will bring us some ice cream...To figure the BTUs, we need the square footage of the house...Slim, how's that little dog of yours doing...I hope they get those props fixed...Where's your mother? Is she with that gorilla?" Bill asks, referring to his favorite photo showing Mother posing with King Kong at Universal Studios. Bill smiles, and I imagine him remembering that vacation at Universal Studios.

Aurora appears on the landing and seems dazed. She holds a glossy brochure with pictures and descriptions of different furnaces. She places the brochure on the credenza, next to Mother's purse, and goes into the kitchen to join Alice.

"I put dirt in the tires you set out for the potatoes," I hear Alice say.

"I've got to call the VA about the bedsores," Aurora says.

"Got the carrots planted for you. I'll do lettuce this afternoon," Alice says. She refolds the dish towels then stacks the towels so all the stripes face up and all the folds face the same direction. Alice and Aurora continue to chatter and organize the kitchen. After the towels are finished, Alice gathers the spices and lines them up on the counter. She returns the spices to the spice rack in alphabetical order. Aurora takes inventory of the canned goods and makes notes on a shopping list.

"Hm, we are low on jasmine rice," Aurora says.

I understand the folding, the alphabetized spices, and the inventory of rice. These things provide control and give structure to a world falling apart. They have this, and I have the belugas.

"Don't you and Tim go to court today?" Alice asks.

"No, tomorrow, for the arraignment," Aurora says.

"Well, let's hope it goes well." Alice comes around the corner with a small bowl and a spoon. "Time for a snack, Billy."

I let Alice have the stool next to Bill and go the couch. The mother moose and calf are now chewing on the birches at the edge of the yard. I watch the mother moose pull down the branches so the calf can reach the tender new shoots and buds.

"Hey, Roadrunner," Bill says. "How do you make holy water?"

"You scare the devil out of it," I answer.

"No, silly, you punch holes in it," Bill says, and we groan.

Alice tries to feed Bill yogurt with peaches, but he won't eat and waves his hands and mumbles about the propeller.

"I'll get you some coffee," Alice says.

"There she is again," Bill says.

I hear the roar of a plane engine and go to the window. I'm absolutely sure it is a C-130. Then I spot a giant plane above the trees and feel a momentary disappointment that the plane is real.

"Here's some fresh coffee for you, Billy. Nice and strong just like you like," Alice says.

I smell the rich coffee and look at Bill. He reaches out shakily when he sees the cup. It's the coffee mug that Mother rescued from the yard sale box, the mug with the air force logo and the picture of the C-130. Alice holds the mug close to Bill's lips and carefully tips the mug. I turn to watch the C-130 hang over the trees as if suspended, as if not moving at all.

"The air force base is having a big training exercise." Aurora sees me looking up at the plane. "There are planes from around the world here, mostly C-130s."

"It's your day, Bill," Alice says. "You'll hear C-130s all afternoon."

"They'd better get the props in sync on that number two plane," Bill says.

For a moment I sense peace in Bill, watching him slurp his coffee from his C-130 mug while he listens and worries about the C-130s rumbling above us. After coffee Bill falls asleep, and Aurora signals us girls to meet in the kitchen.

"I just talked to Tad. He said Bill's condition may soon become worse and possibly unmanageable for us." Aurora pauses. "And for the hospice workers, too."

"How do we plan for the management of...unmanageable-ness?" Alice says.

"We can't," Aurora says.

"How can it possibly get worse?" Alice asks.

"According to Tad,"—Aurora turns and leans on the kitchen sink—"total loss of bowels, pressure sores going septic, inability to communicate, and—"

"Stop," I say. "Please."

I see Alice shaking. Aurora leans more into the sink, almost sinking into it. I think she might faint.

"We'll do the best we can," I say in the calmest, most believable voice I can muster.

"I can't handle this." Alice opens the silverware drawer, takes out all the silverware, and starts to reorganize it. "We can't just manage this willy-nilly, the best we can."

"We are not doing this willy-nilly," I say. "The hospice folks are guiding us. They're working their plan even right now." I hope.

31 May
It's the Vet

We sit up close. Deputies escort Tim and a group of hand-cuffed men, dressed in yellow-gold jumpsuits stamped Prisoner on the back, into the courtroom. The men are told to sit in a row of chairs facing the judge. Tim's shoulders droop, and he stares at the floor. I'm shocked to see the bruises on the side of his face then baffled that Aurora doesn't say anything.

"Tim," Aurora stands and says loud enough for the entire room to hear.

Tim turns to see Aurora, who looks glorious in her teal-blue-green suit, her wild auburn hair tamed into a twist. Aurora winks at him, and Tim smiles. We all stand when the judge is announced.

When it is Tim's turn, he's led by a deputy up to the judge, who informs Tim of his rights. Tim's lawyer comes forward, and the bailiff reads the charges against Tim: child abuse in the form of sexual molestation of a child, his own daughter. The person alleging these charges is Tim's soon-to-be ex-wife, whom Aurora points out to me.

"That's Karen," Aurora whispers to me. "She claims Tim touched their nine-year-old daughter on the leg over a year ago."

I study Karen's face, how she watches Tim, how she smiles when the bailiff reads the charges. Tim enters a plea of not guilty.

"We want him to be released on his own recognizance," Aurora whispers.

"Your honor, the prosecution recommends the defendant be denied bail and remanded to custody. Since his separation with his wife, he has no ties to family or community here and, thus, poses a flight risk," the prosecutor says. "Additionally, the defendant is charged with a crime that's the most despicable of all crimes and most heinous to children."

"Your honor, my client certainly does have family ties here. In fact, the defendant's fiancé and future sister-in-law are here today." Tim's lawyer points out Aurora and me. Aurora stands elegantly and nods to the judge.

As Aurora sits down, the Karen woman, the soon-to-be ex-wife, turns and faces Aurora. Karen's upper lip retreats into a silent snarl. Aurora nods at Karen.

"Your honor, my client also has a good job here in the community," Tim's lawyer continues. "In fact, my client has a long-standing reputation as a good citizen here."

"In spite of all that, these are serious charges your client faces," the judge says.

"Yes, your honor, they are indeed," Tim's lawyer responds. "However, to date, there's no evidence to substantiate these charges. We believe the charges are false allegations resulting from a vindictive spouse seeking legal advantage in a hostile divorce proceeding. Your honor, the defense asks that our client be released on his own recognizance."

There is a pause in the room while the judge glances at Tim's lawyer, the prosecuting attorney, the Karen woman, and Aurora.

"Bail is set at fifty thousand dollars," the judge says. "Next."

"No, no, the bastard needs to stay in jail," Karen yells to the judge.

The bailiff scurries over and escorts Karen out of the courtroom. Aurora sits quietly, elegantly—she is total elegance today, her hands folded on her lap, her face serene.

During the commotion Tim's lawyer approaches Aurora. "As soon as you come up with the bail money, Tim can go home," he says. "Also, when can I expect my fee?"

"Soon," Aurora says.

In the car Aurora settles into the passenger seat and takes several fast breaths, almost hyperventilating. Not knowing what else to do, I offer her a bottle of water.

"That went well for Tim?" I'm not sure what else to say and start the engine.

"Yes. But we don't have the money to post bail. I think we need ten percent in cash to put down," Aurora says. "It's possible we can use the house." She gulps the water, takes several deep breaths, and retrieves her cell phone from her purse. "Yes, I'm calling about my truck," Aurora says. "Do you have an estimate yet?"

Out in the hayfields, I see three moose. It's late afternoon, but the sun is high and bright, and the moose create wonderful moose shadows.

"Of course, yes, I can wait," Aurora says and looks at the landscape passing by.

We drive past classic Alaska houses—split-level, wood, or log construction with wood decks, outbuildings, or detached garages to supplement attached garages, with tall wood piles and large windows facing the Knik Arm, the Inlet, or the mountains.

"How much? About twelve K? Thank you. I'll get back to you." Aurora calls another number. "Hello, I called earlier about posting bail for my fiancé. How's that going?"

We drive by espresso wagon after espresso wagon, each one resembling a carnival wagon and featuring names like the Morning Moose, the Perk-Up Place, or the Glacial Grounds. We Alaskans love our coffee. We drive by a farm with a big red barn and towering grain silo.

"Yes, yes, I understand. Thank you." Aurora looks at me. "Can't use the house for bail."

"Why not?" I ask.

"Same old thing. The house note is over six months in arrears." Aurora sighs. "I've got to call the vet to see how Bear-Bear is doing." The vet's line is busy, and Aurora is quiet until we get home.

Back at the house, the first thing we notice is the blood on Bill's sheets. The putrid smell nearly knocks us over. Aurora goes to Bill, examines the bandages on his upper back, and then pulls the blanket up to hide the blood.

"Go stay with Mama while I change this dressing," Aurora tells me.

"No, I'll help you," I say.

Aurora rummages through a basket until she finds a jar of Vicks VapoRub. She opens the jar and puts a dab under each nostril. A bright menthol smell fills the room. She finds the morphine and puts several drops inside sleeping Bill's mouth. I reach for the box of gloves.

"Abby, you don't want to see this. These are nasty bedsores. It's not the same as poop." Aurora touches my shoulder. "Remember the moose?"

Oh yes, I remember my one and only hunting trip, how Aurora's rifle resounded and echoed, how the moose fell dead—and then the gutting, the smell of the warm blood, the entrails, the red muscles of the meat, the bones showing through.

Aurora sees the horror in my face. She lowers her voice. "I know what to do. The hospice nurse showed me."

I find Mother napping, wrapped in a blanket, her rosary lying next to her hand. I lie down next her and fall asleep. I wake to the sound of the phone ringing and hear Alice answer it in the other bedroom.

"It's the vet, "Alice says when she sees me.

I jump up and follow Alice into the kitchen.

"It's the vet." Alice hands the phone to Aurora, who takes the phone and listens while making notes on the back of an envelope.

"What are his chances? Bad internal injuries. He won't make it without the surgery? How much will it cost?" Aurora writes "$8K" on the envelope.

"Put him to sleep?" her voice slurs. "Yes, do the surgery." Aurora puts down the phone and reaches for a bag of chips.

Aurora crunches chip after chip without tasting or even noticing what she's eating. She begins convulsing sobs, crunches on chips between sobs, swallows her own tears amid the crunching—chip after chip after chip—sometimes a slight choking sound. I sense the universe has now finally overwhelmed her. The lawyer fee. The bail for Tim. The cost of a new furnace. The cost of repairing the truck. The upcoming foreclosure on the house. The copayments for her knee surgeries. Tim all bruised and beat up.

Yet only now, when her dog lies injured so badly that it needs $8,000 worth of surgery or to be put down, does she genuinely cry. Only now does crisis consume her to the point there's no escape.

I've sensed this moment before, on that day when her voice slurred and the music played in the background and I called Anchorage 911 and said the critical words "danger to self or others" and five minutes later, the paramedics pulled her out of the bathtub, unconscious, her wrists slit.

And my heart breaks for her.

1 June
Preflight

Bill picks at the sheets. Aurora sleeps in the big blue chair, and Mother sleeps on the couch while cradling an armful of men's shoes. I trudge into the living room, squinting in the early morning light.

"Roadrunner." Bill sighs. "I'm ready to go, but everyone's still asleep."

"Where are you going, Billiam?"

"Not sure. Haven't got orders yet," Bill says. "We're standing to."

"We?"

"Slim and me."

"Is Slim here now?"

"Yep, he sure is." Bill's voice is surprisingly strong.

I close my eyes for a second and imagine our old friend Slim. Until the day Slim died, he was always ready to go out with the boys to drink coffee or go fishing. I imagine Slim standing there in the doorway, tall and lean and grizzly, wearing his denim overalls and rubber boots, always ready for an adventure, always taking his little Chihuahua dog with him. When I open my eyes after that second, I think I actually see Slim standing in the doorway. Though when I blink, he's gone.

"Say hi to Slim for me," I say.

"Where's your mother?"

"She's over there sleeping on the couch." I wave toward the couch.

"She went to get my shoes, but she never came back," Bill says.

"Which shoes did you want?"

"My flying shoes," Bill says.

I go over to Mother and look at the shoes rising and falling on her chest with each sleeping breath. I select a pair of black leather military-looking shoes and bring them to Bill. He seems pleased.

"Help me put them on," Bill instructs me.

"How long will you be standing by?"

"Standing to," Bill corrects me. "We are standing to. We are ready for action, not waiting for action."

"Got it," I say. "How about if I put your shoes right here under the bed, so when you get orders, you can just jump up, grab your shoes, and go?"

"Good," Bill says. "I think we're only waiting for that prop sync."

I place the shoes under the bed next to the shoes already there, a row of dark leather shoes, once walking shoes or casual shoes or dress shoes, all now flying shoes. The kitchen timer goes off, muffled, from under Aurora's pillow.

"We need to move him," Aurora says groggily from the big blue chair. Her face is blotchy, her eyes puffy, her hair flies out in various directions as if electrified. Oh that wild, wild hair. She sleeps in two-hour shifts between the kitchen-timer rings so she can reposition Bill and sometimes change the dressing. Mother sleeps between flying-shoe deliveries.

"Do we have to?" I ask.

"Yes," Aurora keeps her voice low. "We can give him a little morphine."

She slips a few drops of morphine under Bill's tongue as he watches us. He's too fatigued to object to the morphine or being moved. He falls asleep almost immediately. We roll him to his other side, exposing the dressings on the pressure sores, the red bleed-through showing through layers of gauze, and the putrid smell fills the air. Aurora turns her head and starts to gag, swallows deep and controls the gag. I look away.

"Go do something else, Abby," Aurora says. "I've got this."

I gratefully go back to the bedroom where Alice is typing away on her laptop.

"Palmer and I want to buy Aurora's share of the Homer house," Alice says.

"What do you mean?"

"We're going to pay her twenty-five thousand up front and a thousand a month after that," Alice explains.

Why?" I ask.

"It will help Aurora," Alice says. "Plus the Homer house will be an asset for us."

"How so?"

"It's Momma's intent to bequeath the Homer house to us three girls," Alice continues.

"And that means?"

"That means each of us gets one-third of the house. Palmer and I buy Aurora's third of the house, and she gives up all claim to the Homer house."

"We don't have any right to that house until after Mother's gone," I say. "Besides, Mother may decide to sell the Homer house."

"This would be a way for us to funnel money to Aurora without it being a loan that would never be repaid," Alice says.

"That makes no sense."

"I just want to find a solution," Alice says.

"You can't go buy an asset from Aurora that Aurora doesn't have," I say. "The Homer house belongs to Mother."

Alice swings around and faces me. Her eyes are red and puffy now, like Aurora's eyes. "So what do we do, Abby? What do we do?"

"Well, if you want to funnel money to Aurora, why not just give her money?" I ask. "Why are you hiding behind the facade of buying Aurora's share of the Homer house?"

"Palmer doesn't want to give Aurora money," Alice says. "He says he'll only agree to it if we have some sort of collateral."

"So you're proposing that Aurora's future share in the Homer house serve as the collateral?"

"Exactly," Alice says.

"You're dreaming," I say.

"So what are we supposed to do?" Alice insists. "Sit around and wait for the universe to unfold or emerge or whatever fluffy language you want to use?"

"Explore options?" I say.

"Now you're dreaming," Alice raises her voice. "We need a plan to help Aurora."

"I've said it before. A plan is what *you* need," I say. "Not necessarily what Mother or Aurora needs."

"Yes, it's what I need," Alice retorts. "I can't stand by and watch Aurora lose her house. I just can't! It hurts me too much. Me." Alice taps her chest. "Weren't you supposed to go to the lawyer and arrange for Aurora to get a second chance? What happened to that?"

"I have an appointment this afternoon."

Though I don't want to go because it means trying to help Aurora once again. However, it's a clear, sunny day, and I'll enjoy the drive into Anchorage.

The lawyer's office faces the Inlet in one of the tallest buildings in Anchorage. Sunlight glints off the new windmills over on Fire Island and twinkles off the wave ripples in the Inlet. To the north, the Alaskan Range, snowy and craggy, lines the horizon.

And there she is. Denali, in all her glory, unannounced and unparalleled. I stand and stare at her, like all of Anchorage is probably doing right now.

"Something else, eh?" Ben Brownstone enters the reception area of the law office. He has been Bill's lawyer as long as I've known Bill.

"Hello, Ben," I say.

Ben stares out at Denali. From her desk, Ben's assistant also looks out at Denali. The three of us watch Denali for several minutes, standing there, reverent, almost hearing the words echoing in the streets of Anchorage: "Look, the mountain is out."

"So nice to see you." Ben breaks the silence and leads me into his office.

Ben offers me a chair, facing the window, at a large mahogany table. He opens the blinds so we can look at Denali while she's still out. His eyes are blue, made even more blue against the contrast of his white hair, and though I've known this man many years, those blue eyes always amazes me.

"Eric will be with us any minute." Ben hands me a folder. "Here's the completed documentation making you the legal representative for your mother. Coffee?" Ben pours coffee from a silver carafe on a mahogany tray that matches the table. There's a knock on the door, and Ben's assistant presents Eric, a man wearing khaki pants and a cap that says Gone Fishing. Enrique "Eric" Montano has been Bill's investment broker ever since Bill came into our lives. Eric carries a sheaf of folders.

"Did you see?" Eric says excitedly. "The mountain is out."

We exchange the greeting of the day, pour more coffee, and settle in. Eric arranges his folders. I give an update on Bill. Both men are saddened by Bill's decline.

"So we're here to make a significant arrangement on the estate," Ben says. "As I understand your mother's wishes, she wants to give Aurora a second chance through an early inheritance."

"Which means paying her debts," Eric says. "Do we have an accounting of all the debts?"

I hand Eric my own folder. The long list of debts inside the folder annoys me. No, it angers me. No, it infuriates me. Will there ever be a reckoning for Aurora? Or does she get to constantly go into debt and constantly have someone else pay her debts.

"This is a hefty set of numbers." Eric scans through the folder and hands it to Ben. "Actually, to give Aurora a second chance, we have to do more than pay her debts."

"Your mother indicated to me that she wanted you to figure out how to do this," Ben says and looks through the folder. "As her legal representative, what are your thoughts?"

"I have conflicting thoughts. I don't want my little sister to drain my mother's bank accounts. She has already done enough damage to my mother financially, but I want to honor my mother's wishes," I say.

"According to your numbers, Aurora will need almost a hundred thousand dollars just to cover her debts," Ben says after scanning the list of debts.

Eric nods in agreement.

Nobody ever paid my debts.

"I don't want my mother ending up penniless because of Aurora." I shake my head. "My mother may have good intentions, but it's my responsibility to look after her best interests, not her good intentions."

"This is what your mother will inherit." Eric pushes a green folder toward me.

I look inside the folder to see the amount and gasp.

"Twenty-five years of investing in stock with Frito-Lay, PepsiCo, Radio Shack, and Dairy Queen," Eric explains. "The stocks have gone up and down over the years, but Bill hung in there, and the overall outcome is outstanding, if not incredible, as you can see. I've never understood how Bill selected his stocks. He usually just said something about liking ice cream."

Yes, Bill liked ice cream.

"Here is what Aurora will inherit." Eric pushes another green folder toward me. "Grounded in stocks originating with

Häagen-Dazs and Mrs. Smith's Pies, which means we are talking about Nestlé, Kellogg's."

More ice cream. I'm stunned at the amount.

"Here's what Alice will inherit." Eric pushes another green folder to me. "Microsoft."

"Here's what you'll inherit." He places the green folder on top of the last one. "Intel."

"Here are two special ones." He pushes two blue folders toward me. "A bequest for the Anchorage Arctic Ensemble and a bequest for your mother's church."

"All grounded in remarkable stocks," Eric adds. "Simply based on what Bill liked and, sometimes, where you girls lived."

"Does Bill have any idea that these stocks have accumulated so much?"

"I'm not sure. I know he listens to the stock reports every day, but he invested for the pure fun of it and may have lost track of the monetary worth." Eric pushes a red folder to me. "Here's a codicil for the adult children from his first marriage. They'll each receive one dollar."

Images come to my mind: Bill clicking on the television to watch an old cowboy movie, clicking on the television to watch a golf tournament, clicking on the television to listen to the morning news and watch the electronic ticker tape with the stock report running across the top of the screen. Movies, sports, and stocks were all fun for him.

"Bill has certainly taken care of you guys," Ben says.

"But that's Bill, always doing the preflight." Eric chuckles and sits back in his chair.

"So what are your thoughts?" Ben asks me.

Aurora doesn't deserve this.

2 June
Wedding Bells

My name is Father's Joy. I fight the tide. I fight the moon. I wait for a reckoning, a payment in razor clams. Or perhaps a dead reckoning. Or a simple guess, a lottery: When will the ice break on the Kenai? When will the fireweed bloom? Or perhaps a reckoning of balance. I receive the oyster I give. I push; you pull. Or perhaps a reckoning of white lace on a wedding veil, lace fringed around a white fox like a first snow, a hint of hope that tides ebb and flow and moons come full again. So release that razor. Take the pearl from this oyster.

—Abby Miller, morning pages

Mother Moose–Nurse returns, but this time, she hands out ice cream bars to silly moose calves and happy people walking in and out of my dream.

"Have some ice cream," she says joyously. "We have ice cream for everyone."

The old doctor in the dream sits back in his chair, feet propped up on the desk, licking the edges of his ice cream bar. There are platters and bowls and cases of ice cream bars all around.

"Tell us the truth, and we'll give you an ice cream bar," Mother Moose–Nurse tells me.

The truth. The truth is I don't want Aurora to receive the early inheritance.

"No, that's not necessary. Go ahead and give her one," the old doctor says. "We have more ice cream than we know what to do with."

"Humph," Mother Moose–Nurse snorts. "She doesn't deserve one."

I wake up craving ice cream and get out of bed to embark upon my midnight sojourn of roaming the house and watching Bill breathe. As usual, Aurora sleeps in the big blue chair with the kitchen timer tucked under her pillow. The embers in the fireplace still glow. The house is extra quiet, no kitchen sounds, no furnace, not even the soft whoosh of Bill's air bed. It's cold.

There's no detectable movement in Bill's chest. I lean over and stare at Bill to see if he's breathing.

"Boo," Bill says.

I jump back and nearly knock over the stool beside Bill's bed. "What are you trying to do, give me a heart attack?" I rearrange the blankets.

"What are you doing, checking to see if I'm still alive?" Bill chuckles weakly.

"Yes, I sure am. Could you breathe a little louder so I can tell?" I touch Bill's feet just enough to get a sense of their temperature: cool.

"Where's your mother?" Bill says. Only his mouth moves.

"She's sleeping." I tuck an extra blanket around Bill's feet. He's not even picking at the sheets or clutching the safety rail.

"Go check on her," Bill says, his voice low and hoarse. "She may have gone."

"She's OK, snoring away," I say after returning from Mother's room.

"Not OK," Bill mumbles. His eyes roll up under his lids, and he falls asleep.

What's not OK? I'll ask him later and sleep the rest of the night on the couch. I dream about strong hot coffee but realize it's not a dream and wake up. Smells of the coffee, food cooking, wood fire smoke, and scented candles ride on top of the air. The putrid decay smell lingers underneath. I hear the babble of the television and see Bill watching the morning news. The electronic ticker tape runs across the top of the screen with the stock report. All those stocks. All those years of investing. What a waste to just hand over such a large chunk of those investments to Aurora.

"Psst," Bill says.

"Billiam?" I go over to him.

"How do you make holy water?"

"You punch holes in it," I respond.

"No, silly," Bill whispers. "You make it with pie."

"With pie?" I say. "That doesn't make sense."

"Roadrunner, sometimes it doesn't," Bill says. "But do it anyway." Then he falls asleep.

"Coffee's ready," Alice says.

I get up and pour coffee and sit with Alice and Mother at the dining table. A moose down in the front yard munches on the lilacs. Morning sun glistens and warms the leaves and grass, evaporating the night cold and dampness.

Alice makes lists. She studies her master list that features a list of sublists and arranges separate sublists on the table in alphabetical order: diet, finance, funeral, garden, grocery, hospice, house, medical, wedding, yard sale. Wedding?

"We need more seed potatoes," Alice says and makes a note on the garden list.

"And Bear-Bear," Mother says. "Maybe we can bring him home from the vet today."

"Hm. What list does that go on?" Alice scans her lists.

"Well, what do you think?" Aurora enters the room.

I watch both Alice and Mother look up and transform. Their serious faces turn gentle-soft and shine, almost sparkle. I turn around to see Aurora standing in the threshold of the dining room in a wedding dress.

"You look beautiful," Mother says.

"It needs a couple alterations." Alice pulls out the wedding list and makes a note.

"Could someone tell me what's happening?" I ask.

Why don't I know about this?

"Tim and I are getting married next month," Aurora says.

Tim's in jail and will probably be in jail for several months. More importantly, Tim isn't divorced yet. Aurora turns slowly so we can get a complete look at the dress. Even with that wild, wild hair, she is lovely and beams. Who will end up paying for this wedding, a wedding that doesn't make sense.

"Excuse me, but isn't Tim still married?" I ask.

The dress doesn't fit in the back, and there is about a six-inch gap. Aurora's hair clips hold the dress in place.

"I told you a while back that our lawyer has filed special divorce papers. We can get the divorce right away and do the child support and custody issues later," Aurora explains.

"We can alter the dress with a corset inset in the back." Alice makes another note on the wedding list.

I'm aghast.

"We are thinking about a breakfast wedding down at Kenai Lake then going fishing," Aurora says, examining the beadwork on the bodice of the dress.

The dress is wrinkled all over and soiled along the hem. She probably purchased the dress at Value Village.

"We'll need champagne and flowers and a cake." Alice busily scribbles more notes.

"Can we have cake for a breakfast wedding?" Aurora asks Alice.

"You can have whatever you want," Alice answers.

And Mother can pay for it.

"I'm not sure I can go," Mother says. "I don't want to leave Bill alone."

"Should we do silk or real flowers?" Aurora asks.

"Silk, of course. Cheaper and they last forever." Alice makes another note. "We can go to Value Village and see if they have any with your colors."

"Are you all insane?" I ask.

There's a long pause, and Alice looks down at her list, and Aurora continues to examine the beadwork on her dress.

"Well?" I say

"It's called hope," Mother says.

Hope? It's called delusion.

"Did you have any luck with the lawyer?" Alice picks up the finance list.

"I'm working on it," I say.

I think of all those stocks and what it'll mean for Aurora. Yet it's not so much about money. I don't care if Aurora loses her house or if Tim rots in jail. We're all a product of our decisions, and Aurora and Tim made the decisions that brought them here. I'll be damned if I just let Aurora have all that stock money. There's got to be a reckoning.

I go to the stool and sit next to Bill. It's my place of refuge now. On the television the news reporter is talking about Augustine and its imminent eruption, predicted in days perhaps any day now. Later, a wildlife reporter talks about the annual return of the Cook Inlet belugas, how the belugas were seen at the mouth of the Inlet, not far from Augustine. Hearing about the belugas calms me.

"Show Bill," Mother urges Aurora.

"Look, Bill." Aurora models the wedding dress for Bill, posing and smiling and holding a bouquet of silk flowers. Bill eyes her carefully then realizes the dress is a wedding dress. He doesn't move, but his eyes sparkle and color momentarily flushes across his cheeks.

"You're beautiful." Bill makes a smacking kiss sound and winks at Aurora.

He continues to watch her model the dress, the delight in his eyes unmistakable. Aurora pulls up a chair, sits down beside him, and proceeds to describe all her wedding plans. Bill's eyes never leave Aurora. He's clearly captivated.

What did Bill say earlier? Sometimes it doesn't make sense. But do it anyway.

"I'd better go change clothes." Aurora gets up and walks down the hallway with the soft whoosh of the long satin train flowing behind her. "I've got to get this carpet cleaned. It's brand new and already looks terrible."

The kitchen timer goes off.

"Someone needs to move Bill," Aurora yells from down the hall.

"I'll do it," I yell back.

Bill soundlessly mouths the word, "No."

I rearrange the blankets and start to reposition his hands so Aurora will think he's been moved when I notice how red and swollen his hands have become.

"Sh," Bill whispers weakly. "Don't say anything about my hands."

I carefully place the sheets over him and make a mental note to call the hospice nurse about Bill's hands. I stay with Bill most of the day. He declines food, even ice cream. While he sleeps, the kitchen timer rings every two hours, and we slip a few morphine drops under his tongue to ensure he doesn't wake up and place a few dabs of Vicks VapoRub under our noses and try to turn him.

Tad arrives while Bill is still sleeping, and the rest of us are down in the driveway setting up tables for the yard sale on Saturday. When Tad comes back down from seeing Bill, we are amid a great number of tables and yard sale boxes.

"There are significant changes," Tad tells us. "I'll check on him every day from here on."

"How long will it be?" Alice asks. "We need to plan the memorial service."

"Could be soon, but only Bill knows," Tad says. "I'm surprised he's waited this long."

"We are, too," Alice says.

"I'm going to put in an order for some mittens to help alleviate the pain of the blisters and some dressings that have charcoal in them to help with the smell," Tad says.

"He doesn't have any blisters," I say.

"He will, as the sepsis runs its course," Tad says. "Bill was only awake a few minutes when I was up there, but he suddenly got worried. I'll prescribe something for anxiety."

"Worried about what?" Alice asks.

"Anxiety is natural for the dying." Tad types into his electronic notebook. "Now, as the days go by, it may become too much. Bill is going to need twenty-four-hour care. We could move him to the hospice hospital."

"We're not going to move him. I promised him," Mother interrupts.

Tad puts his arm around Mother.

"I know, but it's an option if you decide you need it," Tad says.

"Mama, let's go get Bear-Bear from the vet," Aurora says. "Alice and Abby can work on the yard sale stuff."

Mother smiles when she hears the dog's name. She's always liked Bear-Bear.

3 June
A Reckoning

Bill sleeps. Bear-Bear pants on his orthopedic dog bed near Aurora's big blue chair. Bear-Bear's stomach has been shaved, and angry black stitches adorn a line down his belly. He looks up at me when I enter the room and gives me a friendly whine in lieu of a heartier greeting. The vet said it would be a couple more days before Bear-Bear could stand on his own. It might take a couple weeks before the 150-pound German shepherd can walk.

It's late afternoon, and we take a break from sorting and arranging the yard sale stuff. When we're done, we'll cover everything with tarps and leave it out overnight. That way we're ready for yard sale action first thing in the morning. Alice makes coffee for our afternoon tea. It's our tradition, coffee, not tea, for tea parties.

We hear Bill moaning into his pillow, and Aurora goes over and examines the dressings on his back. She gingerly peels away the corner of one dressing. She winces at what she sees, and the gag reflex is apparent in her stomach, rolling up to her throat, but she stifles it. Aurora stands back and shakes her head. She retrieves the morphine and administers the drops under Bill's tongue. I count the drops, an extralarge dose. Aurora goes back to her blue chair and reaches down to stroke Bear-Bear's nose.

"It's too much for me." Aurora keeps stroking Bear-Bear's nose. "I'll build a fire to help cover up the smell."

"The home health aides will be here soon for the evening visit, and they can take care of the dressings," Alice says.

"It may also be too much for them, too." Aurora keeps talking to Bear-Bear. "We may have no choice but to move him to the hospice hospital."

"I'm not moving Bill." Mother suddenly appears. "We can take care of him here."

"You mean I can take care of him," Aurora growls at Mother.

The heat of Aurora's response takes me by surprise.

"Have you seen those pressure sores, Mama? Have you seen them? No, of course not, the smell alone makes you sick." Aurora jumps up. "Mama, come look at the sores and tell me if we can take care of him here."

I jump up also, sensing the malevolence in Aurora's movement. I stand near Mother, ready. For what? Aurora jumps up too fast on her brand-new knees, and she yelps in pain just before allowing herself to fall back in the chair with her hair flying out in that electrified way. Bear-Bear whimpers.

"The home health aides are here," Alice announces.

"Good. Mike will know what to do." Aurora slowly gets out of the chair and limps over to the stair landing. "Somebody let Mike in through the patio door. I'm going downstairs."

"Whatever happened to the stair lift?" I call after Aurora. I want to hurt her in any way I can. "You know, the one Bill and Mother paid twelve thousand dollars for?"

I see Aurora's momentary pause. She keeps her back to me and goes down the stairs. I follow Aurora downstairs. She doesn't get to turn her back and walk away. I find her sitting on the bed, rubbing her knee. It's time for a reckoning.

"Mother asked me to go to the lawyer and figure out how to help you," I say.

Aurora changes position to rub her other knee so that she now has her back to me.

"Well?" Aurora keeps rubbing her knee.

"Look, I'm about to share with you how Mother is going give you a large sum of money," I say. "The least you can do is to have the courtesy to look at me while we're talking."

"You're the one who's talking." Aurora adjusts her position so that she faces me.

"Technically, everything Bill has goes to Mother," I begin. "After Mother's demise, we get whatever inheritance has been allocated to us."

"Ditch the pretty language. Get to the point." Aurora looks at her knee.

"We have, however, arranged for you to get an early inheritance," I say.

Aurora glances up at me, and I see her eyes become expectant, anticipatory.

"How much is the early inheritance?" Aurora asks.

"Enough to take care of all your problems," I say. "But, well, as Mother's legal representative, I can't let you have the money for free."

"What do you mean?" Aurora raises one eyebrow.

"There is a price," I say.

A reckoning of sorts.

"What's the price—some type of interest?" Aurora resumes rubbing her knee.

"You agree to a peace treaty between you and Mother," I say. "I don't care what the terms are. You agree to be nice to Mother and make her feel welcome in your home. You agree to forfeit any claim to the Homer house, and you agree to forfeit any further claim to Bill and Mother's estate."

"Would there be anything left to claim?"

"To get what you need now, you will have to forfeit all future claims," I say.

"How much would be left?"

I don't answer.

"When can I get the money?" Aurora asks.

"Actually, you won't get most of the money directly," I explain. "Your debts will be paid straight to your creditors through the lawyer. Once the debts are all paid, an extra amount will be deposited to the account of your choice. After that, it's over. You will not receive another dime."

"How much is the extra amount?" Aurora asks and continues to rub her knee, not looking at me.

So nonchalant. So almost ambivalent. But I sense her eagerness, her expectation in how she rubs her leg, how she sneaks a glance up at me, how her shoulders straightened when I first said the words "early inheritance."

"I'm going to let the lawyer recommend an amount," I tell her.

"How much would be left over? I mean how much would I forfeit?"

"Whatever's left over will be given to Mother's church in Homer," I say.

"Why can't I have all of it?" Aurora looks up at me.

I hate helping her.

"Because you've already gotten more than you deserve," I say.

"She owes it to me," Aurora says simply.

Anger sizzles in me. How can I hurt her?

"You can have the money this last time," I say. "But you must agree to be nice to Mother."

Aurora's eyes narrow, and I think I see hate there. Ah, so the hate is mutual. Good.

"So what's the penalty if I'm not nice? And how will you enforce it?" Aurora says.

"Two ways. First, you will agree to give me Bear-Bear as collateral." I pause to let the words and the sounds of the words sink in.

"You're joking," Aurora says.

"When he's healed and able to travel, I'll take him with me to New Mexico. After one year, if there are no issues with Mother, I'll return him to you. Second, the terms of the early inheritance will be written up and documented through the lawyer," I conclude.

"That's not fair," she objects. "You can't take Bear-Bear."

"Do you want the money or not?"

No, it's not fair, but it may serve as a reckoning.

"Not Bear-Bear. He's my baby." Her voice goes all squeaky as if really talking to a baby.

"Don't be such a dumb-ass girl," I blurt out.

"Ah, when did you become JB?" Aurora says slowly, with her classic lip twitch and narrowing eyes, that faint barest hint of an upturned lip, that trace of a smile that clearly says, boom, I know those words hurt you. Stab, does it feel like a knife?

Inside, I reel from the shock of hearing those words come out of my own mouth. Dumb-ass girl, JB's nickname for me. I was never a beloved daughter because I wasn't a boy. I was always the dumb-ass girl, the greatest insult I could think of to throw at a girl. And I said those very words just now to another girl. Above all, I don't want to be like JB. Dumb-ass girl. Boom, the words hurt. Stab, cut to my core. Oh how I'd always longed to be a father's joy.

4 June
The Yard Sale

It's five in the morning. The bed shakes again, and realizing it's not a dream, I hurry into the living room where Aurora fumbles with the television remote until she finds the local news channel. The house shakes for several more seconds. Mother appears then Alice shuffles in.

The news reporter talks excitedly: Volcano warning underway. Augustine erupting now. Ash plume and smoke heading north toward Anchorage. Aviation Code Red. Tremors occurring all over Cook Inlet. Residents along the coast advised to take precautions. Homer Spit evacuated. The reporter chats on about magnitude, magma, plume density, and the history of St. Augustine.

I hear Bill groan and go check on him. "Hi there, Billiam," I lean over and say.

"What's all the commotion?" Bill whispers, his voice thick and hoarse.

"Augustine is blowing." I look up at the television for a second and see the kitchen lights and images reflecting on the screen. Is that Slim? I turn abruptly and scan the kitchen. No Slim.

"Volcanoes are all very exciting, but we have a yard sale to do," Alice says. "We need to be open for business in two hours to catch the early birds."

After a quick breakfast, Alice, clipboard in hand, presides over fifteen yard sale tables while tremors shake the ground. Mother looks over the tables. She goes over to an old leather purse Bill bought for her in Georgia then a shiny conch shell she got when she and Bill went to Hawaii then a vase from New Mexico when she and Bill came to visit me—item after item telling of her adventures with Bill, each item now marked with a yellow price sticker.

"Abby, can you make the coffee?" Alice makes a check on her clipboard. "But not as strong as you normally make it."

Alice thinks if we give folks coffee, they'll buy more stuff.

"Momma, you're going to be the cashier." Alice guides Mother over to me where I'm setting up the coffee, but Mother stops when she sees a table piled with an array of Bill's hats: fishing hats, winter hats, stylish hats, travel hats, a box of air force hats, a box of Shriner hats, a life story told in hats.

"I want to keep the Shriner hats." Mother unwraps the tissue around one of them.

Yes, of course." Alice takes the box of hats and sets it under the table and points to the coffee service I'm setting up. "This half of the table is the coffee station."

Mother looks back at the table with Bill's hats.

"And this half is the cashier station," Alice says. "Here's your inventory list."

"Folks, we have a problem." Aurora emerges from the garage door. "Mike says Bill's condition is beyond the capability of the home health aides."

"All his clothes?" Mother glances at the inventory list.

"Basically, we need a full-time nurse or to move Bill to a facility," Aurora says.

"I'm not moving Bill," Mother says.

"You want to pay for a nurse?" Aurora hisses. "Make that three nurses, if you take into account twenty-four-hour care."

I bristle at the way Aurora talks to Mother.

"We'll make a plan this afternoon," Alice says.

"We don't need a plan. We just need to get Bill proper care," Aurora flares at Alice.

"I'm not moving Bill." Mother walks to a table with Bill's clothes.

"You may not have a choice," Aurora mutters.

"We'll figure it out," I say. "Let's get this yard sale over first."

"This is a brand-new shirt." Mother picks up a shirt, shakes it out, and refolds it. She shakes out another shirt and refolds it, too. She then pulls out bundles of socks.

"Mama, what in the hell are you doing?" Aurora yells.

"Bill likes his socks folded, not bundled," Mother says.

"Oh hell," Aurora mutters.

"I'll take care of that, Momma," Alice says. "Come over here and do the cashier station."

"This is his favorite jacket." Mother picks up a gray fleece jacket embellished with several souvenir pins. She holds the jacket to her face. Can she smell Bill's Old Spice cologne?

"I think I'll keep this pin from Maui." Mother begins to remove a small pin.

"Here, give me that." Aurora moves over to Mother and snatches the jacket away.

"Mama, come over here and just concentrate on being the cashier." Alice goes to Mother and guides her to the coffee-cashier table.

"All his clothes," Mother mumbles.

"What else did you take?" Aurora accuses Mother.

"It's OK. It's totally natural for people to change their mind," Alice says.

"Give her the Maui pin," I direct Aurora.

"She doesn't need the damn pin," Aurora says.

"I'll get the pin." Alice moves toward the table with the clothes.

"No, I want Aurora to give Mother the pin," I say.

"And I want Mama out of here. I want her out of my house as soon as Bill's dead," Aurora yells. "Fuck the early inheritance. Fuck the peace treaty. I'll sell my truck. I'll sell my soul to the devil. I will sell myself for sex. I'll get the money. I want Mama out now."

I see Mother collapse into the chair at the cashier station. Alice gapes at Aurora.

"You bitch," I yell at Aurora. "I hate you."

"I don't give a fuck," Aurora says.

"I hate you because you can't find the decency to treat Mother like a human being. The only use you have for Mother is when she's gives you money." I actually say it in front of Mother and instantly regret it.

"Hell, you can't be nice to my little Jessica, my little helper, and she's moving to Anchorage in a few weeks." Aurora starts to cry. "I'm going to lose her."

"What in the hell does Jessica have to do with this?" I demand.

"She's part of my family," Aurora cries.

"Get real. Jessica is a teenager you pay to do chores and pick up dog poop," I say. "Jessica is only family as long as you pay her."

"No," Aurora objects. "It's not true. She's family, and I don't want to lose her."

"Lose Jessica? Some stranger you pay? Hell, you just lost your sister!" I yell. "You're nothing but a miserable dumb-ass girl! I'm no longer your sister from this moment on." Once again I'm stunned to hear those words come out of my mouth: "dumb-ass girl."

The last time JB called me a dumb-ass girl, I was twelve years old. That day, JB and I hiked up Bug Mountain to search for bird eggs. My job was to carry the eggs in a special container in my daypack. The hike was fourteen miles up and fourteen miles back.

"I can accept that." Aurora stands straighter, her eyes take on a glazed quality, and she starts to gather items off one of the yard sale tables. "This yard sale is canceled."

I didn't object because I didn't want to be a dumb-ass girl. A total of twenty-eight miles, over tundra and a river crossing, up past the tree line, up to mosquito and bear country. I simply gathered my daypack and my dog Spot and we went.

I realize Mother and Alice must have gone inside, and I run into the house and up to the living room. The home health aides are gone. Bill is awake, wide-eyed. Another tremor shakes the living room. I rush down the hall to Mother's room. Alice sits close to Mother who rocks back and forth and seems to be looking at the walls.

I couldn't keep up with JB, so he hiked up ahead and left me and Spot to fend for ourselves. At the river crossing, the water was cold to the bone. The river itself was wide and shallow with a slippery bottom and fast current. I slipped on the river-bottom rocks several times, and one time slipped so abruptly that I twisted my ankle, but I didn't feel the pain right away because the water was so cold.

"Mother, Mother," I say. "I'm so sorry. I didn't mean to be that nasty to Aurora."

"Yes you did," Mother says.

"Go check on Bill," Alice tells me. "I'll stay with Momma."

"What took you so long?" JB asked me when I caught up with him.

I told him about my twisted ankle.

"Dumb-ass girl," he said.

Then we were off, up the tundra toward the higher ridges, each footstep sinking deep into the tundra and releasing swarms of bugs.

I go into the living room and glance at the television for the latest report on Augustine, and out of the corner of my eye, in the merest of a blink, I think I see Slim.

"It's time to go," Slim says. Or is it the reporter on the television?

"I can't yet," Bill says.

"OK," Slim says. Or is it the reporter?

"Not OK," Bill says.

I twirl around. Bill sleeps a deep morphine sleep, his hands in mittens.

Hike the ridges, JB reminded me before hiking on ahead. Sometimes I saw him looking back at me and Spot with binoculars. Sometimes we smelled bear scat. At one point, Spot gave a low warning "boof," and we both froze and watched a bear lumber out of the alders below and wander away.

"I don't know what to do," Alice says. Alice walks over to the dining table and rummages through her stack of lists. "Aurora is packing up the yard sale."

At the top of Bug Mountain, I told JB I was afraid of the bears.

"Dumb-ass girl," he said.

My ankle throbbed.

"It's a conundrum. We can't take care of Bill on our own. Momma won't let us move him," Alice says.

"We'll figure it out."

"How?" Alice pleads.

"I don't know."

"We need to make a plan," Alice searches through her lists.

"Don't worry," I say. "We'll figure it out."

We didn't find any bird eggs, so we started back to camp, JB moving even faster while I moved even slower on my aching ankle. When I finally got back, JB was cooking on the camp stove.

"What took you so long?" He chuckled.

I told him my ankle was worse.

"Dumb-ass girl," he said.

My own words blurted out, "What kind of dumb-ass father thinks it's OK to take a twelve-year-old girl up Bug Mountain?" I crawled into my sleeping bag. "Besides, I climbed your damn Bug Mountain as good as any boy, better than most adults. So don't you ever call me a dumb-ass girl again," I said.

"And if I do, you'll stop me how?" JB chuckled again.

"However I have to," I said.

And I knew he knew I meant it. With Spot next to me, I smelled the potatoes frying and felt the cramps start in the back of my legs, penetrating, rippling, cramps. I covered my head with the sleeping bag so JB wouldn't see me bite my lip in charley horse pain or twisted-ankle pain. But above that pain and the exhaustion, my JB hate soothed and cooed me to sleep.

"I don't know what to do," Alice says.

"Don't worry," I say again and realize I'm saying more JB words. "Don't worry."

"Abby, you don't understand. I don't know what to do!"

She can't find the answers, the solution, the order, the structure that her world relies upon. Her world has fallen apart.

And me calling Aurora a dumb-ass girl and telling Alice not to worry and becoming JB incarnate—my world, too, has fallen apart.

5 June
Volcano Sunset

> My name is Father's Joy. I go to the Inlet when Augustine erupts to see the volcano sunset. But don't be fooled because it's a false sunset. It's

light diffracting off ash, light bouncing off glass
fishing floats, not a sun letting go of day. If you
doubt it, stand on the cliffs of the Kalifonski, catch
the tide-smell tide-swell. Dare to look across the
Inlet. Squint to see Kalgin Island merge to the
horizon. Quick, before your eyes burn, the tide
turns, always the tide. In one miniscule moment,
see what reflects back. See what explodes. See who
you are before the tide washes back in and it's too
late.

—Abby Miller, morning pages

"Bill is declining fast," Tad says. "You folks can't take care of him
now."

"What do you advise?" Alice asks.

"I can think of three ways," Tad says. "We could bring in
nurses twenty-four hours a day. This is expensive, but it wouldn't
be long term, and the VA will pay for part of it. Another way is
to move Bill to our hospice hospital. The VA will pay for all of
this."

"What is option three?" Alice asks.

"Well, I hesitate to say," Tad begins. "It's actually inappropri-
ate for me to say."

"We need to know all possible solutions," Alice says.

"Based on my experience, Bill should've died a long time
ago. Yet here he is."

"And option three?" Alice asks again.

"Bill's entire body is poisoned from the sepsis. Every movement is agony for him," Tad says. "Not only that, he's very anxious. I believe he's afraid."

"Afraid of dying?" Alice asks.

"I can't say this officially. I say this as a human being who has
seen many people die," Tad says. "I think Bill's afraid of what will
happen to you folks after he dies."

"Oh no," Mother says.

"I think he's hanging on until he knows you'll all be OK," Tad says. "In the end it won't matter. The sepsis will run its course and take him."

"And when that happens," I say, "Bill will die afraid, not knowing about us?"

"Yes, that's what happens," Tad says.

"Oh my God," Alice says. "Back to option three, what is it?"

"Somehow let him know you're going to be OK after he's gone," Tad says.

"For planning purposes, how long do we have?" Alice asks.

"It's hard to tell right now. Normally, eight to twelve hours, but Bill's fighting."

Mother's countenance takes on that slow stalwart look she gets when she walks up the steps with a sore foot. "I'll talk to him tonight," Mother says.

"I think Bill would like that," Tad says. "Perhaps you girls could go away for a few hours and give your mother some alone time with Bill."

"We could drive into Anchorage and go watch the volcano sunset," Alice offers.

"With a million other people," Aurora says. "Forget it."

I know Aurora wants to go. It's what we do. When a volcano erupts, we watch the sunset. When the northern lights are out, we look up. When the reds are running, we go dip netting. Above all, when Denali is out, we stop everything and look at the mountain.

"We could go to the Point," Alice says. "Only the locals will be there."

We drive into Anchorage in icy silence. After parking, we walk down to the Tony Knowles Coastal Trail and hike toward the Point.

"Who are you calling?" Aurora snaps at me when I get out my cell phone.

"Mother," I say. Mother doesn't answer the phone.

"Hell, we've only been gone an hour," Aurora says.

"There are sure a lot of people here," Alice says. "I'd hate to be down at Potter's Marsh."

We see crowds of people along the bluffs and the beach below. Even so, the crowds here measure only in hundreds, while the crowds measure in thousands at Potter's Marsh and at the Kalifonski or Kasilof or Ninilchik beaches.

"Stay high or go low?" Aurora asks.

"Low," I say.

We go down low by the Inlet, close to the water where we can smell and sense the tide. The crowd is unusually quiet for so many people. The quiet is intensified because the planes at Anchorage International are grounded due to the ash in the air that could clog up the jet engines.

"It's strange not to hear the planes," Alice says.

Down to the beach, above the high-tide line, we spread out a tarp with a blanket and join the large group of people already there.

"Maybe Denali will come out," we say and hear others say. I look at all the people along the bluffs above us sitting in camp chairs and people along the beach sitting on tarps and blankets. Everyone faces west, except for an occasional glance north to see if Denali is out.

"I think we should propose a truce," Alice says after we sit down on the blanket.

The evening turns twilight, and light starts diffracting off the dust and glass particles produced by Augustine's eruption.

"Does that mean another stupid peace treaty?" Aurora asks.

It is ebb tide, and I smell the salty, fishy, fragrant mud flats. Perhaps when the tide turns, it will be a bore tide.

"No, it means we suspend hostilities until after Bill dies," I say.

Both Alice and Aurora give me a piercing look as if to say, *How can you say that?* But I did say that, and we look west again.

"We have to make a plan," Alice says.

I'm tired of her plans.

"Just tell Bill we're OK," Aurora says. "Bill won't know if it's true or not."

Deepening pink streaks of cloud layers turn redder as the sun sets. The reddish light reflects in the Inlet, waves flickering like little tongues of fire at the bottom of hot coals.

"He'll know," I say.

Out in the Inlet, silhouettes of the oil platforms become visible, and the gas burn-off torches create more red flicker. Behind us the silhouettes of birches and spruces appear up on the bluffs, interspersed with the shadows and outlines of people facing across the Inlet.

"I don't want Bill dying all worried and afraid for us," Alice begins.

"That's why we should tell him whatever he needs to hear," Aurora says.

The volcanic diffraction emerges in scarlet ripples of orange and red along the entire west sky. Mt. Redoubt turns magenta. Mt. Susitna turns dark pink. Rays and beams of pink and crimson appear. Denali doesn't appear.

"What do you propose for a truce?" I ask.

More streaks appear, each a different hue of red to orange to bright, almost blinding, yellow. The light reflects in the smooth shining mud flats. The wetter, darker patches of mud reflect more fiery, almost blood red and blend into the crimson sky. In that moment the world before us is transformed into one scarlet universe—unreal, surreal, flaming and flickering.

"We could agree to get along and each of us tell Bill that everything's OK," Alice says.

"Sh," someone from another group scolds us.

We fall into silence to match the silence of the crowd because this night is a night of magic only the Inlet can offer. And the belugas. Are you out there, my belugas? It's fire music in the sky. Sh.

We sit transfixed and watch the fiery light all around us. Somewhere, I think I hear music, a Wagnerian opera, where Wotan summons the fire god to cast a ring of fire around his daughter, Brünnhilde, to protect her. Or was it to control her? Is this how it is with us, with Bill? We love him, so we must protect him, control him, even in his death?

The sun dips down below the Pacific Rim and we hear the tide turn, the roll of water coming forward in the bore-tide rush. Behind us a faint ghost of a moon appears, rising, almost spectral. With one reverberating sigh along beach and cliff, the volcano sunset is over.

We walk to the car and frequently stumble because we keep looking back to catch any last fragment of sunset. Sometimes we look north to check if Denali is out because Denali is known to appear with the moon.

"So do we have a plan?" Alice says after we are settled in the Malibu.

"A truce?" Aurora says. "We should've done this a long time ago."

Such a fraud she is.

"Abby?" Alice prods me.

"Sure, sure," I say.

"We also need a plan for his care," Alice adds.

"Mother refuses to move him," Aurora says.

"Then we find twenty-four-hour care," I say.

"That's a big expense for Mother," Aurora says.

"Since when do you care?" I say.

"Truce," Alice interjects.

Aurora drives, Alice facilitates the conversation, and I sit in the backseat and watch for night animals. We spot several moose and a red fox. Animals like to come out after sunset.

"I pray that Bill doesn't last much longer," Alice says. "I've been reading about near-death experiences and truly believe there's a spirit world where our soul goes when we die."

We see a porcupine and a pair of bright-white swans.

"I don't like the idea of a father-figure God in a place called heaven. None of the near-death experiences refer to that," Alice says.

God? We just saw God out there in that sunset.

"I've got to go back to court on Monday," Aurora says. "Tim's pretty nervous."

"Why? Is he guilty?" I ask.

"Bitch." Aurora eyes me in the rearview mirror.

"Truce," Alice says.

I watch the moon reflecting off the snowy mountaintops, the trees, and the shining Knik Arm. How much will court cost? I don't ask. Truce.

"But the people who've had near-death experiences do refer to a place of peace and light. I pray Bill finds that place soon. I'm going to talk to him about it."

What are you going to say to him, dear Alice? *Go find the light?*

We spot several moose and a red fox.

"I'll talk to Bill, too," Aurora says. "I'll tell him Mama and I are getting along better."

Miserable liar. Truce.

"Did you ever find more seed potatoes?" Alice asks Aurora.

"Nope," Aurora replies.

"I think Momma is at peace with Bill dying," Alice says.

Mother knows it's coming but probably isn't at peace with it. I don't say it. Truce.

We drive into Wasilla, Alice and Aurora chatting about death and peace and seed potatoes. As we near the house, we smell smoke. Neighbors are standing in the driveway. Alice pulls in and stops the car abruptly. We jump out. All around the entire lower level of the house, tendrils of smoke curl out from under the windowsills, under the garage doors, and around the entrance doors. There's an electrical smell in the air. We can't see the fire, but we hear its crisp crackle.

"Oh God, my house is on fire!" Aurora yells.

"We called the fire department when we saw the smoke." A neighbor rushes over.

"Is there anyone in the house?" Another neighbor joins in.

"Oh my God, Bear-Bear's up there," Aurora cries.

"You idiot. What about Mother and Bill?" I say.

"What are we going to do?" Alice asks, panic evident in her voice.

"I'm going up there," I say.

I survey the side stairs up to the deck and try to grasp the situation. The stairs lead up to the deck, to the patio doors. The patio doors lead into the dining room that leads to the living room and then to Mother and Bill. The patio doors are probably locked. The fire department will take a few minutes to get here. We can't wait. Why isn't Mother calling or at the window or on the deck? She's probably refusing to leave Bill.

"Aurora, get the ax from the wood pile." I spin around.

"Alice, get the blanket out of the Malibu," I direct her.

"How can I help," asks one of the neighbors.

"Tell the fire department that we're up there trying to get our parents out." I point to the deck.

I reach the steps and bound up two at a time. Flames are visible through the windows on the lower level. I hear Alice panting behind me. We can't see anything through the patio doors. Yes, they're locked.

"Get out of the fucking way." Aurora roars up the stairs, and we jump aside just as she slams the ax into the patio door.

"Again!" Alice directs Aurora. "Harder!"

Aurora hits the glass doors again, this time using her body weight and with such force, the glass doors shatter.

Alice wraps her hands in the blanket and pushes enough glass away so we can get through the doors. Smoke rushes out and stings our eyes. I push through the doors, feeling the sharp points of glass scrape my arms. The room is dark inside, intense with smoke and chemical smell, probably burning plastic and fabric. I make my way into the living room where the smoke seems thicker and is coming up the stairwell from the lower level. I squint hard, my eyes burning, tears pouring from the sting and burn, now my nose burning.

There. Bill lies in the hospital bed, just like always. He's awake, watching me, acknowledging me, recognizing me. Mother sits on the stool beside the bed, the stool pulled up as close as possible. Both Mother and Bill have dish towels over their noses and mouths.

"Bear-Bear!" Aurora yells.

Alice goes into the kitchen and runs the faucet. She comes to me quickly and hands me and Aurora wet kitchen towels, which we tie around our faces to cover our noses and mouths.

What do you think?" Alice asks.

I notice how warm the room is and that the carpet is steaming. Or is it smoking? Bill continues to watch, his eyes above the towel watching our movements.

"I think we don't have much time, a few minutes. Five maybe," I say.

"What should we do?" Alice says, and I feel her panic. "We don't have an escape plan."

"Then make a plan," I say. "And fast!"

"How?" Alice stares at me.

"Just do what makes sense. You're a smart girl!" I pull back the sheets and blanket covering Bill. I sense Alice's increasing panic. "You can't have a damn plan for everything. Let's just do this!"

I see Alice freeze. Think fast. No time to think. Time. I understand Alice understands time and how it fits to planning and how planning fits to structure and how structure holds her world together.

"Alice!" I shout. "It's just like testing a kayak! We have five minutes after our head gets wet to get back to shore. Alice, right now, our heads are wet!"

Alice makes a sudden choking sound. "Got it. Five minutes!" She reaches down to unfasten the catheter tube from the urine bag.

"No time," I say. "Grab the whole deal and try not to yank it."

Alice throws the urine bag on Bill's lap.

"Aurora, get Mother," Alice yells.

Smoke billows up the stairwell, and we hear the crackling grow louder. Mother doesn't move. Where's Aurora?

I reach for the morphine to give Bill a big dose so he won't feel the pain when we take him out, but he makes a gurgling sound, and he shakes his head no.

"It's going to hurt like hell," I say.

He nods. He knows.

"Aurora, where are you?" I yell.

The smoke burn and chemical smell are so strong I have to squint hard and continually blink to bring on tears to wash out my eyes. The wet dish towels don't really help, and I can barely breathe. Alice throws the blanket over Bill to cover his head.

"Give me your arm," Alice says, and we lock arms behind Bill's back. "Give me your other arm." Alice slides her arm under Bill's skinny upper legs, and we grab each other's arms. "It's a fireman carry. I saw it on TV once. Four minutes remaining."

We easily lift Bill out of the bed and begin to carry him to the patio door.

"Hey, Roadrunner, how do you make holy water," Bill sputters from under the blanket.

The pain must be hideous for him, but there's no indication he hurts. We can't really see where we are going, but we know the room and slide our feet, feeling our way.

"Aurora!" I shout.

I make out her shape on the floor next to Bear-Bear. The big dog lies motionless on his dog bed, probably dead from breathing poisonous gases near the floor.

"Three minutes!" yells Alice.

Another crash, and, now, we see the actual flames licking up the walls of the stairwell; burning through the paneling with its lush lacquer finish; working their way to Mother, who sits on the stool near the top of the stairwell.

We hear sirens out in the driveway. Alice and I are near the patio door and feel the air rushing in. A bright flare of light fills the area, and I see the flames swell into the stairwell.

"Aurora, forget the dog. Get your mother!" I yell.

There's no response. I hate Aurora even more in this moment in her inability to protect her own. It's what we do.

"Mama!" Aurora stumbles, probably over the coffee table.

"No, go back!" Mother finally responds. "Don't risk it."

"Mama," Aurora says.

I think I hear Aurora struggling to get up.

"Go back," Mother yells.

"Mama, get off the stool and come to me," Aurora yells.

No response from Mother.

"I'm coming for you!" Aurora yells.

There's so much smoke, we can't see. We hold onto Bill, blind and feeling our way, trying to maneuver through the patio door, and then two huge hands, or is it two huge firemen, take Bill from us, and we emerge onto the deck.

"Go!" Aurora yells, and Mother is shoved through the patio door.

Alice and I grab Mother and pull her onto the deck. Two firemen pick up Mother and carry her down the deck stairs, Alice in tow. Where's Aurora?

The flames crackle and smack. I wipe my eyes with the wet dish towel. "Aurora!" I push myself through the patio door, into the smoke, back into the living room.

The strange acrid smell of burning foam hits my nose. So much smoke, but the flames provide just enough light to see Aurora on the floor next to Bear-Bear.

"We've got to go." I touch her shoulder.

"You hate me. Why are you here?" Aurora strokes the dog.

"Yes, I hate you," I say. "But I love you more. Now let's get out of here."

"Mama hates me so much that she didn't want me to save her," Aurora says.

"Stop being such a drama queen," I say. "She didn't want to put you in harm's way. Now let's go!"

"My poor Bear-Bear," Aurora says. "I've lost everything."

"You can rebuild, get new everything, even a new dog."

"How can you love and hate me at the same time?" Aurora asks.

How can she ask such a stupid question right now? But I feel her confusion, and the pathos of her confusion overwhelms me, like the day she slipped away in the bathtub. Whatever it takes, I must get her out of here.

"We can't replace you," I say. "Dammit! Remember when I got trapped in the fishing net, when that grizzly came at me, when I sent the paramedics to rescue you? Remember? It's what we do. We take of each other. Come on. We've gotta go."

Aurora moves as if to stand up and then hesitates.

"Stop being a dumb-ass girl, and let's get out of here," I say.

Damn. I did it again.

"I'm not a dumb-ass girl," Aurora says.

Just like JB, here I am, passing the dumb-ass legacy onto Aurora. She doesn't deserve that. I don't deserve it. I will end this now.

"You're not a dumb-ass girl," I yell so loud that I know the universe hears it and that somewhere JB hears it. "I just said that because I didn't know what else to say, because I'm scared the floor will collapse, because I'm just plain scared right now."

"You're not a dumb-ass girl either." Aurora begins to stand up. We hear Bear-Bear snort. "Oh my God, he's alive." Aurora grabs a corner of the dog bed. "Let's go."

"I'm not sure we can," I say.

"Of course we can. You climbed Bug Mountain, didn't you?" Aurora says.

"You want to drag him out?"

"Yuppers," Aurora says. "What else would dumb-ass girls do?"

"Be dumb-asses!"

"Dumb-ass."

"You know this dog is heavy," I say as we begin to drag the dog bed.

"Dumb-ass dog," Aurora says. "Hey, this is my brand-new carpet going up in flames."

"Dumb-ass carpet."

"Dumb-ass fire."

"Come on, dumb-ass, let's get out of here."

"Bug Mountain, here we come!"

We hold tight to the dog bed; drag it while trying to crawl, hearing whimpers from the dog; crawl toward the door in the crushing smoke; push furniture out of the way; feel our way, one foot at a time. Bug Mountain, Bug Mountain, Bug Mountain—we can do it. I don't know how we reach the patio door, blind from smoke, dizzy, dragging the damn dog. Someone helps me, blanket around me; something soothing in my eyes; truck noises; water and steam sounds; hissing; a blur of movement; cool, cool air around me; Alice talking; someone saying the fire started in the furnace room; Slim talking; Bill saying, "OK, OK"; Aurora gasping with an oxygen mask on her face; Mother holding Aurora's hand. How did we make it dragging that damn dog? Thank you, thank you, JB, for Bug Mountain.

7 June
Father's Joy

Soft noise, hum of air bed, murmurs in the hall, padding feet, the television on low playing an old cowboy movie, Alice and Aurora chatting in quiet tones.

"Do you want me to make a topper for your wedding cake?" Alice asks Aurora.

The priest pats Mother on the hand, nods to us, and departs. I sit on a stool next to Bill's bed, just like at the Wasilla house. Mother sits in a chair on the other side of the bed. Aurora and Alice sit on the small sofa across from the bed. Bill sleeps, his mouth open, his eyelids partially open revealing the whites of his eyes. Sometimes we hear gurgling in his throat.

"Can you put Bear-Bear in the topper?" Aurora asks.

How silly. Put the dog on the wedding cake. Oh, who cares? It's OK.

"I think I'll make a flower thing for my hair," Alice adds.

"We still need to go to Value Village to look for silk flowers," Aurora says.

"When we go down to Homer for the funeral, we should stop by the Wagon Wheel and look for seed potatoes," Alice says, getting out a small notebook to start a list.

How does she keep track of all those lists? Oh, who cares? It's part of her charm.

Soft color; gold drapes framing the window looking out to the Inlet; lamplight, almost candlelight; soft, warm chocolate carpet; paintings of Alaska sunsets and sunrises and the northern lights and children playing blanket toss in soft pinky light.

All soft and warm and cuddly like a family living room, not a hospital room where we brought Bill last night, where we now keep vigil. One of the hospital nurses comes in to check Bill's dressings and begins to change the bandages.

Tad enters and checks Bill's feet, which are purplish blue with black mottling. The lower calves are also purplish. I reach over and touch his feet: ice cold.

"It's time," Tad says in a tone that tells the other nurse not to change the dressing.

I'm sure my heart skips a beat.

"I'll tidy him up a bit," the nurse says. "So you can remember him all handsome as you say your good-byes."

She proceeds to arrange the bed linens so they look neat, positions Bill's head so his mouth doesn't hang open, straightens the collar of his bed shirt so it looks dignified, gently brushes his hair so his thin white hair lies nice, wipes his face with a warm cloth so the crusty corners of his eyes come clean, and dabs his lips with lip balm so they look moist. My mouth is dry.

"He may wake up for a few seconds," Tad tells us. "It's a precious moment if you can catch it."

Tad assists the nurse in gathering up the medications tray, removing the trash cans, and partially opening the curtains to give Bill a better view of the Inlet and the fireweed starting to bloom in drifts along the roadside. The sky glows in brilliant red and pink. Another volcano sunset.

"We'll be at the nurses' station if you need anything," Tad says and looks over the room before leaving with the nurse.

"The family seems close to you," I hear the nurse say to Tad outside the door. "When he passes, do you want to call the time?"

"Yes, very much so," Tad replies.

I look out toward Tad in the hall. But Tad's already out of sight, and it is Slim who stands in the doorway. Or am I imagining Slim?

We gather around Bill in an awkward, eternal quiet. After all, what can we say, especially after last night? Should we talk about the fire, how the fireman said it started in the furnace room? Should we talk about the dog?

Is that really Slim? I glance at Mother saying her rosary, at Alice and Aurora standing by Bill's bed. Or are they standing to? Don't they see Slim?

Or should we go deep and talk about our rage and our hate, our many sins, and how we are not candidates for heaven. Should we talk about going into a burning building to rescue an old man who had only hours left to live anyway? Did the priest grant Bill sanctity? If he did, will Bill have to go to heaven instead of going with Slim?

I look at Slim in the doorway. Yes, it's Slim there in the threshold.

"Where are you going?" I ask.

"I want to open the curtains some more." Alice goes over to the window and draws the drapes fully open so the Inlet is more visible, flickering in tonight's volcano sunset.

"Across the Inlet," Slim says.

"Why?" I ask.

"To see the rainbow," Alice says. "Every time someone close to me dies, I see a rainbow."

"Because it's my job," Slim says.

"When?" I ask

"Soon after the death, not always immediately after, but soon," Alice says.

"Now." Slim nods toward Bill.

I look at Bill and am surprised to see Bill look up at me. His eyes seem big. He moves his lips. I lean down close to Bill's face, the gurgling distinct in his throat, his breathing coming in short breaths followed by no breathing at all. I put my ear closer to his mouth.

"Roadrunner," Bill whispers. "You are my greatest joy, a father's joy."

I feel the most delicate kiss on the tip of my ear. I am his joy! I am my father's joy. The words—the thought behind the words—oh, rapture, and I feel my face light up, radiant, even transformed. I am my father's joy. Ah, the sweetness of it. I kiss Bill on the forehead.

Alice comes over to the bed and puts her ear close to Bill's face. I see Bill's lips move though I can't hear what he says. Alice smiles a smile that lights her face and becomes radiant. Then Aurora's turn comes, and she puts her ear close to Bill's mouth. Again, I can't hear what Bill tells her, but Aurora smiles radiantly, her face lights up, and for the first time in my life, I see happiness on Aurora's face. Mother pulls her chair up close to Bill. They don't talk, but they have eyes on each other. They're not aware of us girls. Alice and Aurora sniffle. Slim waits in the doorway.

"Now." Slims nods toward Bill.

I look at Bill, who looks at Mother, who smiles back at Bill.

"Good-bye," Bill mouths the words to Mother.

"OK," Mother says and puts her hand on Bill's mittened hand.

"OK." Bill takes in a long gurgling breath and sinks into the pillow, and death takes him.

In the doorway Slim is gone, but I think I hear his voice down the hall. "The reds are running early across the Inlet," Slim says.

Alice jumps up and runs to the window. "It's probably too soon for the rainbow, plus it's hard to tell with this gorgeous sunset," Alice says as she scans the brilliant sky.

Meanwhile, I rejoice. I am my father's joy.

Part 4

HOMER

---

8 June
Across the Inlet

> My name is Father's Joy. My father's name is
> Bill. He called my name in a symphony. And we
> are all here to hear it. Halibut, salmon, beluga,
> swan. Telling time in the tide, volcano sunsets,
> and fireweed blooming. We are all here. Eagle.
> Gull. Moose. Tiptoeing over clam beds, mud flats,
> and glaciers, looking west to Augustine across
> the Inlet. He called my name, and I became my
> father's joy.
>
> —Abby Miller, morning pages

"Yes, but I told you, I love you more," I say after Aurora asks me
again.

"Do you really hate me?"

She's probably asked a hundred times now, but I know she
asks just to hear me say the answer. Yes, I love her, flawed and
manipulative and all that she is and is not, and most of all, I love
her alive.

We pause for a moment in the church parking lot. Two eagles
fly over the church and out into Kachemak Bay dotted with fishing charters and a few sailboats.

"Mama," Aurora says. "I hate to say this, especially right now, but we have to pay the lawyer by close of business tomorrow."

We all turn to look at Aurora, more of a stare. Right now?

"Is it OK if you pay the lawyer and we pay you back in installments?" Aurora asks.

"No, it's actually not OK," Mother says slowly.

Aurora's eyes flicker in surprise. I'm surprised, too.

"We need to pay him, or he'll drop us as clients," Aurora says.

"Aurora, sweetie—" Mother begins.

"We need this lawyer," Aurora interrupts.

I sense her panic. No, it's desperation and then something under the desperation. She's embarrassed. But she doesn't know what else to do.

"You could get a different lawyer," I cut in. "Your lawyer charges a high fee. Correct me if I'm wrong, but I don't see what he does that's so special."

"Aurora, sweetie, you're going to receive part of your inheritance early. It'll be enough to cover all your needs, even the lawyer, plus extra," Mother says.

"But we can't do it fast," I add. "We need about another week to finish the arrangements."

"Then, from what's left of your inheritance, we will deduct everything I've loaned you or you've taken from our accounts," Mother says. "I've accounted for every penny."

"If you want to keep your lawyer and he wants the fifty thousand dollars, he can surely wait another week," I say. "He's playing power games with you. If he can't wait another week, fire him."

"What if he won't wait?" Aurora seems shaken.

Then I see it. Aurora the manipulator is actually the one being manipulated. People have manipulated and used her all her life. Just like those fishermen boys. My protective instinct kicks in.

"Do you want me to talk to your lawyer?" I ask.

"No." Aurora hesitates and swallows. "Bill told me I can."

I'm not sure what she means and though hesitant, she seems, yes, somewhat excited.

"Hey, folks, speaking of Bill, the lawyer doesn't have to be taken care of right now," Alice says. "Good grief. It's Bill's funeral."

Aurora's bottom lip quivers slightly. "You're right. We don't have to do this right now," Aurora says. "Let's go say good-bye to Bill."

We go in the church lobby to greet people as they enter: a hug, a gentle pat on the back, sympathy cards in the card basket. A guest book. The lobby blurs with people. I recognize a neighbor. Then I see Linda, Slim's wife. She and Mother hug. Here comes the gang from the senior center. Here come Bill's fellow Masons and Shriners, who hug Mother and give her a brooch that signifies she's the widow of a Master Mason. Then a group of people comes that I don't know. Mother doesn't know them either. We greet them, shake their hands, and thank them for coming.

We greet the Anchorage Arctic Ensemble when they arrive, shaking the hands of each of the fourteen singers, each singer thanking us for Bill's bequest to the Ensemble, and us thanking them for driving down for Bill's memorial service. When the Ensemble begins the opening hymn, the ushers escort us inside the church and up to the front pew. On the way Mother stops to hug Ben, our family lawyer, and Eric, Bill's investment broker. Another hug to the neighbor. Hugs for Mother's dear friends, Jeanine, Sister Carol Ann, and the ladies from the Guild, and, finally, we reach the front of the church and settle down on the shiny wood pew.

Wood is the only embellishment in the church—the polished, gleaming wood of the pews; the altar; the ceiling beams; the doors; and the great arched windows behind the altar, huge windows, framed in glowing wood and looking out to where the Kachemak Bay meets the Inlet. No statues or stained glass or a giant cross. No embroidered linens or old paintings or brass candelabras. No smell of burning candles or incense. Only the simplicity of the great windows looking out over the powerful and glorious Inlet where we see otters bob in the waves and eagles swoop down to grab a fish, and swaths of light dance on the water's surface.

"Mama," Aurora whispers.

I sense an internal struggle in Aurora, though I can't sense what the struggle is about. Perhaps Aurora doesn't know either. Perhaps that's her struggle—not knowing because she doesn't know what will happen next, either with the house or with Tim or, even, with Mother. Underneath the struggle I sense that hint of hesitant excitement I felt earlier in her. Her future may be unknown, but I sense it's about to change.

"Thank you." Aurora sinks sideways into Mother's arms.

Mother cradles her. Have I ever seen Mother and Aurora hug?

"Welcome to this memorial service for our friend Bill McCray," the announcer, one of the deacons, says. "This service is unique. Instead of the traditional memorial service, the Anchorage Arctic Ensemble has come here today to memorialize Bill by singing his favorite piece. They will sing Rachmaninoff's *Vespers.* Bill was a longtime patron of the Ensemble and attended their concerts whenever possible. Bill told me that the music you are about to hear reminded him of flying a C-130 because it takes a perfectly coordinated team to fly a C-130 and another perfectly coordinated team to sing this music. Both the C-130 and the music were magic for him. As his health declined and Bill could no longer fly even a small plane, Bill told me this music allowed him to fly again, though in a different way. On behalf of Bill, Bill's family, and the Anchorage Arctic Ensemble, we welcome you to this fitting memorial to Bill. We now remember Bill the pilot, the father, the husband, and the lover of music. We pray for Bill's everlasting soul. We pray for the life he has lived and shared with us. We pray that he flies again."

The opening hymn fades out, and the gentle hymn of "The Short Gloria" fades in: "And on earth peace, good will among men." The hymn begins soft, like church bells in the distance ringing a call to prayer. I turn to glance at the people behind me, all these people who brought their goodwill here today to say farewell to Bill. There are Mike Glendale, the realtor, and Cecil Finch, the manager of Eagle Grocery. There are Irene and Joe, close friends of Bill and Mother. On the other side of the church are Stephanie and Diane, more friends of Mother. There's Tad, gazing out the arched windows. He drove all the way from Wasilla to be here.

It was years ago when Bill took me to hear the Ensemble sing this piece for the first time. From the very start, I was amazed to hear voices so beautiful they were like instruments, the violins and oboes especially. It felt like the Ensemble had taken me to another world. Bill told me this "otherworld effect" was created by the repeating alleluias. He was delighted I enjoyed the music as much as he.

"This music shows the miracle of human beings working together," Bill would always say after a concert.

I listen for the start of the repeating alleluias as the chorus begins the bolder hymn of "The Six Psalms."

"Alleluia." The fourteen voices of the Ensemble seem to blend into one voice. I float between the beauty of the music and the beauty of the Inlet. Bill, where are you? Can you hear me? Can you hear the music?

Somewhere I hear the priest enter and echo the alleluia. People in the church echo the priest, and the chorus joins in for one united alleluia resonating throughout the church and out the windows to the Inlet beyond.

Over at the Homer airport, I envision three of Bill's air force buddies climbing aboard a C-130 to take Bill's ashes across the Inlet. What a great send-off for Bill, a C-130 and his favorite music. Is Slim onboard? He must be.

Next, the hymn of "The Resurrection" begins with a haunting tenor solo. Lower voices join in, so low they sound like a murmuring crowd of people. I look around to confirm it's actually the chorus and not the people in the church. The people are quiet.

Mother watches the chorus intently. I wonder what she's thinking about. What's next for her? "I don't know—it's too soon," she says to everyone who asks.

"The time for sorrow has come to an end," the chorus sings. Bill might say something similar.

"I don't want you to grieve for me and be all sorrowful," Bill had told Mother. "Well, a little bit maybe. Then go out and live it up."

I look out the big windows and see Augustine, a faint shadow out on its Inlet volcano island. The volcano still smokes and coughs up ash, and we still feel an occasional tremor. The damage done by the eruption hasn't been determined yet. Augustine will go to sleep now, perhaps for years, perhaps for decades, and erupt another time.

"Alleluia," the chorus sings, and I drift in between layers of worlds, here at the church, back at the Homer airport, earlier today with its snippets of conversation, and right now with my memories of Bill.

I see the C-130 all ready for departure at the Homer airport. The pilot announces, "Seven souls onboard" and declares the direction of departure as, "Across the Inlet."

"He is risen from the tomb!" the chorus sings. I see Bill's buddies, in their old uniforms, guarding the urn of ashes. I hear the low growl of the turboprop engines roar to life as the C-130 accelerates, wheels up. Takeoff. And Bill is flying again. Oh how Bill loved the sound of those turboprops.

Here in this pew, I feel Bill's presence in the music.

"Listen for those low basses," Bill would say. "It's almost impossible to sing that way, yet they do it."

And there's my Bill in the photos and mementos on the table in front of the altar, in front of the magnificent windows overlooking the Inlet. There's the photo of the young airman, of the C-130 pilot. A photo with Slim, the photo with Mother, and the photo with us girls. There's the Shriner hat that Bill treasured and the coffee mug with the C-130 logo. There's a small figurine of a German shepherd to represent Bear-Bear. Then there's Bill, in the urn, in the C-130, now heading out to the Inlet.

And there's my Aurora, passionate and wild, even in a life of crisis. And there's my Alice, able to make passion live through a list. And there's my mother, stalwart and unwavering in her passion for loving us.

Alice places her hand on Mother's hand. What did Alice tell us on the way to the church?

"I think I understand now," Alice had said. "Parents want the best for their children, no matter what, no matter what mistakes they make along the way. For that, Momma, I thank you. I want to be a landscape architect," Alice then blurted out.

We responded in a volley of questions. How? Why? Can you draw? When?

"I don't know." Alice's eyes sparkled when she had said it. Her face lit up, and there was a hint of relief in her eyes. "Bill told me that I don't need a plan."

Landscape architect? Of course. It's all about seed potatoes.

"Now and ever, and unto ages and ages," the chorus sings. The words talk to me, as my worlds drift in and out, slipping from one to another, lingering in this time and that space and back again, ages and ages of memories with Bill. He's gone. He's really gone.

I see the C-130 lift off at the Homer airport, still low, but gaining altitude and turning west to face the Inlet. What's next? Aurora will call the VA and order a marble headstone for Bill. Alice will plant a commemorative garden. I don't know what to do.

"For, behold, through the cross, joy has come into all the world," the chorus continues, first sung by the tenors and basses, then followed by the giant roar of the C-130 flying above us, shaking my senses, with the sopranos and harmonizing altos joining in just as the C-130 passes over us and we all look up to hear the turboprops become part of the music.

"Alleluia," the chorus sings and the repetition comforts me.

"The repeating alleluias are like the tides," Bill had said. "They come and go and come and go, just like life."

Come back to me Bill—be like the tide.

"For behold, henceforth all generations will call me blessed." The bassists sing "The Magnificat." Again the words talk to me. Yes, I am blessed for knowing you Bill. Don't leave me. I'm no longer aware of the others in the church. Are we sitting or standing?

"Every day I will bless thee and praise thy name." The tenors begin the longest, most complex hymn. I see Bill's buddies stand to attention, thank Bill for his military service, praise him for being a good man, and then salute. Thank you, Bill, from me. Bye-bye.

"Bye-bye, Roadrunner," I hear, but from so far away that I strain to hear it. It's Bill. I know it's him.

"Today salvation has come to the world," the chorus sings. The C-130 completes its pass over us and gains altitude to go across the Inlet.

Bill, we'll be OK.

"OK, Roadrunner," I hear behind the alleluias.

The low rumble of the C-130 dissipates, and we look behind the altar to see the plane appear in those divine windows and watch the C-130 head out. I feel Bill's presence so close, yet starting to fade even as I think it.

"And you, Roadrunner?" I hear from that faraway place.

I don't know. There are no answers today except that we will be OK. We will love each other no matter what, and we will take care of each other. It's what we do.

We continue to watch the C-130 as it grows smaller, crosses the bay, and begins its trek across the Inlet, flying upwind from Augustine still smoking. The belugas are there.

"Not we, Roadrunner, you."

I don't know the answer. I only know that I'm a child of the Inlet.

"Your answer is in the music," I'm sure I hear. "And you don't have to do it alone."

Like the tides and the repeating alleluias, the words comfort me. Whatever comes next, I don't have to do it alone.

OK.

I see Bill's buddies release Bill's ashes through the jump door. The wind catches the ash, mingles it with the ash of Augustine, and goes aloft toward the Valley of No Return. After the ashes are released, the pilot announces, "Six souls onboard." And Bill is across the Inlet.

"Rejoice!" proclaims the chorus in the final hymn.

"You are a joy to me," I hear so faint and far away that I lean forward to hear it, more of a sensing than a hearing, the sound becoming fainter and fainter until it's no longer in any world I'm privy to and becomes a wisp of memory in my mind, and I look out across the Inlet and have never seen or sensed the Inlet more brilliant or beautiful or omnipotent.

Ice

I am my father's joy. This was my story. How across the Inlet my father called my name. One day Denali will call me. Ah, sometimes when the clouds break, Denali will appear. Stop to stare at her. Stare all day at her. You will not make her blink. You cannot tempt her. Glaciers spiral down from Denali's six peaks. Wind gusts blow snowdrifts over entire camps of climbers looking for gold or God. Sometimes light rays shine so bright, you become blind.Sometimes in the ice you can hear cries of climbers who died, their bodies and remnants and camp tents now cyclic momentum in the sublime ice. Denali has no rules. Sometimes she allows climbers to reach the top. Mostly when Denali finishes with you, nothing remains except your remains frozen in those icy layers. You, too, may cry or pray for answers, but Denali will ignore you. Or so you think. But she is always there to remind us that there are no answers, only this ice-crystal sword we live under. Only this warning: This is your life. Do not waste it.

—Abby Miller, morning pages

ACKNOWLEDGEMENTS

Thank you to John Thomas who is my writing and critique partner. Thank you to Julia Cameron, author of *The Artist's Way*, whose book inspired me with its concept of morning pages. Thank you to Denise Bitidis, who wrote morning pages with me and helped me discover my creative self.

Across the Inlet was inspired by real events, however, the depiction of the events and characters are fictional. Similarities to actual events or people are coincidental and may be due to the emotional authenticity that I've tried to create. I'd like to extend a special thank you to my sisters, Jan Keiser and Laura Keiser, who shared some of their feelings with me and allowed me to turn them into fiction.

I'll always be indebted to my mother, Connie Creal, who continues to inspire me with her unfaltering faith and my stepdad, Robert Creal, who became my real father.

Most of all, I want to express my deepest gratitude and love to my husband, Ken Summers, who never wavered in his belief in me.

Made in the USA
Middletown, DE
03 March 2015